The Journey to Felicity

Thank you for reading my book
Hope you enjoy it!

NATHAN JEWELL
a k a

Published by:
Nathan Jewell LLC
4957 Lakemont Boulevard
Suite C-4 #250
Bellevue, WA 98006

NathanJewellnovelist@gmail.com

Google Group: the-journey-to-felicity@googlegroups.com

Facebook: The Journey to Felicity, Nathan Jewell

Twitter: @NJewellnovelist

This book is loosely based on actual events. However, most names were changed.

Second Edition December 2014
First Edition October 2013

ISBN – 13 978-1492845201
ISBN – 10 1492845205

DEDICATION

To Annie, my muse, who graced the first part of my life
and J, who graces me every day for the second.

NOTE TO READERS

This novel is my first literary effort. Its writing came at a time when I needed to tell a story. One thing led to another and the first draft was written. Once published, the book gave me a chance to connect with readers I knew personally on a new level. It's the greatest gift I could have received.

Most of my readers have glossed over the book's shortcomings, but it took a skilled, anonymous reviewer to truly identify its faults. Although I was happy just to satisfy my friends and acquaintances, I do want the book to endure with fewer blemishes.

The Second Edition addresses the constructive feedback I've heard: greater character development, easier to read dialogue (especially the Sheffieldish accents), and final scrubbing of typos. I can't guarantee that it's perfect but I feel it should offer a smoother ride.

Enjoy!

NJ

May 2015

ACKNOWLEDGMENTS

This story contains many autobiographical truths that helped me get through the intense complexity and time challenges in writing this novel. Thank you to my dear friend Annie for saving my letters for over twenty-five years.

I accomplished the writing of this book by drawing from personal experiences of people that have enriched my life. Some of these may be more obvious than others. In the end, I'm grateful to have had these memories and to have known these people characterized in this literary journey through time.

I would like to thank the fine city of Westport, Washington who hosted me while writing this book. The pillow-comforting pace, the fishing and the mesmerizing scenery gave me an ideal backdrop from which to write.

Don Campbell was my awesome editor. I was both surprised and overjoyed that he treated me more like a best friend instead of a client when I discussed this crazy idea of writing a novel.

Thank you to all my Alpha and Beta Readers. They gave me the confirmation I needed and clued me into all the blind spots I had on my initial drafts.

And, finally, I could not have done this work without the patience and support of my loving wife and children. I know it will take some vacation and gift bribes to settle the disturbance of writing this novel has had on their lives.

ONE

One

Lower East Side, New York City

"You're going where?"

They were all sitting down schmoozing at the circular dinner table of Seymour and Wilma Stillman's Lower East Side apartment after the Passover Seder. The fragrant smells of roasted chicken and matzo ball soup filled the air.

Seymour's son Marshall spoke up. "Dad, we're going to go to Greece to retrace our roots," he said.

Seymour turned his head in dismay. "What? Do your Israeli roots have weeds? Dorit at the dry cleaners would still love to meet you, you know."

"Dad, I told you, I'm not meeting anyone you set me up with after you hooked me up with that waitress at Ratner's with the three breasts," said a frustrated Marshall.

Seymour raised one eyebrow. "It was a cyst. Besides, she was adorable. She reminded me of your stepmother when I met her."

Marshall, was a twenty-six year old strapping young man with brown hair, hazel eyes and a light complexion. He had his father's mannerisms, had the same duck walk, and imitated his dad's tendency to talk over everybody.

1

He also matched his dad's hot-headedness, which frequently fueled an unexpected outbreak at the dinner table about some girl or his continuing goal of complete independence from the family.

He got his six feet two inches height from somewhere deep on his mother's side of the family since everyone else on both sides of his family seemed to be shorter. Marshall was your stereotypical twenty-something New Yorker: loud, heavily accented, and in a perpetual state of arousal. His loud exterior was complemented with a quiet self-assurance and sparkling hazel eyes that magnetically attracted women.

Marshall's brother, Zach, was two years younger and five feet eight inches tall. He inherited more of his mother's features: black hair, brown eyes and dark complexion. He was quieter, though still heavily accented, and less horny than his brother. Zach was considered handsome by the girls given his European features and muscular physique.

Zach appreciated being under his brother's wing with women. He learned a lot while studying Marshall skillfully dissecting women's inhibitions with his self-assurance and highlighted equipment. But what Zach lacked in self-assurance, he made up for in his ambition and intellect. Zach graduated college with honors and immediately entered the work force at an accounting firm in pursuit of his own independence. The brothers' favorite joke with each other was that Zach got the brains and Marshall got the schlong.

"Where in Greece are you going?" Seymour's brother Moishe boomed into the dinner table din. He was a traditional participant of the Seymour and Wilma Passover Seder along with his wife Rose, whose talking volume contributed to the dinner table's decibel equivalent of a jet engine during takeoff.

"It's at this hotel in Rhodes that Ma recommended," Zach said proudly.

"Oh, this is your mother's idea?" chirped Wilma with a sarcastic lilt.

Wilma and Helen, the boys' mother, were the fiercest of rivals. While both were Jewish, their family origins couldn't be more different while keeping the same faith. Wilma was an Ashkenazi Jew, one who descended from Northern European Jewish communities; in her case it was from one in Bialystok, Poland. Helen's ancestors were Sephardic Jews, descended from Western and Southern European Jewish communities remotely dispersed after the Spanish Inquisition. In Helen's case, it was one from the Greek island of Rhodes.

Seymour's roots were muddled. His family was originally from an Ashkenazi community in the Soviet Republic of Belarus, but moved to Tel Aviv, to a more free-spirited Jewish community, in his twenties before immigrating to the United States five years later to work as a peddler.

Helen and Seymour met at a hospital while she was on duty at Montefiore Hospital and he was there with a broken leg playing soccer. Their relationship catapulted on mutual lust, ignoring the social norms in the Jewish community. Back then, their relationship was perceived with racial overtones. In those days, Ashkenazim and Sephardim did not mix, lest were perceived as inferior. It eventually became a sticking point between them.

Things were often tense between Wilma and Seymour's children ever since she had an affair with their father and drove him with her Ashkenazi culture to divorce Helen six years ago. The boys were raised in a loving home with two caring parents until Seymour's attention and body parts were quietly lured away by Wilma's more familiar upbringing and hypnotic Eastern European cooking. After a bitter turf war, Zach and Marshall's parents eventually divorced when Zach was in college and Marshall was apprenticing to be a plumber.

The whole breakup did not come as a complete

shock. Since Zach was in high school, his mom's craving for women's equality and his father's macho Soviet ways were at loggerheads. Marshall and Zach would often escape to the bowling alley in Yonkers to blow off frustration at the situation. Zach and Marshall loved their parents individually but could never completely forgive their father for running out on his marriage with their mother.

"I hope you're going to get a villa where your mother and I stayed on our honeymoon," Seymour wished aloud. "I think it was the Fontana Hotel in Lindos. How I remembered that, I can't tell you. I recall it was a beautiful spot overlooking the Mediterranean Sea. There was this staircase in our room that led to a loft area dominated by three large windows from which you could see for fifty miles. I got so caught up looking at the view, I didn't even see your mother laying half-naked on the bed below until she yelled down for me. She was wearing this red silk negligee and she..."

"Seymour!" Wilma shouted.

"*Wil...-Ma!*" he retorted in his favorite Fred Flintstone impression. "Okay, okay, I got a little carried away. At least there were some good times with your mother. So, when are you going?"

Zach couldn't believe it himself when he declared, "The week of Memorial Day. I just have to square it with work."

Two

Lower East Side, New York City

The next morning, Zach set off on his regular routine to work. He had been tirelessly saving up for his own apartment; until then, he still lived with his father and stepmother.

He loved the walk to the train station. The first sight he usually caught leaving his 1950s era apartment building was the natural beauty of Tompkins Square Park. That morning was crisp, and the park's cherry trees bloomed with bright pink flowers creating a sweet floral scent.

The last three months had been especially grueling for Zach, but this day, April 15, felt like the last day of school. Although most Americans rued the day, others, like Zach, actually cherished it. For Zach, it meant a break from tax returns for a while, no more eighty hour work weeks, and some time to get his social life moving. He had been so focused on getting through tax season, his social schedule felt like a room filled with paper scattered by a gust of wind through an open window. There was the occasional date or set-up by his meddling father, but his mind was in such disarray, it never added up to anything.

That morning, he walked down to St. Mark's Place and into the Athena Diner to pick up his first cup of coffee. It was also a good opportunity to use one of Zach's small handful of words he knew in Greek with Dmitri Kourabas, the owner.

"*Kalimera*, Dmitri," he said in his best Greek accent.

"Hey Zach! Good morning to you, my friend. Thanks for getting my taxes out last week. I know I'm always late giving you my information."

"No problem Dmitri." He waited. "Say, I'm planning a trip to your mother country."

"To Greece? Really?" He thought for a minute. Although Zach was not a family member, he felt a kinship to Zach because of their shared heritage. "Hey, I've got good news for you. My cousin Krystos owns a highly rated restaurant in downtown Athens called the Zegras Family Restaurant. He makes a fish that would bring you to tears."

Zach was relieved to have an insider's connection in Athens. "Sounds great! We plan to stay a few nights in Athens before flying over to the island of Rhodes."

"Be sure to visit the Parthenon, the Acropolis and the Olympic Stadium. I'll call Krystos and let him know to be on the lookout for you. He'll treat you right."

Zach was grateful for the advice. "*Efharistó* Dmitri, I'll make sure that those places are on the list. Thanks again! I'll see ya tomorrow!"

Zach walked a few more blocks until he was at his train stop on Astor Place. The ride was usually an easy twenty minutes from station to station. He clicked through the entry gate and walked down to the platform passing a bum who was splayed out sleeping on a cardboard box. The scent of urine was pungent and burned within Zach's nose.

Before long, the *Lexington Avenue* train arrived and Zach joined the throng trying to board, but the graffiti-covered train was already packed with commuters. Zach pushed he way through but could barely grab a hold onto one of the bars near the door. Although this would have severely invaded the personal space for anyone else in the world, Zach accepted it as normal. People in seats were already reading their papers and listening to tunes on their Sony Walkmans. *Thank God this is only a twenty minute trip.* Arriving at Nassau Street, he made his way off the train and up to the street level to finish his commute to work. Upon reaching the busy street, he stared up at the majestic Twin Towers before him, the morning's golden sunrise gleaming off their windows. *Another day at the world's largest building. How cool is that?*

Myers, Morik, and Mitchell was a regional CPA firm that focused on Wall Street-based clients. Their offices took a portion of the sixth floor of Two World Trade Center. To secure a job there after graduation, Zach was singularly focused through his time at the state college to make solid grades. He nailed the interview and thought it was awesome to work in the towers. He started off as a worker bee, but raised himself up from the pack to be seen as a future partner candidate. He had now notched two seasons under his belt, and was recently promoted to Senior Associate Tax Accountant. His clients were mostly midsized investment firms and their owners. Duncan Arpad was his manager and closest work associate.

Duncan came from a wealthy lineage. Former New York City Mayor Fiorello LaGuardia's uncle was his great-great-grandfather. It sounded compelling at office parties if he could actually say it while soused, and he liked to weave this fact in his mantra when squawking his mating call. Duncan ignorantly thought that all the women in the office had a crush on him. For the ones he could entice, he used the office facilities as an extension of his bedroom. During one of his after-hours rendezvous, one of the senior partners caught him with the receptionist after-hours in his office. That episode created a career devastating scar in his personnel file.

"We made it!" Duncan cheered as he watched Zach pass by his cubicle. "Tax Day is finally here and now I can get back to my real life outside of this prison!"

Catching Duncan in his cheery mood, Zach felt that now was the time to iron out any issues with his approaching trip. "Speaking of which, I want to remind you about my upcoming vacation. I also got to get away from this place for a while."

"I perfectly understand. Hey Z, I forgot whether you were taking your trip during the Memorial Day weekend or not. I was going to invite you again to my parent's place in the Hamptons that weekend. I know how much fun you had last year. All my college friends from Dartmouth will be there. There is this one chick, Ashley Lewis, that wasn't there last year. Zach, you'll be guaranteed a blow job!" He put his tongue through his cheek simulating the motion. "You know what I mean!"

Duncan promoted the same prospects last year. At that time, Zach was new to the firm and took Duncan up on the invite since he did not want to upset his boss right away. Duncan, coming from an Ivy League school, had a different flavor of school friends. Nevertheless, he met the most interesting girl at the party. Her name was Sheila Daniels; she was stunning. The combination of her rich chocolate skin and her preppy yachting attire was captivating. The encounter drove Zach to ask her out on a date. However, after exploring her perspectives through dinner and drinks back at her apartment, Zach ended the relationship abruptly. Her holier-than-thou attitude transformed her from captivating to revolting. It was an ugliness he was not willing to accept.

"Sorry Duncan, I'll have to pass. Unfortunately it is during the time that my brother and I are going to explore our roots in Greece. I think Greek women in two-piece bathing suits under the hot Mediterranean sun trumps your Dartmouth girls in any competition."

Duncan raised his shoulders. "No problem, Z. I

know how much this trip means to you and Marshall.

Three

Jane's Café at Lord & Taylor, Manhasset, Long Island

Marshall and Zach had a monthly ritual; on a Saturday evening, Zach would take the train up to Marshall's apartment in Riverdale and from there they would go out to the dance clubs in Yonkers. The next day, they'd drag themselves up and have lunch with their mother.

During those Saturday nights at the clubs, Zach would repeatedly end up being Marshall's wing man. While Marshall discoed to something like "Everybody Have Fun Tonight" by Wang Chung blaring over the smoke-obscured lights with the over made-up, over boozed-up women in tight jeans, Zach would keep her companion company. It was a comfortable arrangement for Zach; he lacked the machismo to directly approach women. He honed his own skills watching Marshall at work with the ladies.

Marshall had his successes over the past months, often bringing home one of these bimbettes for his pleasure. Their animal mating dances would usually keep Zach awake all night on the pull-out bed as he would hear the combined sounds of Marshall's bed creaking and the bimbette's shrieking moans of pleasure. One time, Zach could swear that he heard one of the girls shriek out

"Cheers!" when their lovemaking session was over.

That night, both Marshall's bimbette and her wingwoman came back to his apartment. The wingwoman, known to everyone at the club as "Kathy Disco", was Zach's take-out food for the night. Kathy really wasn't Zach's type, but she had the requisite curves and smells to satisfy his constant sex drive. Zach preferred the more conservative type but was interested in meeting a wide range of women so he could better understand what excited him.

Kathy brought some psychedelic mushrooms with her which Zach had never tried before. She explained that it made light act like prisms so the room sparkled like rainbows. Zach was conventional but adventurous, so he tried some. Shortly after eating them, he spent a good fifteen minutes captivated by the wispy streaks of color flying off a candle before Kathy pulled him away and rode him like a mustang.

■■

Zach woke up early the next morning with a major headache. A nearly nude and panty-less Kathy Disco was still comatose on the pull-out. This morning, he wasn't real impressed with himself. *Kathy had the sexual stamina of a marathon runner, but there was little left to give substance to any conversation. No matter, I really don't want heavy conversation with her anyway. Toss another one into the deadwood pile.*

Marshall came out of his bedroom at mid-morning wearing only cotton boxer shorts while scratching his hairy chest like a male gorilla.

"Good times." He winked at Zach.

■■

Later that morning, Zach and Marshall drove out to Long Island to meet their mother, Helen Perakakis, for lunch at Jane's Café inside the Lord & Taylor's in Manhasset.

Helen was wearing a flowing purple silk dress and her signature large black-rimmed glasses. She was trim and had the perpetual ten extra pounds she insisted were solely applied to her hips. Her big curly hair resembled Cher in the movie *Moonstruck*. She was picking through her salad as her hungover sons stared into space.

"What's with the both of you? You can barely lift your heads off the table!"

"Ma, I danced my legs off" Marshall spouted.

"It was a late night," Zach added.

"And a late morning," Marshall smiled.

"Marshall, what's with all the fun and games? When are you going to get more serious like Zach, the rising corporate executive?" Helen scolded.

Marshall pleaded, "I am serious, Ma. We met some very respectable young ladies last night."

"Speak for yourself," Zach grunted.

Helen dismissed them and changed the subject. "Boys, when you go to Rhodes, you have to visit the old Jewish neighborhood surrounding the Sephardic Synagogue. All your ancestors are buried there!"

"Do you have any living ones still there?" Zach asked encouragingly.

Helen reached back in her memory. "Not that I know of. Most of them moved to either New York or Seattle."

"Seattle? Why there?"

Helen straightened herself in her chair as she counseled her adult children. "A lot of the Sephardic Jews that emigrated from Rhodes landed in New York and looked immediately for jobs. The Eastern European Ashkenazi Jews didn't even recognize my ancestors as actual Jews, which made things hard for them. Most of the Sephardim from Rhodes were fish merchants. They all came to New York through Ellis Island and tried unsuccessfully to get jobs at the Fulton Fish Market. Then, they heard about opportunities in Seattle's expanding Pike Place Fish Market. Many of the families eventually moved there to try their luck and wound up settling in the Pacific Northwest."

"Ma, why did your parents decide to stay in New York?" asked Zach.

"Don't you remember? I told you that my father was a fur merchant and he had good ties both with the Greek community and the Ashkenazim. We stayed here but it was tough for me since I was excluded by both groups until I met your father."

Marshall raised his voice in disgust, "You were discriminated by your own people?"

Helen motioned with her hand for Marshall to quiet down. "You have to understand it was a different time back then. "True" Greeks didn't recognize me as being Greek and the Ashkenazim didn't acknowledge my Jewish heritage. My father had earned both groups' respect, but, as a woman, I felt I had no way to earn it. I grew up as an Orthodox Sephardic Jew. In my upbringing, women's rights were considered secondary to the men. It was the same in the Greek-American community where women were expected to be home taking care of the house and children."

"Why did Dad treat you equally?" Zach asked.

She laughed to herself remembering those years with him. "He was a horny, good-looking young stud from Russia who emigrated here from Israel in the early days of its independence. His liberated spirit back then gave him this grandiose view of the world. He appreciated that I was an independent thinker who challenged women's unequal rights in society."

She leaned in and whispered, "He also liked that I could drive him crazy under the sheets." She smiled and pulled away to gauge their reaction. "Hey, stop smirking!" Her mind flashed to a picture of a young, virile and hairy Seymour Stillman coming out of the ocean at Long Island's Jones Beach wearing a tight bathing suit.

Then, her memory turned wicked. "But that was long before he met up with that *hooer*," she said like she was spitting nails. "The sheer mention of her name upsets me."

Zach jumped in, "Ma, don't go there. You only upset yourself when you talk about Wilma." Helen scrunched her face in outrage. Marshall settled her down. "Yes, Zach said her name. Please calm yourself. At least you helped me shy away from the thought of you and Dad together in bed. *Ewwww*."

"It will have to be another brain cell you'll have to destroy in Greece," Zach quipped.

Helen took a few major breaths as if she was in yoga class. "All right, I'm done talking. I hope your trip gives you a better appreciation of your Grecian heritage. But since you have half your father's pale-skinned Russian genes, make sure you take plenty of suntan lotion with you. The sun is deceptively strong there," she added.

Four

Boynton Road, Sheffield, South Yorkshire

"Felicity, will you stop looking at pictures of Mum!"

"O' Ellen, shut yer cake 'ole!" Felicity responded. Ellen laughed hysterically. It was their favorite saying to each other and it perpetually helped to suppress the tension between them.

The girls spoke in a Sheffieldish accent where the letters *h* and *g* somehow left the alphabet and words were commonly smashed together or shortened. Many words sounded like they were replaced with the sound *oo*. For example, the word "come" sounded like *coom*.

They were two very attractive girls in their early twenties. Ellen Williams was twenty-four years old, about five feet six inches tall with ample bosoms and a curvaceous bottom. She had a dark complexion with brown, shoulder length wavy hair and brown eyes. Her sister Felicity, two years younger, was much shorter. She was only five feet one inch tall, but was a well-proportioned copy of her sister. Felicity sported a different look than her sister, with flecks of blonde in her straight, neck length brown hair to highlight her deep blue eyes and lighter complexion.

Felicity remembered how it was with her mum alive.

Growing up, they lived near a river and wood, and in their teens, she and her sister would stay out hiking until it was dark. She could still remember her mum's beckoning call for a "wash and a hot chocolate" before they went to bed. The girls would lie awake talking long into the night telling jokes to each other until their cheeks flushed with laughter.

The girls lived in a modest row house in the South Yorkshire city of Sheffield, a small working-class city in Northern England between London and Scotland. During the 19th century, Sheffield gained an international reputation for steel production. Many innovations were developed locally, including crucible and stainless steel, fuelling an almost tenfold increase in the population during the Industrial Revolution.

They shared the house with their father George who was a taxi driver by trade. George Williams was fifty years old, six feet tall, husky, with a pasty complexion. His ancestry went back to the early settlers of Sheffield. For the last two years, their father had lost the will to drive the taxi anymore when their mother, all too quickly and painfully, succumbed to breast cancer. The three survivors had struggled with their adapting thoughts and emotions, each in their own way.

Their mother, Sophie, was the matriarch of their family. She had a Southern European heritage with French and Italian ancestors in her family tree. She had been a passionate mother and wife; she dealt with all the minutiae of running a household, and cared deeply about everyone's personal feelings and life's goals.

Ellen stared lovingly at her sister. "You got to get over your grieving! You know why Mum named you Felicity, don't you? It's because once she set eyes on you, she knew you'd give her happiness every day of her life."

Felicity calmly reflected on the past two years. Her mother had been a vibrant, fetching and well-endowed woman when she got her cancer diagnosis. "I'm going to fight it," she'd invariably say. And Sophie attacked it like a lioness. She endured endless radiation treatments and suffered through the nausea of chemotherapy.

Felicity remained Sophie's constant companion during all of it. She would make her mum tea and milk to calm her stomach, help her dose out her medications, and made sure she didn't miss any of her doctor appointments. All the activity made Felicity feel that she was actually contributing something to ease her mother's burden and not acting like a bystander to her ultimate demise.

In the year of her cancer, Felicity and Sophie became extremely close. They both shared their deepest secrets and Sophie helped her daughter cope with a future without her. "Don't settle in love," she said to her daughter. "Your heart will tell you when it's right. I knew it was destiny with your father and me when all those voices inside my head stopped objecting. It created a very calm feeling, like I didn't have to be worried ever again about being alone in this world. Your father took me to a mental state where I was safe, confident, and appreciated for who I was. I hope you find that in your life, my sweet Felicity."

Ellen brought Felicity out from her trance with a snap of her fingers. "Felicity, we need to start up our holiday trips again." It had been unforgettably hilarious when Felicity passed the legal drinking age of eighteen and the two of them would go vacationing at some Mediterranean beach locale to flirt with lads and work on their suntans.

Ellen enjoyed laying out on nude beaches so the blokes could check out her well-stocked equipment. She had ample bosoms and she was proud of her figure. She felt it was her physical attractiveness that could pluck herself out of the humdrum routines in her life. All her friends envied the stories of her sexual encounters since she could consistently charm the most eligible men to her bidding.

Her complete familiarity with her own body's urges drove her yearning to be as one with nature, especially on holiday. She singularly sought out nudist beaches since she treasured the freedom of not wearing any clothes. Felicity, however, was regularly more conservative in her freedom of expression, but accompanied her sister on these trips anyway since she cared more about being a friend and wingwoman than being restrained by her own inhibitions.

Felicity thought long and hard about Ellen's invitation. *Maybe it's a good idea to take a respite from this grief for a while. I've been killing myself over Mum to the point that I'm losing out on the best years of my life.*

"We'll see," Felicity said thoughtfully.

Five

Sheffield, England

Felicity and Ellen commuted to work on the downtown Sheffield city bus. It was a one-bus trip from their house to the Sidney Street office of Graham Cutlery where they both worked. For their daily journey, the bus ride typically required only twenty minutes door to door. The ride was eternally calming; Sheffield had more trees per person than any other city in Europe, creating a park-like vista before reaching downtown. Sometimes, when the weather was fair, the girls would ride their bikes to work. They loved to race along the sweeping neighborhood hills, weaving in and out of cars, challenging each other to reach work first. Sometimes, they would compete as if it were both competing in the Tour de France, pulling out the best in each other.

Graham Cutlery established itself in 1898 when its founder, Howard Graham, returned from the Crimean War. The company had retained its family ownership since inception, and this able leadership built Sheffield's reputation as a marquee hub for the finest cutlery in the world. Although their standards of quality never wavered, Graham's status at the top was recently being challenged by cheaper Chinese competitors. This created a trend;

Sheffield used to be a booming steel hub, but today, the quiet factory streets were sorry reminders of failed decisions by well-meaning Sheffield businessmen.

From the bus stop a few blocks away, the girls walked down the uneven paving of Sidney Street towards their building. The street was lined with brick industrial style buildings that hadn't been remodeled in fifty years. They stopped at the Graham office entrance. Freshly applied paint coated the office entry doors in a vain attempt to make it appear stately and thriving.

Felicity and Ellen made their way down a long and poorly lit hallway back to the cramped clerical office that they shared with three others. Once inside, their office mates Carole, Lindsay and Claire looked up while busy with their paperwork.

"Where's the gaffer?" Felicity said referring to their boss, Titus Graham.

"Oh, he's in a super-secret meeting on 'redundancy'," Carole said while slowing down to emphasize the last word.

Felicity had worked at Graham for the last four years since completing secondary school and vocational training in office management. She did her best to keep on Titus' good side. It was a real challenge since he was such a cranky old bugger. Titus did have an eye for the ladies and, to the girl's credit, often strutted when one of them complimented him on his attire or bawdy jokes. After work, when the girls got together at the pubs or nightclubs, they worked on their material to keep Titus happy and themselves gainfully employed.

"What are you thinking will be the results of this so-called redundancy meeting?" Felicity slowly questioned.

Felicity worried that staff layoffs would soon be coming. Businesses in the area were struggling, and she would overhear complaints now and again around the office about their company's Chinese competitors.

"Don't know," said Carole, "but the ladies in the

Shipping Department say cuts are expected across the board. You know those ladies' knowledge of company intelligence is constantly ahead of anyone else."

"Well I hope they spare us," said Felicity with a sigh. "Me sis and I can't afford to lose our jobs right now."

Later that morning, Titus Graham walked very slowly and seemingly in a daze into the clerical office wearing a face as if he had been sucking on a lemon for the past hour. He acknowledged the presence of the ladies, then moved on glumly to his tiny corner office and quietly shut the door.

The ladies soon huddled up. "We didn't get our daily *mornin' luvs*. That can't be good," said Lindsay.

"He don't look right in the 'ead," Claire postulated.

Ellen started fretting. "Someone's going to be sacked!"

"Who's it going to be?" cried Lindsay.

"Well, I'm sick and fed up of worryin' 'bout it," said Claire with a frown.

A tense fifteen minutes passed until the corner office door opened a crack so Titus could announce the verdict.

"Claire, can you please come in here," he said slowly without emotion.

"O', crap!" cried Claire.

Six

The Lunatic Laura Nightclub, Sheffield England

The girls decided to take Claire out to console her on her redundancy news. After work, they walked down to the Lunatic Laura Nightclub on the corner of High and York Streets. The place was a landmark made famous as the debut location of the chart-topping singing group, the Human League. The club was renamed after a particularly whacked-out groupie named Laura dove headfirst into the band's bass drum during a concert, putting her in a neck brace for six months.

The crowd was pretty sparse that night. As they walked into the club they saw a three-piece local band, Fondoondee, playing on the stage on the far side. They played covers of popular hits like "West End Girls" and "Walk Like an Egyptian". The girls sat on the opposite side of the club, near the bar, recapping the day's events while drinking pints of Smithwicks Ale. Claire had the lion's share of the alcohol. Her accent was in full flower.

"Claire, I'm sure another job will come your way soon," said Ellen encouragingly.

Claire shook her head with a frown, "Don't know. T'local economy is bein' challenged b'all t'ose Chinese coomp'nies sellin' t'ose cheap knock-offs. W'girls are t'ones feelin' t'squeeze."

Lindsay challenged Claire, "Didn't you say you had an uncle who ran a metal works in Doncaster?"

"*Ahhhh*, he's daft as a brush," replied Claire raising her eyes to the ceiling. "I t'ink 'e drove 'is business into t'ground 'n lost his 'ouse as well. No job t'ere."

When the band finished their set, the three lads approached the girl's table. They all wore similar black denim jackets, solid black shirts and tight jeans with black boots.

"Did you girls like our set?" lead singer Donnie probed with a bright smile.

Ellen imitated a crazed groupie and squealed, "I got all a flush with your singing, especially your rendition of 'Brand New Lover'." She pulled Donnie closer and played with his jacket.

Felicity pulled Donnie away from her sister's game playing. "Do you know 'Lessons in Love' by Level 42? It's me favorite."

"I think… so," Donnie replied while seeing that his band mates were nodding their heads. "We'll definitely play it in our next set."

Over the next two hours, the girls got pretty plastered and acted silly. They danced with each other and flirted with the band members. Felicity felt sorry for Claire but was content they could at least make her laugh. She was scared to think what she personally would be feeling if she was the one laid off that day. *With Dad still drinking and not back in the taxi, how much longer will the money from Mum's life insurance last?*

Felicity stared at Ellen and Donnie pawing at each other. *Ellen is right. We really do need a mental break, especially now that we just survived the latest cuts. All this negativity around me will most definitely drive me into the ground next to Mum.*

Ellen had moved to a secluded booth to duel with Donnie's tongue, so Felicity waited until Donnie had rejoined his band members for their next set before she came over and slid into the booth next to her sister. "I've been thinking about what you said yesterday. I think I'm ready for our holiday. I need to start thinking more about me and not about things I can't control. Let's talk to Dad. If we're sure he can stay out of bed and off the booze while we're away, I'll go ahead and make the travel arrangements."

"I'm so chuffed," Ellen said with a grin.

Seven

Boynton Road, Sheffield England

Felicity worked the early shift the next day so she could stop by the grocery store before dinner on her way home. She wanted to make her father's favorite meal that night before it got too late. Felicity did most of the cooking, and her sister helped out setting the table and cleaning the dishes. Shepherd's pie was her signature dish and her mother used to be so pleased to give up her cooking duties for the night when Felicity prepared it.

She quickly wheeled around Perry's Greengrocers and caught the bus home straight away. Hurriedly throwing off her jacket, Felicity focused on dinner preparation. Shards of onions, carrots, mushrooms and potatoes flew off her Graham cutlery as she expertly combined the vegetables with the rest of the ingredients before putting the large pot into their small but functional oven. Forty minutes later, she slowly opened the oven door and smiled as the heavenly aroma wafted out of the kitchen.

The fragrance of the entrée meandered upstairs and into the nostrils of her father who was taking one of his now-regular naps. The attraction from the scent levitated him from the bed as if he was being pulled up by a ghost.

He made his way down to the dining table just as Ellen arrived home from work.

George was just going through the motions of life like he was outside Heaven's Gate where his beloved Sophie lay waiting. Two years ago, he watched cancer take his soulmate and disintegrate her into a shell of a woman before she was fifty. Her battle with the disease had also taken its toll on him. He now was two stone, or twenty-eight pounds overweight and walked with a hunch.

After Ellen pulled off her coat and set the table, they all sat down to eat. Before they gorged themselves, they said their prayers expressing their collective wish for Sophie's eternal peace. George silently ate his shepherd's pie as if it was therapy. While he stared at his plate, the girls scrunched their faces at each other as if communicating telepathically.

Felicity stared at her sister. *Okay Sis, it's time. Ask!*

Ellen sighed. "Dad, what did you do today?"

George talked while chewing. "Somt'is, somt'at."

Ellen was frustrated at her dad's evasiveness. "Did somt'is include getting out of bed?"

He turned his head to face her. "*Oh*, bollocks!"

Ellen moved around the table to take a whiff of her dad's aroma. "Dad, you know you smell worse than the rubbish bin?"

George stared sideways at his eldest daughter. "Leave me alone."

"Dad, I'm not asking these questions to upset you. I'm asking so you can start to realise you need to pick yourself up. Mum's not coming back!"

George stared at the table, and then bored into Ellen's eyes, "It should have been me! She didn't deserve what she got."

"No. but she's been dead for a year. When's enough, enough?"

"When I say so!" he said, slamming his fork on the

table. He sighed and thought for a while. Felicity pushed another helping onto her father's plate to calm him.

He raised his eyebrows in sorrow. "I know you're right. A year is a long time to grieve. But living in this house only makes it worse."

"Well we can't even think of a new house until you're back at the taxi service bringing in money like Felicity and me."

Silence ensued. Felicity and Ellen waited until their dad finished his pie to ask in unison "Dad, we need to talk to you about something."

George still remained lost in his thoughts but eventually looked up and nodded. Felicity looked straight in his eyes and said loudly, "Dad, I really need your full attention right now."

George fired a concentrated glance at Felicity and responded, "What is it, Kitten?"

"Dad, Ellen and I want to get away for a few days holiday but we're worried about leaving you here alone to take care of yourself."

The thought of taking care of himself was now scary for George but he'd never admit it. "Oh, go on! I'm doing just fine."

"Dad, you're not," Felicity said frankly. "You're still brooding around all day drinking or taking naps. When are you going back to work full-time?" she pleaded.

George reached for an excuse under the heated examination of his daughters. "I'm ready now but Sal at the taxi company stopped calling me for shifts."

"Well, don't just take that!" Ellen yelled at him like a child. "Go on down to the office and have a chat with Sal. Tell him that you're over the grieving and you're ready to go back to work full-time. Dad, we could really use the money. Yesterday, we were just barely spared from the company's latest cuts and we desperately need to get away. But it will cause us to take a little dip into the Holiday Fund."

George tried to maintain his composure by deflecting the subject. "Oh, what do you girls know about money? When me Sophie was alive, we regularly had ample money in the Holiday Fund." He started drifting again. "You know, she never complained about anything. She always kept a positive attitude and felt that things worked themselves out." He started getting more emotional. "She was the sweetest, most thoughtful creature on God's green earth…" George started whimpering.

"Dad, get a grip!" Ellen angrily snapped.

He righted himself in his chair, resigned to his daughter's well-meaning intentions. "You're right Ellen. I have to get out of this dungeon I've gotten meself into. Maybe…," he pondered, "I'll call up me brother Percy and see if he's up to going fishing together at his cabin by Chapman's Pond."

"Great idea, Dad!" the girls sang out in harmony.

Eight

Paradise Bowling Lanes, Yonkers, New York

With just a week until their Mediterranean trip, the two brothers focused on getting themselves ready. Marshall went to the Heavenly Body Salon in Yonkers so an attendant could rip off all his back hair using hot wax. Zach went to the bookstore and bought a travel book and another one on typical Greek phrases. He and Marshall practiced mixing them into their daily conversations.

By now, they had made their travel reservations and their itinerary was set. Their plans were to spend three days in Athens and then hop over to Rhodes for the rest of their trip.

A couple days before flying off, they drove up to their favorite hangout, Paradise Lanes in Yonkers, to bowl some frames. There, they started brainstorming their trip strategies with the proprietor, their favorite cousin Alex.

Marshall said proudly, "Although it was inspiring to hear about what Ma said about our Greek ancestry, between you and me, my focus for this trip is strictly the Greek dishes—on the plate and in my bed."

"I'm with ya there, bro, but there's more." Zach was

flipping through his Greek phrasebook and attempted to say a word. "My trip is going to be about *oikogenatalia*–family."

"That's *oikogeneia*, Zach," chuckled Alex.

"Whatever," Zach said with a smirk. "As my Greek friend Dmitri recommended, I definitely want to see some of the historic sites in Athens like the Acropolis, the Parthenon, and the 1896 Olympic Stadium."

Marshall made a pose. "Yeah, I wanna see some of those Greek god statues so I can do some personal comparisons."

Alex jumped in, "Especially the ones that have had their balls cut off."

"I heard that there are topless beaches in Rhodes," Marshall stated wishfully.

"I'd go topless!" Zach offered with a grin.

"Yeah." Marshall closed his eyes and conjured up a vision; *a whole beach covered with naked skin steaming with fragrant coconut oil under the hot Mediterranean sun.*

Zach closed his eyes as if Marshall's vision would jump into his head. He then walked over to his brother, held him by the shoulders and preached, "Moses, take me to this land of milk and honey!"

Marshall smiled. "I can hardly wait!"

Nine

Dirty Laundry - A Lingerie Shoppe, Sheffield, England

"That shows off your bosoms nicely," said Ellen staring at Felicity with pride.

They were in the lingerie store, Dirty Laundry, trying on fun frocks for their trip. It had been a whirlwind jumble of events after making the decision to go on holiday.

After their dad picked himself up and arranged to be at Uncle Percy's house for some fishing, the girls set a plan in motion to get more fit. Both girls religiously rode their bikes back and forth to work every day. The hard commute up and down the suburban hills of Sheffield toned the girls up. Neither of them had much weight to lose, so the increased exercise gave them even more definition to their womanly curves.

Felicity sped through her household chores as if ironing and washing were Olympic events. When she looked in the mirror, she saw hints of her new muscled frame.

Felicity also splurged at the hairdressers and dyed her hair fully blonde. She liked herself that way because it reminded her how sunny and playful she used to feel before her Mum died. *With a bronze tan, my blue eyes will pop*

31

on this trip.

Her new look raised her mating prospects. She never had a problem with the local lads; however, she tired of them. They all were the same; most were either stuck in a lifetime rut, or running as far away from Sheffield as they could.

Her dates were predictable. They would pick her up in whatever car they could find and take her to the pictures. Then, when the lights were low, they would chat up while trying some supposedly strategized move. Felicity would counter with her famous slow karate chop to deflect their attempt, leaving them to kiss for a while.

After the movie, the lad would take her to a pub for dinner and drinks and attempt to dazzle her in his raucous Sheffieldish dialect. She would see through the whole scheme and leave the lads with their tail between their legs. She rarely slept with these blokes unless there was a serious burning in her loins or she allowed herself to get too drunk to know better.

She finalized the air and hotel reservations for the trip with her travel agent. She was thrilled that they were able to secure one of their favorite places, the Lindos Hotel. It was in the middle of a row of seaside inns with a gorgeous view of the Mediterranean Sea.

She also browsed through bookstores looking for a holiday page turner. She found one, *The Prince of Tides* by Pat Conroy. She loved reading on holiday since it transported her to places she'd never been. The newsagent recommended the book as a gripping roller coaster of emotion. It sounded like a chance to mentally get away for a while.

The sexy lingerie was Ellen's idea. Ellen was so thrilled with her own figure's final perfections, she pulled out some of her old skimpy two-piece bikinis to prove how they now fit her. She later chided with Felicity that the swimsuits were not likely to be worn much anyway between the nude beaches and the expected after-hours *boinking.*

Ellen had her own reasons for retreating. The challenges at home with her father, and the stress of maintaining employment at work drove negativity into her head like ear mites. It was all she could take before her emotions would spontaneously combust.

Felicity gazed at herself in the dressing room mirror. She was ready to deserve better than the blokes in Sheffield and anticipated a meeting with an exotic international hunk in Rhodes. She made flirty poses and laughed to herself. *I may not have Ellen's Maserati seduction engine, but my Jaguar one should do just fine.* As she walked out of the dressing room, she remarked to the store clerk, "I'll take it!" It was a black negligee. *I hope I get to use it.*

Ten

En route to Athens, Greece

Marshall and Zach's trip to Greece started off a bit rocky. Trying to cut costs, Zach had booked passage for them on Sparta Airlines, a low-fare charter company. Sparta flew junkets to Greece from JFK once a week on a rented Boeing 747 jet. Because the price was so reasonable, the flight was very popular and people were packed in like Zach's daily commuter train.

Since Zach waited long until after tax season to book the tickets, he and Marshall had to settle for the worst seats on the plane. They muttered when they found their seats in the middle row of the smoking section. They were suddenly dreading the overnight flight to Athens.

On the other side of Marshall sat a heavyset businessman that had obvious sleep apnea problems. The big man's sleep pattern had a routine—he built up wheezes until his eyes popped opened, signaling an expectant explosion, and then gasped for his next breath. Just in the man's act of breathing, he'd continually shake a rubbery and highly annoyed Marshall aching for at least one wink of sleep. Marshall heckled the man's actions without relief. He leaned into Zach on his other side.

On Zach's other side, sat a rail-thin, greasy-haired

man with an oily mustache and balding hair pressed flat with a bad comb-over. He spent the entire trip chain-smoking thick Macanudo cigars and blowing smoke rings into Zach's nostrils.

Zach wore a hooded sweatshirt which he pulled over his face like a mummy to block the smoke. The guys turned toward each other to get away from their neighbors, eyeing the armrest between them like a warrior's prize for a coliseum duel.

"Hey bro, I'm dying over here. Don't take my armrest too," Marshall pleaded.

"Well, I can't rest either breathing in what the Marlboro Man here is blowing." Zach responded.

"Rock, paper scissors!" the shouted in unison.

A sexy flight attendant came by with drinks as the game was staged. She smiled brightly at Marshall to catch his interest.

"I'll take some of that action. Ten dollars on Mel Gibson over here", she smiled over at Marshall.

"You're on!" Zach gleamed.

They both counted to three. Marshall held two fingers out while Zach held his hand stretched out. Marshall simulated a cut with his two fingers over Zach's stretched hand.

"Scissors beat paper!" Marshall announced.

They counted again. Marshall held two fingers out while Zach showed a closed fist. Zach slammed Marshall's two fingers with his fist.

Zach smiled. "Rock beats scissors. Last one for the armrest."

They counted a final time. Marshall showed an open hand while Zach displayed a fist. "Paper covers rock," Marshall exclaimed. "Thank you very much."

Marshall grabbed the armrest leaving Zach to pout while sucking in secondhand smoke.

The flight attendant smiled widely as Zach forked over a ten spot.

The movie on the flight was *The Princess Bride,* a classic fairytale with swordplay, giants, and an evil Prince. Zach loved Billy Crystal in the movie who played Miracle Max, a retired wizard with a heavy New York accent. He couldn't help but think that his own life paralleled a fairytale, hoping to find answers about his ancestry and insights into his future. *It about time I got away from my nudging parents and the Alcatraz of an office. I don't know what is ahead but at least I'll finally have the freedom to make decisions as I please.*

They made it into Athens at dawn the next morning. They both were mentally fried and couldn't wait for a long nap.

■■■ı

The Hotel Socrates in downtown Athens was a budget hotel with spartan amenities. It was located on Aharnon Street in the center of the city. When the guys arrived at the hotel, their room wasn't ready, so they crashed on stiff metal lobby chairs.

When considering hotels for the trip, Zach thought that the two of them would barely use their Athens hotel room. Therefore, he weighted their vacation funds more to the resort hotel in Rhodes. The only redeeming feature of the Socrates was that its central location allowed them walking access to the tourist sites.

The hotel was sandwiched on a busy street between a gyro stand and a nightclub. The hotel name was printed in old Greek style on the square awning above the entrance; the sign looked cheesy giving the entrance a forgettable appearance.

At mid-morning, Zach woke up groggily in the lobby with a crick in his neck from sleeping in a balled-up position. He struggled to move his head and finally stretched his neck using circular movements. Scoping out the dimly lit lobby, he realized a deadness in activity. All he could see was a couple of elderly folk sitting at a table in the eating area playing a card game. He turned to Marshall who remained draped over a cheap yellow vinyl couch like a dead starfish.

In the early afternoon, their room was ready. Zach and Marshall carried their heavy suitcases up four long flights of stairs to their room. Their hotel room was tiny, drab and stifling. There was barely enough room for two thin twin beds. A TV hung from the top of the wall facing the beds to avoid taking up any more of the limited floor space. A central light sporting a cracked globe hung from the low ceiling. There was a simple rectangular sconce over each bed and a small night table between them. On the opposite side of the beds hung a picture of the Parthenon; upon Zach's further inspection, he noticed it was a completed jigsaw puzzle with two pieces missing. When he moved to look out the window, the only view he had was the rooftop utilities unit of the building next door. *Paradise, this ain't,* Zach drily commented to himself.

Marshall gave a quick glance over the room's accouterments, smiled, and then summarily crashed on the nearest bed. Feeling claustrophobic, Zach decided to check out the stores and restaurants near the hotel.

Looking around outside the hotel entrance, Zach witnessed that all the stores seemed to be closed. It was a Sunday and the whole area was eerily quiet. However, he spotted a few restaurants open for a snack. He tried out his Greek skills at a small café by asking for *dolmades.* By the time he got back to the room, Marshall was awake and watching the TV.

"Zach, I can't find any English-speaking channels." He pointed to the set. "These guys talk so fast I can't even catch one Greek word. What did you find outside?"

"It's dead out there. A couple of food places seem to be open though."

Marshall rubbed his hairy stomach underneath his

shirt. "I'm starved."

Zach remembered Dmitri's invitation so he picked up the phone and got through to the Zegras Family Restaurant to confirm it was open for dinner. The restaurant had a dinner party that night but was able to squeeze the guys in.

"We're set for dinner, bro!" Zach said proudly.

Marshall rose from his bed. "What are we waiting for?"

"Marshall, be prepared that this city smells just like the Jersey Turnpike from all the diesel fuel from the buses. Walking around, I could hardly breathe!"

Marshall turned to his shoulder and lifted his arm. "Can't smell worse than that." He reached into his toiletry bag for his deodorant.

"By the way, the front desk said the nightclub is closed but will be open tomorrow. So tomorrow, let's plan on doing some tourist sites and check out the Greek social scene in the evening."

■■■

Athens streets were gridded like a labyrinth unlike the rectangular shape that Zach and Marshall were familiar with at home. Each street seemed to run into each other haphazardly. It was as if the original city architects never had an overall plan and worked fully independently from each other.

The guys meandered up and down various streets looking for the location of the Zegras Family Restaurant. Zach was excited to give Dmitri his personal critique of its food. He was also quite partial to any place that started with the letter Z. After circling the same street a few times, they finally found the restaurant.

Eleven

Zegras Family Restaurant - Athens, Greece

Marshall and Zach asked for a table on the patio overlooking the city but were told it was reserved for a private party, so they sat inside.

A thin, young waiter came to the table. "Welcome to Zegras'. I am Damien. I'm here to serve you. Here are your menus."

The dimly-lit restaurant seated five tables outside and fifteen tables inside with a bar on one side. Each table had a salmon colored table cover with matching cloth chairs. A lone painting of a flower vase hung on the far wall. Greek music tinkled through scratchy speakers. Wall sconces and small lights attached to the industrial foam ceiling tiles provided a yellow glow.

Marshall and Zach scanned the menu. They both settled on the stuffed tomatoes with spinach and cheese for an appetizer. Zach ordered halibut and Marshall splurged on lobster for their entrees. Growing up in a Jewish home, they guys never ate shellfish in the house and their parents discouraged it while eating out together. It only drove Marshall's sense of defiance and attraction seeing lobster on the menu. The barbaric act of cracking open the shell and stabbing at the flesh abated his internal rebelliousness.

The stuffed tomato appetizer arrived cold. The guys thought it was strange and questioned whether it was the normal way of preparation. Marshall was so hungry he practically inhaled it anyway. Zach feared eating the dish. Instead, he focused on the decor and compared it to Greek diners like the Athena Diner back home.

They waited an additional thirty minutes for their entrée. Marshall dug into his lobster like a medieval ogre but stopped quickly as he discovered that the fish was gritty and dirty. Zach's halibut arrived tough and cold with an odd odor. They called Damien over and requested new dishes.

When Damien tried to clean the lobster right there on the table, Marshall's anger erupted. He demanded to see the manager. After another fifteen minutes, Krystos, Owner and Head Chef, arrived at their table. Krystos was beefy–three hundred pounds on a light day, and was sweating profusely through his hairy torso. Drips of sweat trickled off his balding head.

"My son Damien says you two Americans do not like my cooking!" Krystos boomed in his broken English accent. "Look over there in corner. I get two-star Michelin rating. The best in all of Athens!"

Marshall thought the sign was a fake. "Well, it wasn't the best today," Marshall defended. "My lobster was sandy and gross. My brother's fish smelled like your farts and it was tough as my shoe!"

"Hey, you insult my cooking! I take you Americans outside and I throw you off terrace," Krystos threatened.

Marshall sized up Krystos–*like a sumo wrestler. He didn't look like he moved too fast. A couple of punches at that overhanging belly and he'd fold over like a fir tree.*

Marshall abruptly got out of his chair ready to accept Krystos' threat. Zach jumped up between the two.

"Hey, calm down! Krystos, we're sorry to insult you. We didn't mean disrespect. We just got here from New

York City and your cousin Dmitri Kourabas told me this establishment was the finest place for fish in Greece." Krystos stepped back and Marshall sat back down.

"*Ahhhh*, Cousin Dimi!" He calmed down and he reached into his decaying memory. "You should have said something earlier. He call me about two people coming to Greece."

Krystos looked over the plates. He inspected the lobster, tasted a piece of the tail and promptly spat it out with a grimace. He then poked Zach's halibut and smelled it. It was rubbery and the aroma smelled like his armpits at the end of a work night.

He nodded like a bobblehead as he spoke. "All right, Krystos busy with private party on terrace. I rushed meals out before my 'quality' check. Okay, here's what I do for you, friends of Cousin Dimi." He looked around so no other patrons could hear. He leaned in and whispered, "I replace meals and get you bottle ouzo on house if you keep quiet."

The guys looked at each other and shrugged. They appreciated the gesture and were too hungry to argue further. The guys had always wanted to try ouzo so they accepted Krystos' offer.

The new plates came out fifteen minutes later. The lobster was clean and succulent and the halibut was flaky and fragrant, freshly scented with oregano. Marshall walked back to the kitchen entrance to thank Krystos for the revised fare. After closing the kitchen, Krystos came out with his promised full bottle of ouzo. By then, all the diners had left the restaurant.

Krystos opened the bottle and poured generous servings to himself, Zach and Marshall. "You like ouzo?" he barked.

"We've never had it," Zach replied.

"Never had ouzo? The drink of gods? You two true virgins!" said Krystos with a smile. The liquor was clear with a sweet licorice scent. Zach sniffed a few trial times before getting ready to drink.

Krystos stepped in between Zach and his glass. "You don't sniff ouzo. You drink it, like so!" He grabbed his glass and took a major swig followed by a two second burp. Marshall and Zach imitated Krystos by simultaneously chugging down the liquid. They stared at each other as the initial sweet licorice taste rapidly led to the sensation of swallowing lit butane gas. They both gasped.

Krystos reveled in his role as drinking teacher as he traded ouzo shots with the guys until the bottle was empty. By then, the three of them were absolutely sloshed.

"You boys okay for Americans. Maybe one of you can take out my daughter Aphrodite while you're here. She speaks good English and needs to meet smart boys like you." Krystos slurred.

Zach pondered through his fuzzy brain what Krystos' daughter would look like. He gauged Krystos' size and hairiness, and deferred to Marshall for the honors of her company.

Marshall, now completely drunk, was on autopilot. He slurred, "How about tomorrow night?"

Zach furthered the arrangements. "There's a nightclub by the hotel."

Krystos agreed to have Aphrodite there at the hotel lobby the next night at eight o'clock. Krystos then called his brother Plato over from the bar to taxi the guys back to the hotel. When they arrived back at their hotel, they slowly staggered up the four endless flights of stairs to their room. Both of them immediately passed out after plopping on the beds like Mexican cliff divers.

■■■ı

"*Aaaarrrrgggggg!*" Zach woke up at ten the next morning with the worst hangover of his life. His brain felt as if someone stuffed a barrel of tumbleweeds between his ears. His body ached in places he didn't know existed and he stared at the wall trying to remember the previous night's dinner. He inspected the conditions of the clothes he slept in as he wondered how he made it to bed.

Marshall was snoring loudly. He commonly talked in his sleep and most of his words were unintelligible. However, while Zach was getting off of his bed, he distinctly heard Marshall exude a *grrunnnt* and then "Oh, Aphrodite" with an audible *coo* as if she were right there in bed with him.

Zach stretched his eyes open and roused Marshall. "Wake up bro! Today is the day to see the sights of our freaking homeland!" he announced. Marshall put his pillow on top of his head. "Give me a minute to come back to reality. I was having such a nice dream."

Zach reset his expectations that they would get themselves ready for touring before noon. They both weren't moving too fast.

The hotel offered a free breakfast but they arrived several hours too late, so the guys sauntered over to the stand next door and grabbed gyros. The spiced lamb inside the warm pita bread aroused his sleepy senses. Marshall liked the creamy tzatziki sauce and Zach remarked that his shirt liked it too. They both sighed as the meal triggered their interest to finally get moving to see the sights.

Zach played tour guide and announced, "All right, it's already two o'clock; we don't have much time to the see much. I'm hoping we can do the Acropolis, the Parthenon and the original Olympic Arena before it's time to get back to the hotel."

"Yes, for my date with Aphrodite," Marshall smiled wryly.

Twelve

Athens, Greece

"Take my picture, Zach!" Marshall beamed as he stood in back of a headless goddess. He posed trying to make his head replace the one omitted on the statue. They were touring the Acropolis Museum. The high ceilings and the white marble walls gave the museum a dramatic presence. Rows of broken and restored statues lined its sides.

"Wow, that must've hurt!" Zach exclaimed as he saw the Doryphoros statue with its genitals worn down.

They walked through the Parthenon on the Acropolis and gazed in sheer admiration. The Parthenon was the remains of a temple dedicated to the Greek goddess Athena, the patron goddess of the ancient city of Athens. It was built a little before 500 BC, and sat on the Acropolis, a hill overlooking the city.

It was a warm, sunny but smoggy spring day. The temperature had reached eighty five degrees when Zach took a break to sun himself on one of the large benches outside. Zach reflected on the moment. *I've never felt this happy to be Greek, to be part of a culture that created this magnificent structure. It was so ahead of its time in architecture and art.* He imagined living in the ancient time, wearing togas and learning mathematics from the inventors.

He stood up on the bench and checked the time. "Hey Marsh, let's get to the Olympic Stadium before it closes!" he yelled over.

■■■

The Panathenaic Stadium hosted the first modern Olympic Games in 1896 and remained the oldest stadium in the world. Reconstructed from the remains of an ancient Greek stadium, it was the only stadium in the world made entirely of white marble. Walking up to it from the street, the guys were overwhelmed by the immense structure, with rows upon rows of benches seemingly ascending up to the sky. An entrance plaque stated it could hold 80,000 spectators. On the stadium floor, a tight oval track edged the field. Inside the oval were spaces for a number of track events including: the long jump, javelin throw, and pole vault. One side of the stadium was gated but the other side was free and open to the public.

The guys were as awed as devout Catholics visiting the Vatican. Zach remembered when he had the privilege to personally see Bruce Jenner win his Olympic gold decathlon medal in Montréal in 1976 while on summer Jewish travel camp. The Olympics were in his blood.

Envisioning the ancient competitions, Zach looked over the field and challenged Marshall to a contest. They were constantly competitive with each other, whether it was playing HORSE out on the basketball court, Strat-O-Matic, the baseball simulation card game, or making bets at the bowling alley. The sight of the stadium accelerated the flow of their competitive juices. They agreed that the loser of the bet had to drink a half bottle of ouzo in three gulps straight down. They both recalled the morning's hangovers. The incentive was in place!

Since the arena was fairly stark, they felt they could only hold running and jumping events. The three events they selected were the hundred meter, the four-hundred meter and the long jump.

A smattering of tourists were milling about on the track. Marshall coerced a college-aged kid wearing a University of Michigan sweatshirt and his friend to agree to be judges. The guys placed a judge on either side of the race course so one acted as the starter and the other determined the winner.

As they were assembling the competition, word-of-mouth began to spread amongst the tourists. They were starting to collect their own side bets with heated interest. Odds opened with Marshall getting the majority of early action on account of his greater size and seemingly louder authority. Zach heard the rumors and knew he had to make a quick start at the first race since the hundred meter dash was his best shot of the three events.

They both stepped to the line as the starter screamed, "One, two, three, go!" Zach took a quick lead as Marshall pumped wildly to catch up. They were even at the midpoint line when Marshall started breathing heavily and eventually dropped to the ground with only twenty-five meters left to the finish. First round, Zach!

They took a full ten minutes to catch their breath before the second event. In the meantime, the crowd was growing as word got to the street that there was betting action on the competition. Individual bettors in the crowd coaxed the guys to participate in their own wagers but Zach and Marshall only took slices of bets when they didn't have to pay if they lost.

The next event was the four hundred meter dash, one full lap around the track. Zach remembered that Olympic athletes typically complete the race in about forty-five seconds so he felt he could kill himself for at least that long. Zach looked over to Marshall and the starting line. Marshall sneered angrily back at Zach trying to psyche him out. When the starter shouted, "Go!" Zach took off as he did for the hundred meter. Marshall, however, was Steady Freddie, keeping a strong but consistently moderate speed. The difference in pace allowed Zach to extend his lead as he hit the slight embankment of the first turn. He eagerly turned back and could see Marshall well behind calmly pushing forward. Zach's exhilaration got the best of him as his heart and breathing accelerated beyond control. By the time he reached the three-hundred meter mark Zach was wheezing heavily. He looked back to gauge his lead and tumbled over his feet.

Marshall saw Zach go down; Instead of helping him up, he patted his brother on the back, then cruised to the finish. The ever-growing partisan crowd cheered in delight. Tied up!

Marshall walked back to check on his brother's condition and said, "This scene is crazy! Look at all these people!"

Zach only had a knee scratch but took almost fifteen minutes to recover his wind. By that time, the stadium was starting to get dark. The building crowd started to grow restless as if they were overpaying customers.

The guys set the rules for the long jump. Three attempts. If a foot touched the white jump line, that contestant's jump was disqualified. The long jump area had about fifty meters for a runway in front of a jumping platform which extended into a sandy pit twenty feet by ten feet. Someone had previously painted marks on the side of the pit indicating the various distances.

Zach jumped first. One judge was lined up at the jump platform, the other was assigned to measure the distance. Zach ran hard and fast until he met the line with his shoe and launched into the pit. The distance—a mere six feet. Marshall's fans jeered Zach's weak attempt.

Marshall's first turn was better—eight feet, and he grinned to taunt his brother. Zach followed with his second attempt. Although it was better than his first, the jump platform judge said he fouled.

Marshall's second attempt was better than his first— nine feet, and his faithful cheered in gratitude. Before his last attempt, Zach stared at the runway and visualized a proper body arc and stretch. He took off, leapt, stretched and fell into the pit with a firm nine and a half feet! A new leader! Zach's minority followers sporadically applauded.

Marshall reached the starting line for his last attempt with the betting crowd now chanting his name "Mar- shall! Mar-shall! Mar-shall!"

Marshall took off down the runway. The crowd noise grew as he flailed his arms and snorted. With bulging eyes, he lifted himself from the platform like he was jumping between rooftops. He glided up and made flapping movements with his arms propelling him halfway into the pit area. He crashed down with a guttural scream and plopped into the pit spraying grains of sand in all directions.

All eyes went to the measuring judge who signaled the distance of ten feet to win the event! Marshall exulted at the judge's ruling and that the competition was finally over. However, in the distance, the jumping platform judge was waving his arms and shaking his head frantically.

"He stepped over the line!" the judge announced.

The boisterous crowd booed at the decision while a sprinkling of tourists put Zach on their shoulders.

After some minor grumbling to the judge, Marshall came over to Zach and pulled him away and hugged him tight. "That was awesome! How'd we do on the take?" Marshall asked.

"I won twenty dollars and a whole bunch of Greek drachmae," Zach replied

Marshall patted his little brother on the back. "Good, now you can buy the ouzo!"

Thirteen

MONDAY, MAY 25, 1987

The Bronx Discotheque, Athens, Greece

On the way back to the hotel, Zach found an open liquor store and used some of the wager proceeds to buy the earned bottle of ouzo.

Upon entering the hotel room, Zach spotted three plastic cups. He swiftly opened the twist-off ouzo bottle. He wanted Marshall drunk before he met Aphrodite.

Zach barely remembered the offer from last night and didn't see any pictures of Aphrodite around the restaurant. His vision of her was a version of Krystos with breasts. On the other hand, Marshall maintained a wet-dream image of Aphrodite; his mental picture was a starlet in flowing robes standing amongst rose petals. Zach smiled in anticipation. *I guess we'll see which of us has the right vision!*

Marshall stared at the bottle and cups. "All right, let's get this over already." Marshall beckoned to Zach who poured the half bottle into three cups on the small night table. Marshall downed the first cup with a smile— and then gagged. Zach encouraged him to drink the second one right away so Marshall grabbed the cup, held his breath like he was about to dive into a deep lake, and then gulped the drink down. *Buuuuurpegog.* Marshall started looking pale. He still had one more cup to drink.

Zach thought of letting Marshall slide out of it but then thought the better of it. He started to remember all the times in their childhood when Marshall beat him in contests so he was going to make sure to savor this one.

Marshall stepped away from the tiny table and declared, "I need a break. I'm going to shower and dress, and before we go downstairs, I'll do the third cup."

After Marshall was ready to go downstairs, he raised his last glass of ouzo high in the air, shouted "*L'chaim*" and gulped it down in one swig. It was ten minutes to eight when Zach reminded Marshall of their plan to meet Aphrodite in front of their hotel and walk next door to the nightclub.

Twenty minutes later, Plato arrived with Aphrodite. He opened the door for her very professionally. Marshall turned as she exited the car, craning his neck for his first glimpse. What he was presented with was a large, colorful look-alike of Krystos Zegras, the massive restaurant owner. Zach looked over at his brother gathering in the vision. *Two points for me!*

Aphrodite was hefty. "She looks like a defensive tackle!" Marshall murmured under his breath. Aphrodite also looked a bit punked out. She had pink and black hair with heavy makeup and well-manicured eyebrows. She wore matching earrings and a necklace made out of black beads and plastic shapes of a rectangle and a triangle. Her undershirt was neon green with pink trim that highlighted her hair. Her dress top had black and gray prints of skulls and crossbones. Her dress was short and poofy, but thankfully for Marshall, was complemented by fully covered black leggings.

As Marshall slowly walked up and introduced himself, he gauged her to be about twenty years old. She spoke English well but with a sultry tone. She was tall, five feet ten inches, and seemed sure of herself despite the extra poundage. She seemed eager to meet the guys and practice her English. Her smile improved her look immeasurably.

The three of them casually walked next door to the nightclub. Marshall especially liked the club's name, the Bronx Discotheque. Aphrodite was familiar with the place so had dressed appropriately. Inside the club, the ceiling and all the walls were black, creating a Goth-like mood. Zach noticed about ten tables located near the bar and black vinyl booths surrounding the dance floor. The bar took one entire side of the club.

At this hour on a Monday night, it was pretty empty. There were only about ten people milling about. Zach asked Aphrodite what she wanted to drink. She ordered a screwdriver and the guys stuck to local beer. "Rhythm's Gonna Get You" by Gloria Estefan loudly reverberated through the room.

The club got busier as the night progressed. Marshall was content playing his mating game with Aphrodite. As the ouzo and beer made its way through his system, Marshall thought that Aphrodite was starting to look halfway decent. When the deejay put on "I Wanna Dance With Somebody" by Whitney Houston, Aphrodite squealed with delight and pulled Marshall onto the dance floor.

Zach saw their coupling as his opportunity to take a bathroom break. As he walked along the bar, he couldn't help noticing some strange behavior amongst the crowd. The guys and girls seem to be pretty patient in putting the moves over each other. Zach panned his view over to a group of girls bunched tightly over a bar table. One of the girls pulled herself away and gazed back at Zach. With her white blonde hair and her disco clothes, Zach dubbed her the Disco Princess. Her ice blue eyes stayed with him for a second as he moved toward the restroom.

He hyperventilated next to the urinal as he garnered the strength to approach the princess. He stared at a mirror. *Well, no time like the present. This is why you came to*

Greece. Go for it!

He left the bathroom, took a deep breath, and made his way back over to her. On further inspection, she wore a fun Madonna knock-off dress that was black with red frills. As he approached, she maintained his glance and then started talking hurriedly with her companions. One of them smiled back at her with a high-pitched giggle. Zach quickly diverted his route to her table and ordered a shot of ouzo from the bar to compose himself. *If it's only one shot, I can deal with it.*

With the liquid courage fortifying his confidence, he made his way back over to the girls. Stopping in front of Disco Princess, he gave her his most assured smile, and asked her to dance.

Meanwhile, Aphrodite and Marshall had taken a break from their own dancing and had sat back down at their booth. While finishing their drinks, they observed Zach and Disco Princess make their way onto the dance floor. "Addicted to Love" by Robert Palmer blared out of the speakers. Disco Princess danced provocatively. She energetically swayed back and forth enlarging Zach's magic mushroom. Zach suddenly became conflicted between enjoying the dance and not showing everyone his growing hard on.

"Your brother has some nice moves," exclaimed an impressed Aphrodite.

Marshall had his eyes on the other dancer. "Yeah, and the girl he's with is pretty hot herself. Do you know her?" he replied.

"Yes. She's one of the regulars here."

Marshall was puzzled seeing such a gorgeous knockout untethered from an expected throng of men in heat. "She's so sexy looking, why aren't guys hanging all over her?"

"She's a lesbian," Aphrodite said matter-of-factly.

"What?" Marshall said with puzzlement.

"Yes, and so are her companions. They're all

lesbians. See those guys there?" She pointed over to the other tables. "They're nancy-boys," she said without derision in her voice.

Marshall started shaking his head. "I'm not catching this," he pleaded.

Aphrodite said slowly so Marshall could fully understand, "Didn't you know? This is a gay club!" Marshall's eyes widened with surprise.

He suavely collected himself. "Are you gay?" Marshall cocked his head closer hear her answer.

"Sometimes. Sometimes, I'm not," Aphrodite returned with a radiant smile.

"Do you think Zach knows he's dancing with a lesbian?" Marshall pondered.

Aphrodite threw open her hands. "Why does it matter?"

"Because I am familiar with that signature mating dance of his," he schooled. "He's trying his best moves on her."

"*Oh...*"

Marshall winked at Aphrodite knowingly. "Let's help him out."

Aphrodite and Marshall went back out onto the dance floor. Zach immediately danced his way up to Marshall and boasted, "Isn't she spectacular?"

"Yeah, but she's not buying what you're selling, bro," he said through the loud dance music.

"*Huh?*" Zach replied but he couldn't hear through the bass beat. The song ended and Disco Princess pulled Zach away to her table. Zach called to Marshall, "Gotta go. See you later."

Back at the table she introduced herself as Heather from Sweden and pointed to her perky companion. "This is my friend, Mindy from Russia." Mindy was black haired, cute, and also wore clothes à la Madonna.

"Hi, my name is Zach from New York City."

"Mindy and I were chatting, Zach from New York

City, and we wondered if you wanted to join our little party?" Heather made puppy dog eyes encouraging Zach's consent.

"That could be arranged," he said in his most nonchalant tone.

"By way, you stay at hotel next door?" Mindy asked in a Russian-laced English accent. "If so, can we come over?"

Zach thought about the expected conclusion of Marshall and Aphrodite's date. He tried to encourage an alternative location to Heather and Mindy. "How about your place?" Zach offered instead. "My brother at the booth over there is looking like he might need our room for the night."

Mindy followed Zach's gaze over to Marshall. "He with Aphrodite!" she announced to the other girls. She looked back at Zach. "All right! She first-class Greek goddess." Mindy smiled. "*Hmmm*. Okay, here another idea. I met guy last night, Justin from Australia. I know he has two-room suite. I bet he host party for us. Wait here. I call his room."

While Mindy went to use the pay phone near the bathroom, Zach sized up his chances with Heather. *She is stunning but things are progressing almost too easily for me. Is it the ouzo or my American accent? Mindy's really cute too. I might even have a chance for a career-first threesome with Mindy and Heather. Nah, Mindy just slept with Justin from Australia last night so they'll probably pair up. I guess I'll just have to suffice with eating Swedish dumplings. This is almost too much for me.*

Mindy came back from the pay phone. "Is ok," she said. Heather then grabbed Mindy's hand and walked out of the nightclub with Zach following close behind. From across the hall Zach signaled to Marshall, "You got the room for the night. I'm good!" He smiled putting both his thumbs up.

Marshall looked at Aphrodite with a smile. "He's good," he repeated to her and then he laughed.

■■■

Justin from Australia sized up Zach as he opened his hotel room door. "G'day mate." He was thin and wiry with a skinhead haircut. His Australian accent was barely decipherable. Zach thought he seemed a bit older than him, close to thirty years old and had aura of worldly experience.

Justin invited them all into his suite. The living room was small, but comfortable for the four of them–two blue cloth and wood sofa chairs flanked by a matching loveseat. In front of the U-shaped configuration was a rectangular wood coffee table which had a mirror laying on its surface with four lines of coke neatly lined out on top. There was a bedroom off the living room with an adjoining bathroom inside. Right past the entrance was a little kitchenette with a microwave oven, a stove and a sink.

"Care for a line?" He asked casually.

Zach had tried cocaine twice before. The first time was before a Dan Fogelberg concert during freshman year in college; the second, on New Year's Eve with Marshall and two bimbettes. He carefully weighed the situation and faked a casual "sure." He proceeded to snort one of the lines on the coffee table, using a five-hundred drachmae note he found in his pocket.

They took turns doing the lines and Zach's nose started feeling numb. His nostrils felt like huge garages and each inhale felt as crisp as a Minnesota winter day. He became hyperaware of his surroundings.

Heather started kissing Zach intently and he immediately got hard. Mindy was kissing Justin and it left Zach strategizing how he could snag the only bedroom for him and Heather. Heather must have been reading his mind and moved toward the bedroom. Heather announced, "I have to use the bathroom. Mindy want to join me?" Zach wasn't ready for her to get up. *Why is it that women always have to go to the bathroom together?*

While his man muscle went back down to normal, Zach got up and grabbed a water glass from the kitchenette. He ran the faucet for a while and drank a half a glass of water.

When he turned back away from the faucet, Justin was standing right in front of him. Without pretense, Justin grabbed Zach's crotch and wriggled his fingers. Zach was in shock. He slowly fumed, "What the fuck are you doing?!"

"Oh come on now, mate. I saw you getting a bit excited there with Heather. I thought you were just getting warmed up for me!"

"I was getting warmed up all right!" Zach screamed, "For *her!*"

"Oh, then you'd be waiting forever for her, mate" Justin said. "She's strictly a lesbo. She told me that last night! She's shacking up with Mindy tonight."

"Then why were you and Mindy licking each other's tonsils before?" Zach asked with his chin stuck forward.

"She and I had a poke last night but she's really a lemon. I didn't plan on shagging her tonight. Last night I told her I wanted to play hide the salami with a looker and *poof;* she brought you right to me room."

Zach sat down on the couch trying his best to deal with the circumstances. He was so puzzled, he needed to know more. He got up, went to the bedroom door and checked the knob. The door was now locked. As he put his ear to the door he heard Heather moaning from inside the bedroom.

Zach turned his head back and forth repeatedly. Justin broke Zach's consciousness. "Hey mate, I thought things were cool since you were hanging out down at the nightclub. "

What does that have to do with anything?" Zach stared at him with sarcasm.

"Well mate," he said confrontationally. "Since it's a gay club, I had this wild idea that you were primo talent!"

"A gay bar?" Zach said doubtingly to himself. This situation was all unfamiliar territory for Zach. He had never met a gay person before in his life and didn't know how to process his jumbled logic and emotions. He then jumped up abruptly and stated in an Aussie accent,

"No offense mate, but I gotta go. Thanks for the blow! Don't be sad if I don't give you a hug."

He stormed out of the room. He then walked down one flight to his hotel floor. As he neared the room, he noticed Aphrodite's leggings hanging on the knob so he knew he was going to have to find alternative sleeping arrangements for the night.

Fourteen

Fontana Hotel, Rhodes, Greece

"Now we're *talkin'!*" yelled Marshall in his most bravado New York accent as he looked out over the pool at the Fontana Hotel in Lindos, on the island of Rhodes. *"Bronze up!"* he said motioning to Zach military style to provide him the suntan lotion.

It had been quite the ordeal for the two guys to get the chance to sit on those plush blue padded chaise lounges by the poolside. Zach was beyond exhaustion.

Last night, after seeing the leggings hanging on the hotel door, Zach made the climb up the four flights of stairs three more times until the doorknob was bare. It was almost four o'clock when he finally went to sleep and then woke two hours later to catch the early morning flight to Rhodes.

The guys sleep-walked onto the single-aisle Olympic Airways turboprop plane and fell into their seat. Zach felt like he just blinked and they were already landing in Rhodes. Everything moved in slow motion as they entered the taxi to their hotel. Standing in the hotel lobby, he barely knew how he arrived.

The Fontana Hotel was located in the municipality of Lindos, a peninsula that jutted out into the Mediterranean Sea located on the mid-east side of the island. Its exotic beach locale made for a special honeymoon for Zach and Marshall's parents. As youngsters, they had heard so many stories about the place that the hotel became the required landing spot for the guys' Rhodes leg of their adventure.

"So what's the plan, Stan," Marshall joked to Zach.

"Yo, bro, I'm good for a while at least until our room is ready."

Marshall pointed at a nude middle-aged man with a paunch. "Hey, check out Chief '*Showmacock*' over there."

Unbeknownst to the guys, it was clothes-optional at the pool. There were families and a smattering of older women laying out in the sun or frolicking in the clear water. Zach thought it was strange that parents were nude in front of their children. He tried to adjust to this new perspective. *I guess that Europeans are freer with their bodies than us stick-in-the-mud Americans.*

The weather was ideal. The blinding hot sun radiating off the pool, when combined with the suntan lotion, made Zach feel like he was the main entrée in the oven on Thanksgiving Day. He got up dripping from sweat, and made his way to the shallow end of the pool. There, wide steps led Zach into the icy water. It took a few minutes for his body to adjust to the temperature. He was quietly lingering in the cool water when he saw the Chief making his way over to him.

"Hi, I'm Martin from Brussels. You are American, no?"

"Yes," Zach replied awkwardly. *Something about talking with a naked stranger prevents me from giving you my name.*

"I've been practicing my English on this trip. Do you mind chatting for a while?"

Zach didn't really want to engage in chatter but

toughened up. "No problem, English is my best language." *Okay, this guy seems nice enough to at least divulge my name.* "I'm Zach." He cautiously reached out his hand to his nude English student. He tried keeping his eyes focused on Martin's face and hoped he didn't call him "Chief". He considered Martin's features–above the waist. He estimated him to be over fifty. He had salt-and-pepper hair and a black goatee that gave him an artist's look.

Zach thought that as long as he was helping Martin with his English, he might as well get some intelligence about the hotel's female prospects. "How long have you been staying at the hotel?" Zach asked.

"We've been here for a week and we leave to go home tomorrow," Martin replied.

"What do you think of this place?"

"We have been really enjoying ourselves. I travel a lot for work so it is nice spending quality time with my wife and children."

Zach tried to steer Martin to his point. "I noticed lots of families. Have you seen any single women at the pool since you been here?"

"Haha. I remember my single days." He started dreaming off. "There was the stewardess I met in Ibiza… Ah, *weleer.*"

"*Huh?*"

"That means *in old days.* That is in Dutch, my native language. Now, getting back to your question, you know all I have seen here is families. Believe me, if there were young ladies around the pool, I would have noticed."

Zach frowned. He changed the subject to what was burning in his head. "You mind if I ask you something personal?" Zach moved closer and whispered, "What happens if you get excited while 'you're just showin' off'," he raised his eyebrow knowingly and smiled.

Martin went into a rehearsed explanation. "My nudity is a part of who I am. I think that the human form is beautiful and I have no problems with other people being naked around me. I only want respect for my wishes."

Zach tried to get Martin out of his prepared mantra. "But what if you get…'the blood flowing'?"

"Believe me; my hormones in my fifties are much different than what they were in my twenties. I also have a different perspective about nudity than just tying it to sex."

"Sorry, I just perpetually tie nudity to sex. I think every time I had sex I was nude," Zach joked.

Martin saw how uncomfortable Zach was behaving just talking with him. He leaned in and whispered, "But since you'd be a *new-dist*, I would get a towel ready." He started laughing at his own wordplay.

Zach chuckled then looked around at the pool seeing kids playing without bathing suits on. "How do you feel about your children running around naked?"

Martin stopped laughing and went back on his virtual podium when Zach mentioned his children. "I've raised my children to have a healthier attitude about themselves and others. My children have a natural curiosity about their bodies and the bodies of others. When they suppress this curiosity, only problems occur."

Zach didn't care much for the nudity spiel but appeased Martin by saying, "I never thought about it that way." He took a breath. "Since there doesn't appear to be any young females at the pool for an American stud to consider, where do you think we can go for entertainment?"

"The evening shows here were very enjoyable. They have both belly and Greek dancing. I would check with Eddie the concierge. He seems to know things."

"Great, thanks. It was really nice meeting you, Martin. Enjoy the rest of your stay."

"You too. Remember to have coverage if you ever want to 'air' things out!"

Zach walked thoughtfully back to the lounge chair next to Marshall. "It appears that this hotel is mostly for families. If we want any female action, we better find Eddie the concierge."

"All right, we'll talk to him after we've settled into our room."

■■■

Zach and Marshall's room was actually a recently built, two-bedroom villa located a hundred yards away from the main building.

When they walked in, they inspected the place. It was sheer heaven for two cash-strapped guys. It also didn't hurt that they coerced both their parents to chip in for the cost of the hotel once they conveyed that they were staying at their honeymoon locale.

When Zach walked further into the living room, he noticed it had an orange cushioned sofa and matching rattan loveseats that complemented a coffee table and a small desk pedestal TV/VCR. Around the L-shaped corner, there was a functional kitchenette with a stove, sink, fridge and eating nook.

Marshall had raced upstairs to snag the choice of the two bedrooms while his brother was scoping the main room. The master bedroom was more ornate and had a king bed. It also had French doors leading to a small terrace looking out in the distance to the sea. The other bedroom was simpler having only two twin beds.

After showering and feeling more human, Zach and Marshall meandered down the stone walkway past the pool to the main building. To the right of the receptionist stood a black-haired, swarthy-looking, dark-complexioned man who looked straight out of a foreign film.

"My name is Ediz, but you can call me Eddie. I'm from Turkey. What can I do for you gentlemen to make your stay with us more enjoyable?" He spoke in a slightly Turkish-accented English.

"Eddie, I'll tell you what you can do," Marshall blurted in a mob-styled phrasing. "Tell us where we can meet beautiful babes. All I see around here are well preserved wrinkles. I'm not trying to meet Mrs. Robinson here!"

Eddie didn't understand the Mrs. Robinson reference but he did get the point. "Who stays with us changes from week to week," he shrugged. "Just two weeks ago, the hotel hosted the Portuguese Swim Team here for a European swim meet. Those women were *spec–tac–u– lar!*" He then dreamed off…

"Attention Eddie–back to Earth!" Marshall made a grand gesture with his hands around the main lobby, then stopping and pointing at the pool area. "Looking around the hotel now we don't see any young females here except for the Chief's wife over there. Any recommendations?"

"Okay, okay." He looked both ways and quietly motioned the guys to follow him. Then he stepped around the counter, grabbed a map and found a grouping of furniture they could sit around and talk quietly.

"The place to go is St. John's Bay. It's a clothes-optional resort just a thirty minute walk along the coast. Make sure you show up early because you'll both want to get chaise lounge chairs before they're all taken."

"Why there?" asked a now interested Zach.

"It's an ideal setting for the young ladies. The bay has a romantic cove nestled in front of the blue Mediterranean Sea. The resort has a snack bar and nice background music. Most of the folks are locals just there to suntan in private."

It sounded exclusive to Zach "Does it cost anything?" he asked.

Eddie reassured them. "I'll set you up. I know Dominick, one of the cabana boys there. He owes me a favor."

"Sounds great!' He changed the subject. "Oh, and by the way, can you tell me more about the belly dancing?"

Eddie went into his concierge personae. "The hotel has belly dancing tonight and Thursday. There is Greek style dancing on Wednesday and Friday. The belly dancing is a lot of fun for the tourists. The dancer is my cousin Suzan. If you come, I'll make sure she gives you a special show."

"Awesome!" the guys celebrated in unison.

Fifteen

Zorba's, Fontana Hotel, Rhodes, Greece

The belly dancing was performed at the hotel's bar called Zorba's. The bar was constructed as a square structure located between the pool and the main building. It had a rectangular lower tier with a dance floor area surrounded by twenty tables. The hotel supplied a band for both Greek and belly dancing. The band included a big drum called a *tabla*, Turkish nay flutes, and an *oud*, a Turkish guitar with a deep wooden belly, a short neck, and a backward slanting peg box.

Waiting for the show, Marshall showed the bartender how to make a Long Island Iced Tea. When the show started, Eddie surprised both guys by being the one playing the tabla. The band played some warm-up Turkish tune to get the forty people milling around the bar into the mood.

Twenty seconds into the second song, Suzan, Eddie's cousin, made her dramatic appearance. Suzan was a voluptuous and seductive young woman with black hair tied back under a thick red fabric headband. Her exotic makeup and red lips blended perfectly with her red and silver costume. She wore a heavily decorated bra supporting more than just her breasts, as strings of beads suspended from it were dangling teasingly above her navel.

"She looks like a Greek Wonder Woman," Zach marveled. She was wearing a loose red shawl tied to one of the Wonder Woman-type arm sleeves which made swirls around her like a cloud of dust. Well below her navel were tight-fitting silk pants that flared at the bottom.

Marshall and Zach's heat-seeking love missiles sprang into action like pointer dogs on the scent of prey. Both guys sat there stunned, mesmerized by her rhythmic swaying. Eddie must have briefed Suzan on his promise to the boys because she highlighted her first dance with a personal display for them. She wore two sets of tiny silver symbols called *zills* in her hands and clicked to the music as she swayed her hips around their table.

"Look at that stomach control," Zach stared.

Marshall declared, "I want to be her lover for life."

The band took a break after her fifteen minute show. Eddie stopped by their table to see if the guys appreciated the performance.

"Amazing!" Zach tweeted. "I couldn't take my eyes off of her."

Marshall looked down and inquired with a wry grin, "Is she available for a quiet romantic interlude with a sensitive American?"

Eddie pointed to the band. "Sorry, the oud player over there is pretty protective. Besides, she doesn't know much English. What would you talk about?" He smiled.

"No problem there, I speak the language of love," Marshall responded.

Eddie cut Marshall's hormones from rising, "I think you will do better tomorrow at the beach. Remember, get there early!"

"We can't wait," they sang together.

Before the next set, Marshall and Zach had already finished their third iced teas. "The bartender is starting to get the hang of it," Marshall said.

"*Shhhh*, the show is starting again," Zach demanded.

Suzan took to the small dance floor and swirled around the crowd. *She's a good flirt. What is she thinking as she wiggles those hips?*

Martin from Brussels was there with his wife and two kids. He waved to Zach from the other side of the dance floor. Then, Martin's two kids pulled him onto the dance floor and they all tried to belly dance. Martin took off his shirt and let his large belly jiggle for all to see. Zach couldn't hold back a smile.

Soon, Suzan had made her way over to Zach and Marshall. She beckoned them to the center of the dance floor. The high pitched sounds of the flutes filled the area. As the crowd cheered on, Eddie got up from his tabla and enticed Marshall to pull off his shirt and wear a plus-size sequined bra. Eddie then quickly snapped the bra on Marshall and the audience roared watching his hysterical arm and hip swivels. Zach almost passed out, he was laughing so hard.

After Suzan's set, Eddie brought Suzan over to Zach and Marshall's table. Zach stood up and kissed her hand. She nodded her approval with a tickled laugh. Zach looked over at the oud player who was staring back intently.

She barely understood English, so Eddie translated. "You dance so beautifully. Would you like to join our table?" Marshall beamed.

Zach saw the oud player approaching quickly. "Oh, it's getting late. We better be going."

Marshall was surprised with his brother. "What? It's still early."

Zach rolled his eyes and raised both eyebrows. He said in Pig Latin "Marshall, Suzan's *oyfriendbay* is going to kick you in the *ummichstay*!"

Marshall quickly looked up and reached out to the *oud* player's hand to shake it before he could do anything further. "You have a beautiful girlfriend here. I'm sure the two of you will make beautiful baklava together."

Sixteen

St. John's Bay Resort, Rhodes, Greece

It was a late-night for both Zach and Marshall. After the belly dancing, Zach was too keyed up to fall asleep. He reflected on the trip with its fun times and agonizing sexual encounters. Gauging his recent track performance, he was beginning to doubt whether he would shack up with anyone. At this point he thought he would even be happy with one of the bimbettes back home.

At one o'clock in the morning, Marshall was still awake and hung out downstairs in the living room scanning the TV channels. He found an old *Odd Couple* TV episode with Tony Randall and Jack Klugman, but they spoke only Greek. Growing up, it was their favorite show, so he was amusing himself with it.

They pushed themselves to bed at three A.M. Since they were motivated to get up early, Zach set the alarm clock in his room for only four hours later. The plan was to get themselves together, eat breakfast and be in their lounge chairs at the St. John's Bay Resort by nine A.M. so they could catch up on their sleep in the sun.

■■

The hotel had a varied and delicious breakfast spread

that was included with the room charge. In addition to a flavorful assortment of breads and yogurt, there was a cooking station for personal-order Greek frittatas made with egg, fennel, tomato and spinach. Marshall and Zach overfilled their plates, immensely enjoying this "free" meal.

Both Zach and Marshall had pounding headaches from the drinking and lack of sleep, but decided to skip drinking coffee, thinking it would only keep them from sleeping in their lounge chairs at the resort.

The thirty minute walk down the coast to St. John's Bay was completed in a mental minute. They wore out whatever was left of their strength just to get there. At the resort entrance, a steep ridge lay between the resort and the supporting town, giving it ample seclusion from any curious onlookers in the area. Unfortunately, it was a pretty overcast and chilly morning.

Upon arrival, Zach sought out Dominick, the cabana boy in Eddie's debt. They found him dressed in a logoed collar shirt and white shorts putting out cushions for the chaise lounges.

"I not know why I do this; is no beach day," Dominick said to Zach in his broken English. He walked back to his station, found the day pass ink stamp and rolled it over the guy's left hands. The stamp was emblazoned with the capital Greek letter *sigma*.

The entire area looked like an oasis from *The Arabian Nights*. Pebbly sand blanketed the beach for about two hundred yards surrounded by craggy hillsides that extended out into the water creating a quiet bay. There was a large pier to handle yachts and an ancient church in the corner of the bay at the end of the road.

There were only two rows of chaise lounges laid out so Marshall made sure to snag one near the water. No one was relaxing in this area yet since it was too early and cold; but Marshall grabbed two towels from Dominick for each of them. The guys then covered themselves up and crashed into unconsciousness.

TWO

Seventeen

St. John's Bay Resort, Rhodes Greece

"Could I borrow a bit of your s'n cream?" Felicity asked with a smile.

"Who? What? Why? When?" Zach muttered as he roused himself from his comatose state.

"Do you speak English?" Felicity asked very slowly and carefully.

Zach looked up and shielded his eyes from the burning sun. He sat up and looked around. The place was now packed! Rising slowly from his resting spot, he surveyed the scene. He verified that every lounge chair and beach towel was draped with topless women. *So this is what heaven looks like.*

"S'n cream, please," Felicity prodded.

"The what?" Zach replied, but was still only barely conscious.

"You know?" Felicity started making suntan applying motions to help Zach understand her request.

Her request sank in. "*Ooooooooooh,* suntan lotion!" He thought for a second. "Right here in my bag."

Felicity let out an audible sigh. "Thank God you speak English. I was hoping you weren't one of those Greek come-on boys."

74

Zach never heard English spoken with such an accent. "Yeah, I speak English. But whatta you speakin'?" Zach grinned.

"Bloody English as well. The original kind!" Felicity replied proudly.

Zach moved away from focusing on her speech to the sight of her delectable and unshielded breasts. It was the first time Zach had peep access on a first encounter and the world seemed to stand still. He looked left–*boobs*. He looked right–*boobs*. They were everywhere–*boobs, boobs, boobs. A wonderful playpen of boobs. I can now clearly visualize a water slide emptying into a sea of just boobs.*

Zach regrettably left his dream state and grabbed a tube of suntan lotion and handed it over. "Hi, my name is Zach and uh…" He pointed next to him, "…this passed-out individual is my brother, Marshall."

"I'm Felicity and this…" She turned her head to her right. "…ignoring person is me sister Ellen." Ellen raised her hand up obligingly.

Zach sized up Felicity. *She is really cute. She seems small, but wrapped in such a perfect package. My God, her skin looks like lightly roasted marshmallows. Man, a blonde, blue-eyed goddess appears next to me like a dream. My prayers have been answered.*

Felicity had been staring at Zach since she arrived at the resort and purposely pulled up to the chaise lounges next to him. *He has an international look with that dark tan. I'm relieved that he speaks English, or whatever he calls that. I'm glad I was able to successfully execute the suntan ruse to wake him since I'm getting so bored of Sis ignoring me while she is into her own world.*

Since Zach was already awake and had the plan for targeting the bosom population, he figured he could, for once, place Marshall into the wingman slot. *If Marshall could just keep Felicity's sister busy, I'd have a better chance with her. But first, I can't wait to see his reaction to this paradise.*

Zach walked quietly to the other side of Marshall's lounge chair and put his mouth by Marshall's ear.

"Marshall!" he screamed. Marshall reflexed from the noise. He then quickly quieted down but loud enough for Felicity to hear, "We're being attacked by an army of topless superwomen! One even has me in her grasp! Help!" He smiled at Felicity, "I'm going down... down... down!"

With Felicity laughing, Zach turned his attention to Marshall. He was still groggy. "*Oooooooohyeah!*" he yawned without really wakening.

Zach continued, "Okay, Marshall, this is your brother speaking. When you open your eyes and look around you, you will behold the sheer paradise you have been seeking."

The hypnotic suggestion popped Marshall's eyes open. He robotically sat up and turned around. He was speechless. He slowly stood up, scanned the beach of sheer toplessness and looked back intently at Zach.

"This is the reason why the aliens abducted me and placed me on this blue orb of Earth!" He kneeled on the sand and playfully kissed the ground for Felicity's amusement.

"Amen, bro," replied Zach.

Zach quietly tried to get Marshall's roaming eyes to focus. "Marsh, I need help here. I've already made a couple of winning points with our luscious neighbor over here. I just need you to cover her sister with your array of serves."

He slowly stood up and ogled at Ellen's gleaming skin. "No problem bro. I'm on it," he said grinning.

"Okay, let's see if we all can get acquainted in pairs over lunch."

Marshall and Zach both faced Felicity as Zach acted like he was a royal announcer. "Felicity, I officially present to you my, now awake, brother Marshall."

"Hi Marshall," Felicity said with a perky smile.

Zach rubbed his tummy and led knowingly, "I'm a little hungry. Would you like to grab a bite at the snack bar with me?"

Felicity looked thoughtfully, and then said, "Be right back."

Felicity went to the other side of the lounge chair where she had whisper access to her silently tanning companion. "Okay big sister, you were the one who encouraged me to come here. Please get up and make nice with the natives."

Ellen gingerly turned around and stood up. Her bronzing naked body glistened in the hot sun. She selectively examined Marshall and then curtly declared "He'll do." Marshall's jaw dropped to the ground.

Felicity faced the guys with a big hand gesture. "And please let me introduce you to, the one and only, Ellen Williams!" she smiled.

"Oh, Sis, stop your mithering!" Ellen said with a smile.

Eighteen

Snack Bar, St. John's Bay Resort, Rhodes, Greece

Felicity asked, "So, where you lads from?"

Felicity and Zach were standing in line at the snack bar while Marshall and Ellen got acquainted by their lounge chairs. Felicity put on a tank top which significantly helped Zach focus more on the conversation.

"We're from *Nu Yawk Sittay*," he replied.

She hesitated to better understand what he said. Thinking she recognized the city name as New York, she said "I always wanted to go there. Me and me sister have never been to the States."

Zach couldn't place Felicity's accent, so he inquired, "Where are you from?"

"Sheffield." Felicity responded expecting Zach to know it.

"Where is that?"

"The northern part of England." Zach was still puzzled so she ventured out, "between Scotland and London."

Zach made a face as if she was from the moon. "They all speak like that there?"

Felicity defended her land of the Queen, "Like what?

78

I can barely understand your assassination of the English language." Felicity realized that if she wanted to better communicate with this man across the pond, she had to speak more clearly to him.

"Hey," he smiled, "so, I don't talk like a professor."

Felicity smiled at their common destruction of proper English. "I think it sounds cute," Felicity flirted.

Zach smiled and changed subjects. "Do you mind me asking about..." he hesitated, "...your freedom to go topless? Bear in mind, I have absolutely no problem with this particular behavior. I'm just curious."

Felicity never had to explain her state of undress to a man before so she noodled on it. She said while thinking it through, "We love the sun down here in the Mediterranean. The locals treat the nudist resorts as normal. It was strange at first, but me sister taught me to be more comfortable with me body."

And I'm already comfortable with it.

They picked up gyros for themselves and their siblings and walked back to their lounge chairs. As they neared, they saw Marshall chatting up to Ellen. Ellen appeared engaged in the conversation; Felicity and Zach exchanged glances and smiled knowingly.

"Okay, here's chow!" Zach reported. Nodding at Felicity he said aloud, "I think we're going to find a private spot over on the pier to get to know each other a little better."

Marshall and Ellen both looked up at them and smiled their agreement.

■■

Zach and Felicity found a quiet comfortable spot. The pier was currently empty of yachts and pleasure craft. Sunbathers, in various degrees of nakedness, dotted the structure.

While their physical attraction brought them

together, it was their mutual interest in each other's culture that kept them engaged. They talked for hours about their lives and what brought them to Greece. But their free flowing conversation dug deeper, to their cherished feelings about family, religion, work and entertainment tastes.

Felicity shared thoughts about growing up with limited means but not realizing it since they were happy living together as a family. She intimated her dreams of living a better life, one free from the illness that took her Mum. She teared as she revealed her genuine concern about her dad, his challenges coping with life as a young widower.

Zach explained how his dad let his marriage go to pieces by letting his ethical guard down; how he loved both his parents dearly despite the mental effort it took to mitigate their mutual tensions. He shared his goals for greater independence to be a partner in a growing CPA firm and not struggling to make a rent payment. They compared favorite music groups, Level 42 vs. the Doobie Brothers, and movies, *Educating Rita* vs. *Body Heat*.

At the end of their conversation, they both came to quickly realize that, even though they came from completely separate cultures, they had much in common.

Later in the afternoon, Felicity jumped in the chilly bay water and encouraged Zach to follow. He did his best Olympic dive and joined her. They swam together toward the rocky outcropping lining the mouth of the bay. Halfway to the ledge, Felicity challenged Zach to a race to the finish. They playfully raced with all they had and reached the ledge together in a frenzied hand grab to the finish.

Zach jumped onto the ledge and then pulled Felicity up. Zach stared at her with her shapely, petite body and nipples stuck pointedly out from her tank top. Zach pulled her close in and kissed her firmly.

"I was wondering when you were going to do that,"

Felicity cooed with flushed cheeks.

They envisioned exchanging lips, tongues and other body parts for hours, but both didn't want to rush things. They still didn't know how much time they had together.

They blurted out simultaneously, "When are you heading back home?"

"Okay, you first," laughed Zach.

"We just got here yesterday," Felicity said. "We're here until Sunday."

"Great! We don't leave until Saturday afternoon," Zach replied with a sigh.

Nineteen

Fontana Hotel, Rhodes, Greece

After that afternoon's swim with Zach, Felicity noticed her sister was fully dressed and giving her the secret signal that she wanted to leave. Felicity was curious to know how Ellen got along with Marshall. *Ellen's interest in Marshall might determine how much time I get to have with Zach.* Ellen mentioned that the two of them had a good platonic connection on the surface, but it was the building underlying sexual tension that needed a little cooling for a while.

Zach mentioned about the Greek dancing at the hotel and thought it would be fun for the four of them. Since their hotels were close by, Felicity offered to walk over with Ellen. The walk allowed Felicity and her sister to compare notes.

Zach's kiss seemed to unclog all of Felicity's tense mental pathways that had built up over the past two years. As she silently walked the ten-minute stroll with Ellen from their hotel to the Fontana, she sought guidance from her eternal confidant on meeting this "New Hunk City".

Mum, you are my sounding board since I got past those confused months as a teenager. We moved past the mother-daughter

82

relationship and matured as soulmates before…it all went to pieces. All those silly and unforgettable times. Mum, can you hear me? You told me what I'd feel like when I met someone special. What can you tell me about this New Yorker?

Felicity broke the quiet with her sister. "I really had a great time with this bloke, so don't screw it up for me," Felicity warned.

"I liked Marshall, too." She raised her eyebrows. "I think he might well provide the requisite services I've been seeking on this Greek holiday!"

"All right then, let's make nice with *duh Noo Yawkuss*," said Felicity mimicking Zach's accent.

■■

Zach and Marshall met them out in the reception area of their hotel. Zach wore a black printed silk shirt, tight fitting pants with black dance shoes. He looked a little like John Travolta in *Saturday Night Fever* but shorter. Felicity noticed that Marshall's pants were so tight, nothing was hiding. *The way Marshall and Ellen's libido trains are chugging head-on, the wreck will be a sight to behold!*

Felicity wore a cream silk top over a short beige skirt; she felt it would best accent her tan. Ellen wore a frilly lace top with her breasts crushed together like commuters on a third-class Indian train. It was her primary mating dress which had a "no-failure" rate to date. Felicity shook her head. *Marshall will be no match for her.*

The four of them made their way over to the bar. They sat down at one of the tables outlining the dance floor, and a cocktail waitress dressed in a Greek toga walked over to take their drink order. Felicity had a piña colada and Marshall asked the bartender to make Ellen and him two more of his special Long Island Iced Teas. When the drinks came, the waitress put four additional shots of tequila on the table with salt shakers and lime wedges.

"What's with the shots?" Marshall asked.

"Compliments of the tabla player," The waitress responded as she pointed over to the stage.

Marshall looked over to a waving Eddie as he was getting seated. He raised his shot glass and then looked at both Felicity and Ellen. "Here's looking at the two loveliest tourist sites in all of Greece!"

Zach showed Felicity the proper method of tequila shot drinking. He made a square with his thumb and forefinger and picked a lime wedge in the same hand. Then he poured salt on that thumb and held the shot glass in his other hand. He quickly licked the salt, downed the tequila in a gulp and then bit into the lime as fast as he could.

Ellen really got into the new drinking game. She quickly ordered another round as the band started playing.

Although the music seemed the same, the aura surrounding the dance floor for the Greek dancing was very much different than it was for the belly dancing the night before. For the Greek dancing, it was more of a group dance instruction session than a show. Eddie was the host of the evening, smartly attired in traditional Greek dress. He wore a short-sleeved white button-down shirt, a blue and red vest, and light gray trousers fitting into calf-high white boots.

He introduced the Greek dance as the *sousta*, a traditional dance commonly performed on the Greek islands. He brought out Suzan and another pretty Greek woman to demonstrate.

Suzan looked completely changed from the previous night. She and her dance partner wore a Greek traditional dance dress: gold leaf adorned headscarves, white blouses buttoned up high and covered by a short black and gold printed vest open to show their white shirts like bibs. Below their vests, they wore bright red scarves with fringes hanging down. Their white poofed ankle-length pants were covered with a printed linen drape that looked like a table runner.

Eddie demonstrated the simple dance movements of the sousta. The dance had two variations. In one, a dance line formed with everyone facing the same way with their hands on their neighbors' shoulders; the second was a two-person dance with couples following behind each other.

Zach and Marshall were familiar with the dance from socials at the Sephardic temple. It was invariably a showcase moment for Zach when the dancing started during Sephardic festivals. He was an exceptional dancer and joyfully toyed with Felicity on the floor.

"I'm very impressed with this secret talent of yours," Felicity cooed.

"One of the side benefits of being forced to go to twenty Sephardic bar mitzvahs." Zach retorted.

Zach and Felicity agreed to keep a safe distance and maintain a careful surveillance on their siblings. On the dance floor, Ellen and Marshall were both degenerating into primal behavior. Marshall acted like a male prairie chicken that drummed its feet in stylized dances and made a booming call that can be heard for over a mile. Ellen responded like a new queen bee that had the instinct to kill off all of her sister siblings ensuring she remained the unchallenged monarch of the hive.

As Felicity and Zach stared at their siblings' foreplay, they appraised its outcome. Felicity believed Marshall was a solid bet as a sexual up-and-comer, but knew that Ellen was the reigning champ. Zach compared it to a steel cage wrestling match between Professor Toru Tanaka and Gorilla Monsoon, which meant absolutely nothing to Felicity.

The dancing was sidesplitting, and it created a silly vibe amongst the four of them. Towards the end of the dancing, Marshall demonstratively grabbed Zach and made a sweeping motion to clear out the dance floor. Seizing the night's peak moment, Eddie followed by distributing easily breakable plates to the crowd. While the guys were rhythmically swaying shoulder-to-shoulder in the middle, Eddie instructed the crowd to simultaneously throw their plates down at the edge of the dance floor.

"*Opa!*" the crowd cheered in unison as a crescendo of plates smashed on the floor. Felicity and Ellen rushed out to Zach and Marshall to hug them as they bowed to a round of applause. Then, the ladies went off to the loo, as the guys were now calling it. It gave them a chance to discuss their next moves.

"Ellen has already commanded that we will be going back to her hotel room," Marshall said with confidence.

Zach concluded that he and Felicity would have their entire villa. "Mind if I take your room?" Zach asked. He craved the space of a king bed for his quest of Felicity.

"Only if you make sure the housekeeper changes the linens in the morning," Marshall quipped.

When the girls came out of the bathroom, the guys shared their plan for the hotel room pairings with the girls. Ellen assumed as much but Felicity hesitated a moment. This pause caught Zach off-guard. Marshall and Ellen ignored them and immediately left, walking arms around waists. Zach and Felicity sat alone.

"You look like you don't like these arrangements?" Zach said.

"It's not that. I'm just worried about me sis. I've seen her acting like this with blokes before. She has the tendency to lose control at these times."

"So does Marshall," Zach confessed. "I hope there isn't a catastrophe. I'd hate to get deported from Rhodes before this smile gets permanently etched in my cheeks."

Twenty

Fontana Hotel, Rhodes, Greece

Zach led Felicity by the hand back to his villa down the curved pathway past the pool. Felicity's mind was both clear and confused. She felt safe and comfortable with Zach but, in the back of her mind, she wondered where her feelings for him were going to lead. Her recent depression over her mum's loss reached as deep as a North Sea oil well. Her mood had only recently risen up enough to enjoy life again. Meeting Zach raised her outlook so rapidly she remained on unsteady turf.

Zach led her into his villa. The place was luxuriously spacious compared to what she and her sister could cull from their holiday fund. He led her over to one of the orange loveseats in the living room and they got comfortable snuggling. The sexual tension between them started to percolate; she recognized that although she really craved Zach, she was hesitant to just rush in.

Zach picked up on her silent cues. "What's up?"

She defrayed the subject. "I don't know, but I don't picture this scene as being identical to me hotel room right now," Felicity shared.

"Yeah, I'm sure the pillows are shredded already," Zach quipped. "I just hope all the windows stay intact."

She drew him in. "Zach, just so you know, me and me sis are different in that way."

"In what way?"

"She just wants sex for the feeling. I'd rather have the feeling for the sex."

His eyes opened quizzically. "Please don't tell me you don't have feeling for sex?"

She blushed, "Yes I do, you twit, but me mind is in a bit of a jumble at the moment. Things are happening too fast in the feelings department." She smiled pleadingly at him.

He reached over and kissed her deeply. She kissed back and they lay on the loveseat kissing while Zach moved his hands across her breasts.

"Steady sailor," she warned.

"*Huh?*" Zach's mouth gaped open a bit. Now he was confused.

"Can we just take it easy? It's about all I can handle right now."

Zach took a deep breath and recalibrated. "That's cool. Let's just lie here and *shnuggle.*"

Felicity felt relieved that Zach understood her feelings so clearly. *Most guys back home would've acted like wankers and immediately blow the situation up badly. But Zach seemed to handle this slowdown of progress without major incident.* It made Felicity relax in Zach's arms and start to open up about her feelings.

"It's just that I'm just finally starting to get over me mum's death."

"Were ya close?" Zach asked tenderly.

"You're going to turn on me water works." Felicity took heavy breaths to gather herself. "We were inseparable. We used to finish each other's sentences."

Zach gauged whether he wanted Felicity to tell him the details of what happened to her mom because it might take their conversation down an unrecoverable path. But she was finally opening up and they seemed to be talking with each other so easily, he decided to venture with the topic anyway. "What happened to her?"

Felicity took a deep breath and blew it out. "She was as healthy as you and me. The breast cancer just took hold of her and wouldn't let go. The radiation and the chemo weakened her to a shell." She started tearing up. "She fought tirelessly hard, but her system was so weak at the end. She died of liver failure last May. Since then, I've barely been living me life, really, just going through the motions, preventing meself the chance to really feel...I haven't wanted to feel anything." She stopped.

Zach caressed her as she pumped tears out of her eyes like a faucet. They were quiet for a while after that.

Felicity broke the silence. "Please just hold me tonight. I think all this emotion has been building up for a while."

Zach pulled Felicity off the loveseat and led her upstairs to the master bedroom. He picked her up and gently carried her over to the king bed. While Felicity lay on the bed, Zach then stood perfectly tall and said with a German accent, "I have *prrre-scrrrrribed* total bed rest for *zis* patient, but first I would like to demonstrate my bedside *manna!*"

Twenty-one

Fontana Hotel, Rhodes, Greece

The next morning, Zach woke up a bit disoriented and saw Felicity snuggled opposite him on the bed sleeping soundly in the fetal position. He squeezed his eyelids a few times to focus on what had happened last night.

The Greek dancing was a riot. I can't remember when I've had so much fun. Felicity made it special and was so laid-back with everything. I had all hailing frequencies open trying to read her signals. When she put up that "Do Not Cross" sign on me, I could've said "the hell with it" but something is strikingly different with her. Instinctively, I went for the longer play. Now that I'm not so horny for a moment, I'm glad I did.

Zach started to think about what it would be like to lose his mom. *It must've been really traumatic for her. I hope I don't have to deal with that for a while. Ma is my emotional Sherpa guide, at least when she's not feeling so sorry for herself over her divorce.*

Felicity sweetly grumbled next to him starting to rouse herself. "Hi, handsome!" she peeped.

"How're you *doin'*," he said in his heaviest New York accent.

She giggled, and then turned her head formally. "I am doing very well, thank you. I think I dropped the

90

mental load on you last night." She locked eyes on him gauging his reaction.

"That's okay. I can't imagine how difficult the last two years have been for you." He jumped off the bed. "How about a road trip today?"

"I'm right for that. What do you have in mind?"

"I haven't done any exploring on the island except for the beach. There are some historical places I have to see while I'm here." He had an errant thought hit him. "I think we should first check in with Marshall and Ellen."

Felicity pictured the aftermath. "If we can see through the carnage."

They casually dressed and made it down to the lobby restaurant. They were just sitting down for breakfast when they saw a disheveled and panicked Ellen bolting towards them.

She was out of breath. "Come quick! We need to get to hospital straight away. Marshall had an accident!"

"What?" Zach raised his voice "Where is he?"

She was panting. "Rhodes...General Hospital." She finally gathered herself. "We need to go right now!" She waved them to the lobby entrance.

"I'll get a taxi," said Felicity jumping out of her seat and running towards the lobby.

"No need, the one I took from hospital has the meter running. Come on!"

They quickly jumped into the taxicab for the twenty minute ride while Zach and Felicity tried to extract the full story from Ellen.

"I feel so bad," Ellen said slowly between long breaths. "It was me fault. We got carried away."

"What was your fault? How'd you get carried away?" Zach and Felicity said in unison.

She steadied herself as she replayed the scene for them. "Well, you saw that Marshall and I were feeling pretty amorous last night on the dance floor."

"Ellen, you were frothing at the mouth." Felicity

scolded.

"Thanks, Sis. Well, we got to our hotel room and made a bit of a tumble straight away. We were having a good old time of it when Marshall pulled out this magazine article he had brought from his villa."

"What was it about?" Felicity encouraged.

"The article was titled 'The Ten Most Challenging Sex Positions'."

Zach was startled. "What? He never shared it with me. I'm not sure I'm gonna like where this story is headed," Zach groaned.

Ellen took a deep breath and slowly went on. "So we looked at the list and first did a couple of positions called 'The London Bridge' and 'The Wheelbarrow'. Then we tried 'The Backdoor Cartwheel'. "

"What was that?" Felicity asked.

Ellen struggled with how to explain it. "You remember Sis how I was so good at cartwheels in gymnastics class? That talent really came in handy because, while I was doing a cartwheel he'd be doing the nasty."

Zach contorted his face. "Is that...how he got hurt?"

"No! That happened this morning."

"Okay, I don't know if I'm ready for more," Zach conveyed. "Felicity, are you ready?" Felicity shushed Zach and encouraged Ellen to finish the story.

"Well," she started, "we both got up at eight o'clock. We started remembering how much fun we had last night so we decided to continue where we left off. Marshall was ready to tackle the one position we didn't do last night."

"Oh God, what was that?" Felicity looked at her sister sheepishly.

"The article called it 'The Incline Leg'. They didn't recommend doing it. " She started to use her body to try to describe it in the tight confines of the taxi. "Well, he was on the bed…"

"Do I really want to hear this?" Felicity openly questioned.

"Oh Felicity, stop your mithering. I'm just trying to explain what was happening."

"Go on then!"

"Well, 'The Incline Leg' required a bit of gymnastics expertise from both of us." She tried to imitate the position with her fingers. "Marshall laid down with his knees up and I sat down on his John Thomas and *pop*! He let out a yell that you must have heard all the way at your villa."

"*Oooooooooooooh*!" Zach doubled over in the taxi.

"They're now doing emergency surgery on him."

"What kind of surgery? Are they cutting it off?" Zach screamed.

Ellen steadied Zach. "No, you bloody wanker. The doctor told me it's only a temporary setback. He'll be okay soon," Ellen reassured him.

Twenty-two

THURSDAY, MAY 28, 1987

Rhodes General Hospital - Rhodes, Greece

"That vixen broke my *schmeckie!*" Marshall hollered.

"Hey, Marshall, I heard that the male octopus cuts off his schlong after mating. Consider yourself lucky," Zach chided.

The three of them found Marshall in bed in a semi-private room on the second floor of the two-story medical complex. He was resting comfortably and had an IV drip into his arm for the pain. His broken frank and beans were safely mending under the covers. Zach motioned to the girls to leave him alone with Marshall and he walked over to the side of the bed. He immediately wanted to get Marshall's side of the story.

"Marshall, what's with the article?"

"Oh, that. Cousin Alex gave it to me. I never thought I'd use it until Ellen started whispering what she planned for us. She's unbelievably talented."

"Lay it on me, bro."

"She got very interested in the article since most of those positions were new to her. In the hotel room, she was on me right away. I never met a sex acrobat before. She could do things that I didn't know were physically possible. Zach, I had the most incredible night of my life on God's green Earth, but this morning even I went too far," Marshall admitted.

"What happened?" Zach prodded.

"Well, I woke up with a hard-on just thinking about last night. So, when she confidently said we should try the 'Incline Leg' position, I said, 'Bring it on!' "

"Marshall, please don't give me the play-by-play, but tell me one thing, did it really... snap?"

"*Ooh maaaaan*! I can tell you that it was the worst sound I ever heard in my life." He put his finger inside his mouth and pulled on the side cheek. "Like a *'pop'*. Then, the pain followed. I swear, I thought full castration was my destiny."

"*Ewwww*. I'm sorry, bro. What's your...status?"

"Not too bad. I think the nurse hand-signaled that I'd be out of action for a month. That I can live with, but I need to take a break from Nadia Comaneci Lovelace out there."

"She's broken up about it," Zach smiled.

"She's broken up? I'm the guy that's really broken up."

Zach started snickering causing Marshall to giggle too. Marshall tried to hold it together "Don't make me laugh. My sutures!" He rang for more painkillers.

"My condolences. So, when you getting outta here?"

"They want to keep me here overnight to make sure the sutures hold." He impatiently rang the nurse again.

Just then, a doctor walked in. He spoke English but it was heavily Greek-accented. "My name is Dr. Sebastian Cavos. I perform your surgery."

"Doctor, what's the...*sitch?*" Marshall inquired.

The doctor looked over his chart for his name. "Marshall...you had what is medically called a penile fracture," taking care to slowly pronounce the term. "It occurs when a membrane called the tunica albuginea tears."

Marshall tried to blot out the high school hygiene

class penis picture appearing in his mind. "Okay, okay. I really don't wanna know the medical details. Just let me know when I can go back to…" He used his hands to simulate the sexual act.

"Well, the good news is that the surgery was successful and you should be able to return to sexual activity in about a month."

"Hey Zach, it sounds like I'm only on the 30-day disabled list. I'll be back for our Saturday night haunts in only a month."

"Could've been a lot worse," Zach reassured.

Ellen bolted in carrying flowers she bought at the gift shop she saw at the entrance. She opened her arms for a hug and a kiss, "*Luv*, I feel so *terriboo!*"

He pecked her back. "That's what we get for pushing the limit," answered Marshall.

While Marshall and Ellen were consoling each other, Zach excused himself to speak to Felicity, who was waiting by the door. His needed to change his plans with her since Marshall was remaining in the hospital overnight.

"I need to stay here with Marshall but I'd really prefer to hang out with you," Zach admitted.

Felicity completely understood. It really didn't matter where she was, as long as it was with Zach. "Okay, let's all stay here at hospital for a while and see how he's doing. Then, we can both take it from there."

Next to Marshall's room, Zach saw an unattended linen closet. "Hey, I've got a goofy idea." He looked around. "Up for some fun?"

■■■

Ellen was in Marshall's room gently stroking his arm when a man and woman dressed in full scrubs and masks entered the room. Marshall sat up immediately.

The man looked authoritative due solely to the

scrubs since you couldn't see any of his other features. He stared at Marshall's chart for quite a while. He then spoke English almost too fast but with a beautiful Greek accent. "My name is Dr. Stavros Pousta. I just stepped out of a break from surgery for a consult with Dr. Cavos. This is my nurse Lydia Munaki." Lydia waved.

Marshall sat right up. "Is everything all right, Doctor?"

"I understand you had a little accident today."

Marshall cowered and looked down. "Yes."

"Yes, can you tell me how dis accident happened, please?" He let Marshall compose himself so he could tell the tale.

"Well," he called the surgeon to come closer. "I was trying some new sex positions."

The surgeon appeared perplexed. "Sir, I'm sorry, I don't understand."

Marshall tried to replay "The Incline Leg" position for with his fingers.

The surgeon allowed Marshall to go through the whole sexual episode then said, "Yes, thank you. That was very helpful. Now Marshall, I will now let my dear assistant do a full inspection of the area. May you please remove the blanket and sheet, and pull up your gown?"

Marshall laid back on the bed and blushingly complied. He was getting uncomfortable with Ellen observing the examination since every move he made caused her stomach to convulse from guilt.

"I will now ask Lydia to grab your scrotum while you cough." Lydia assumed the position and the surgeon continued. "Will you please cough, Mr. Stillman?" Marshall complied as Lydia's hands clutched his dangly bits. Marshall was embarrassed and turned on at the same time.

"Lydia, what do you think?"

Lydia gently inspected Marshall's cyclops. "I think it's a wonderful specimen." She held her emotions tightly in check. "Even though it's black and blue, I can see how the ladies find it irresistible," Lydia couldn't contain herself. She bellowed a laugh and quickly left the room.

With all the painkiller circulating his veins, Marshall hadn't really understood what was going on until the nurse left the room. At that moment, another nurse stepped inside and said in a raised voice at the surgeon, "Who are you? I don't recognize you!"

The surgeon took off his mask revealing Zach's face to his brother. He pleaded forgiveness to the nurse, *"Me synhoríte!"* then dashed out of the room over to Felicity.

Marshall yelled after him. *"Ah!* You're killing me, Zach!"

■■■

The hospital staff were good sports about the prank and allowed the four of them to stay into the evening in Marshall's room. Marshall kept complaining about the pain just so they could inject him with more pain medication. The nurse found them a deck of cards so they all played gin rummy by Marshall's bed. They broke into teams of "lads and ladies" with the loser required to speak in the winner's accent for the entire next game. It caused all kinds of silliness as Marshall and Zach tried to speak with a Yorkshire accent and failed miserably. It actually became a language training session that only taught them how similar they all really were.

That night, although Felicity was really tempted to push Ellen back to their hotel room away from her and Zach, she invited her to join her and sleep over at Zach's villa. Ellen remained troubled about the "incident". Remembering Marshall's black and blue swollen boloney pony killed any loving mood for both Felicity and Zach for the evening. When they reached Zach's villa, they headed up to the master bedroom while Ellen stayed downstairs watching television. Hanging out in Zach's bed gave them both more time to assess how they were feeling.

"It looks like tomorrow is our last full day in Greece together," Zach reported.

"I've been thinking about that," Felicity responded.

"I think Marshall will be released from the hospital tomorrow, thank God. With him resting in the villa, I was thinking we could go rent a moped and sightsee around the island."

The thought of holding onto Zach for the day excited Felicity. "Sounds tempting."

Zach sensed her heat rise. Zach moved in closer and kissed her deeply. "You know, I've never met anyone like you," he said as Felicity nearly launched six inches off the bed.

"Neither have I. Is something happening here more than just a chance holiday encounter?"

"Don't know. But I'm unprepared to think about that. I still would like to have one more day of your '*loovly coomp'ny*'."

"Looks like you're picking up proper English for '*an Ameerican*'."

Zach and Felicity penetrated each other's gaze. Neither one knew who made the first move, but before either one of them knew it, they were in each other's arms pressed against one another. Zach kissed her mouth, her neck, going lower. How he cherished the wails of passion Felicity was murmuring. Hotel guests and Ellen be damned, he immersed himself seeing how deafening he could make her scream.

Twenty-three

Fontana Hotel, Rhodes, Greece

The next morning, Felicity woke up before Zach. She turned to see him curled around a pillow. *He looks so serene, so peaceful. Yesterday seemed like a dream. What started out tragically had ended pretty hilariously, then heavenly. I'll never forget Marshall's face when we played that prank. I have to give him credit, he handled it pretty well. It was all good for a laugh. Zach, in every way, can really bring out my naughty side.*

After breakfast, the three of them taxied back to the hospital to pick up Marshall. His sutures had held and he was pronounced fit to resume normal activities except those requiring his bandaged jack-in-the-box in any excited state. Ellen was still feeling a bit guilty and agreed to keep Marshall company at his hotel for the day while Felicity and Zach went off on their moped excursion.

There was a moped rental place between Zach and Felicity's hotel on the hotel strip. The mopeds available were Yamaha OJ50s with a single throttle on the left handlebar. They were three gear vehicles that were rated at thirty mph at top speed. The core frame resembled the letter "J" and had a large black padded seat just big enough for the two of them.

They planned their day to reach the Old Town of

Rhodes on the northeast point of the island and return before it got dark. It was over thirty miles away and they tried to keep off the main highway so they wouldn't be run down by all the trucks that commuted from Lindos. Taking side roads made the traveling quieter and the open ride more exhilarating. They frequently stopped at scenic vantage points to take photos and made it into Old Town by noon.

They walked around the town streets and eventually came up to the Kahal Shalom Synagogue. The synagogue was the only remaining one used for services on the entire island of Rhodes, and was the oldest in all of Greece. Zach's mother had frequently talked about going to Sabbath services there during her honeymoon.

The synagogue was built in traditional Sephardic style as an indication of the island's Jewish ancestors. The Jews of Rhodes were primary descendants of the Sephardic Jews who fled Spain during the Spanish Inquisition. As they walked into the main sanctuary, they marveled at its ornate but simple structure. The main sanctuary featured a huge crystal chandelier in the center of a wide arch supported by cylindrical stone beams. The floor featured black and white stones arranged in an elaborate zigzag pattern. When they looked up, they saw an area called the Women's Balcony.

"Why do the men and the women pray separately?" Felicity asked.

"In the Jewish Orthodox religion, the men and women pray separately so they can focus on their prayers and not on each other. Looking at you here I understand this requirement more completely; it is hard to focus on anything else right now."

Zach explained that even the spoken language was different in the Sephardic synagogues where they speak *Ladino*. "Ladino is a combination of Castilian Spanish and traditional Hebrew with Turkish and Greek phrase words mixed in. A Sephardic Yiddish as it were."

Zach was fairly protective while talking about his religion as they toured the main sanctuary. "My parents were pretty strict with us about getting bar mitzvahed and preserving the Jewish religion in our lives." Zach's family grew up following the less-orthodox Reform denomination but was still was very tied to their religious and cultural background. He felt being Jewish was more a part of who he was rather than what he chose to believe.

Felicity showed Zach a tourist plaque that described the fate of Rhodesian Jews during the Holocaust. It read: "The Italian government's anti-Semitic laws in September 1938 caused 2000 Jews to flee Rhodes–half the entire Jewish population in September 1943. The Italian military surrendered control completely to the Germans. On July 18, 1944, the male Jews of Rhodes age 16 or older were ordered by the Germans to appear with their ID cards and work permits. The men that were assembled that day were brutalized and threatened. After taking all their valuables, on July 23, 1944, the Germans loaded 1673 Jews onto overcrowded boats and they spent eight miserable days traveling to the Greek mainland. From there, they were boarded into cattle cars and sent to be exterminated in the Auschwitz concentration camp."

"How bloody awful," Felicity exclaimed.

Zach talked straight with her about his anti-Semitic fears. "Being Jewish in those times was like a death curse. Even today, I feel discriminated because I am Jewish. It's a big issue. Maybe that's why I think I've stayed in New York where there are almost two million fellow Jews. At least I don't feel like a minority."

Felicity reflected on Zach's religious background. She had never met a Jew in her entire life. She thought there maybe was one synagogue in Sheffield; but if so, Jews were a microscopic minority of the regional population. All the people she knew were part of the Church of England. However, she seemed more intrigued about Zach's religion than repulsed.

The synagogue had a small gift shop which compelled Zach to buy Felicity a memento. He settled on an *oju*, a pendant of silver encasing a blue glass orb with a black center that looked like an eye.

"It looks like an evil eye," Felicity guessed.

"It's actually the opposite. In Sephardic culture, it is used to ward off the evil eye. It's like carrying around a rabbit's foot or a four leaf clover."

"So by giving this to me, you'll always protect me?" Felicity asked.

"I'll eternally have my eye on you," Zach smiled.

Twenty-four

Fontana Hotel - Rhodes, Greece

Zach didn't talk much on the way back to their hotels on the moped. He seemed deep in thought. She was also. It was their last night together. She thought about how she could make it special.

After returning the moped, Zach first escorted Felicity over to her hotel lobby, then walked back to his villa.

While walking up to her hotel room, Felicity reflected on her day. *Holding Zach tight around the waist on the moped was both thrilling and erotic. It was if I was acting in my very own foreign romance film. The synagogue was striking but felt very strange. It's hard to imagine people hating you just because of your beliefs. My eyes watered to think that so many of them were sent to the gas chambers...*

Felicity opened the hotel room door surprised to see Ellen alone. It raised her concern about her prospects for a magical night with Zach. "Sis, why aren't you with Marshall?"

"We needed a break from each other so we split up."

"Were you intending to get back together this evening?"

"He was tired so we didn't make plans. I think

without our motors revving, we both lost interest. How was your day?"

"Sublime," she said evenly. She started to rethink her evening plans by hearing how uncomfortable things went with Marshall and her sister. She rolled through all the possibilities in her mind and then settled on a course of action. She looked at Ellen with pleading eyes. "I need a favor from you."

"Go ahead Sis."

"I am politely kicking you out."

Ellen tried to understand. "*Oh*, let me think about this for a minute…"

Felicity rushed back, "What's to think about? For all these years when we're out at the clubs, who supported you so that you could get the sexy bloke while I carry on with his companion no matter what he looked or acted like?"

Ellen defended herself. "I thought you enjoyed those hookups?"

"Sometimes, but many times not," Felicity confessed. "I did it for you! Now that I found someone I've really connected with, you have to think about it?" She stared at Ellen and started to cry.

"There, there Sis". She took a deep breath. "I didn't know you had fallen to this extent. Look, Marshall and I are only gymnastic partners." She hugged Felicity. "Okay, okay, where can I find Zach? We need to have a little chat over this new plan of yours."

"He went back to his villa to shower. I said I'd be over straight away. I had planned to pick up me new nightie and sleep over there. But now that Marshall is there mending, I'd prefer to have Zach back over here," said Felicity.

Ellen nodded. *Mmmmmmm. Okay, this is serious.* "All right, let me get me things in a bag and go over there. I'll gently advise Zach to come back here and I'll stay the night over there."

"Thanks, Sis. I love you. This makes up for a lot."
she smiled.

▪▪▪

Thinking that Zach may be upstairs showering or
Marshall could be sleeping, Ellen pounded on the villa
door with a loud succession of knocks. After a while,
Marshall groggily came to the door.

"Hi Marshy, mind if I come in?" She didn't wait for
an answer and walked right in.

Marshall was lost for words. "*Uh... oh...* Ellen...
wait... okay." Ellen barged right past him.

"Is your brother here?"

"Yeah, he's in the shower."

"Thanks."

Ellen walked straight upstairs. In the bathroom, she
heard water from the shower bouncing off the tub and
Zach singing "Sweet Freedom" by Michael McDonald.
She opened the door and entered the steamy room. Zach
couldn't see her behind the shower curtain.

"Marshall, what you doing? Couldn't you just hold it
in?" he screeched through the shower.

"No Zach, it's me, Ellen," she yelled over the
running water.

"What? Couldn't you wait until I got out?"

"I need to talk to you."

"Did something happen to Felicity?"

"Matter-of-fact, yes! I'd like to discuss it with you."

"Fine." He turned off the faucet and calmly
requested, "Can you hand me a towel now, please?"

Ellen was still slightly sore at Zach after he played
the embarrassing joke on Marshall in the hospital. She
decided to even the score. She reached the towel inside
the curtain, and then quickly pulled back the entire
curtain to see a shocked, naked Zach.

"Whoa now!" Zach reached down and covered his
crotch with the towel. "These boys want to live another

day; one Stillman may be temporarily disabled, but the other will remain perfectly functional for the near future."

"That's what I wanted to talk to you about." She walked out of the bathroom and encouraged him to follow.

Zach put the towel around his waist, covered it with the hotel-supplied robe and followed her. Ellen waited for him sitting on the edge of the king bed in Marshall's room. Zach sidled up next to her and said "What's going on?"

"I just left me sister the happiest I've seen her in over two years. And it's all because of you. But if you think I came all the way over here to congratulate you, you have another thing coming. I've come here to warn you not to hurt her."

"I never would…"

"Not physically–emotionally! She is wound up so tight, if you pull her string she'll spin on the floor for an hour."

Zach considered that. He was so absorbed in his own feelings he didn't realize how fragile Felicity was. "I get it. I'm emotional, too. You don't really know me but I'm not here to take advantage of her. I have my own issues to deal with. Look, I came on vacation to have meaningless sex with a variety of women I suspected I'd never see again. It wasn't my intention to meet someone like Felicity who has grabbed at my heartstrings. I've been struggling between savoring the moments and, at the same time, worrying about any future with her past tomorrow."

Ellen could read Zach's sincerity. "Okay." She hugged him. "Bring a change of clothes, don't forget protection, and make your way down to me hotel room. Be careful for both your sakes. Now go! She's waiting for you."

Twenty-five

Felicity's Hotel Room, Rhodes, Greece

Zach walked slowly over to Felicity's hotel. He thought through the game plan. *She's vulnerable. She smitten with me and wants to be patient and careful. I'm getting turned on all day as she had those curvaceous chest protectors tightly pressed against me on the moped. My emotions are spiraling. I don't know what to think.*

He reached the hotel and walked down the main floor to her room and lightly knocked on the door.

"It's open," Felicity called from the back of the room.

Zach slowly pushed the door open to see a long hotel room filled with candlelight. When his eyes focused in the distance, he saw Felicity wearing a stunning black negligee.

"*Wow.* I just want to burn this vision into my memory banks forever," he said with an open mouth.

"*Howdy* cowboy! Ready to ride the bronco?" She mimicked a Texas drawl. Zach relaxed and broke up laughing.

"Yes, ma'am," he followed her lead.

"Well, come over here now and give Daisy Mae a kiss."

Zach ran to her and they did a simultaneous hug and kiss combination. While kissing, he slowly picked her off the ground. They seemed to melt into each other like a warm two-flavor ice cream cone. She led him to a small kitchen table where she had prepared a standing bucket of ice holding a bottle of champagne. She pulled out two champagne glasses from the kitchenette and said formally "You may have the honors," as she passed the bottle for him to open.

Pop! Zach opened it with a snap and a wisp of vapor. He poured the champagne into the two glasses and held one out for her as he raised the other one in a toast. "To a remarkable woman!"

"To a devilishly handsome man," she replied.

They drank the toast and she walked towards the bathroom and turned. "Zach, could you give me a little help with me negligee?" Zach slowly ambled over to the bathroom. When he was near it, he was able to see that Felicity had lit more candles surrounding a bubble-filled oval tub.

"Delighted to be of service, ma'am!" He marched imitating a servant. He gently helped her off with her negligee and she returned the favor by helping him off with his clothes. They both walked over and dipped into the tub. The water was tepid so they ran the hot faucet to get it to an optimal temperature.

Zach went in first and Felicity laid on top of him facing forward so she was knitted into the fabric of his body.

"What am I going to do with you, Felicity Williams?"

"I don't know. I was thinking the same thing about you."

His eyes did sweeping glances of her luscious breasts sitting in the bubbly water like lily pads. He quietly shared his feelings. "You know, these last few days have been happiest in my life."

"They've been mine too," she replied.

Although he usually tried to be careful sharing his feelings with women, Felicity's petite touch and erotic breathing opened him up. "I confess, your honor. I came here on vacation to selfishly work out my issues."

"What are they?" Felicity encouraged.

"It seemed like every woman I've ever dated has been supplied to me by either Marshall or my father."

"You don't seem happy with that arrangement."

"Not really. You know, if I didn't take the initiative I'd never have met you."

"You seem to forget it was me who asked you for the s'n cream."

"You got me there."

"You know you weren't on me radar either. I was just looking for a diversion away from being just me sis' traveling companion."

"So that's all I am, a diversion?" Zach said with a smile.

"Yes, but a heavenly one indeed." Felicity reached up and tripped the tub drain switch and the water level started to lower.

They lingered a bit longer, then slowly got out of the tub. There were two robes hanging on the back of the bathroom door. They put them on and climbed onto the bed. At that point they were all over each other. First, kissing and exploring each other's bodies, then using their hands and fingers. She reached out for his joystick and he became rock hard with her touch. He gingerly stepped off the bed to grab a condom from his trousers.

When he slowly entered her, she was like molten lava. They both roared with delight as they helped each other reach orgasm. They crashed on the bed with a heavy sigh and lay motionless for a while.

"I think that the US/UK relations are now at an all-time high," Felicity quipped.

Twenty-six

Rhodes Airport, Rhodes, Greece

"I can't believe this fairy tale is finally ending," said Felicity. The four of them were in the main waiting hall of the Rhodes Airport waiting for the guys' puddle jumper to take them to Athens and then to a charter flight back home.

Felicity felt a deep and calming happiness that she had never experienced before. It was if she had taken a magic pill; she had finally put the despair over her mum's loss into their proper resting place in the file cabinets of her mind.

Felicity and Zach's lovemaking went on late into the night and carried into the morning. She thought their actions felt pre-ordained as if her whole life's teaching led her to this current clarity of thought. She was sleepless most of the night trying to prepare her for the time when she and Zach would part. She was hoping that this was not the last time she would ever see him, but even so, it was all worth it.

"What's so interesting in that paper you're buried in, Marshall?" called Ellen.

"Hey, it's been a week without reading about the New York Yankees' scores. My addiction now needs feeding!"

"Guys and their fascination with sport. I once knew a bloke that couldn't come into work until noon if the Sheffield Wednesday Football Club lost the prior day."

Zach tried to clarify. "Sport is a religion in New York City, especially in our family where Marshall and I are split between the New York Yankees and Mets. By the way Marshall, how did the Mets do?"

"They won 4-3 with Daryl Strawberry hitting two homers. He's having a hellava year for them. You know, right now both the Mets and the Yankees lead their divisions."

"Wouldn't it be great if they ever met in the World Series?"

The guys went on and on, engaging with their obsession. Felicity guessed it was the only thing they felt comfortable talking about at this time. Zach had been pretty quiet most of the day. That morning, his body did most of the talking, but when she tried to prod him on his feelings, he remained stoic.

They exchanged phone numbers and mailing addresses; Zach immediately made an excuse that he wasn't a good writer, especially about his feelings, although he did promise to answer if she wrote him.

"Where does that leave us?" Felicity asked.

"To be decided," Zach said wondering, and leaving her speculating as well.

The boarding call blared into the cramped holding area. Ellen and Marshall were smiling and laughing with each other. They were recapping the previous night, when they spent time healing open and internal wounds oozing from the casualty of their circus sex acts. They admittedly used each other and finally acknowledged the toll it took on them. Ellen acknowledged her own grief from losing her mum and confessed that it manifested itself in her aggressive mating rituals. With one more day left in Rhodes after the guys departed, Felicity hoped that she and Ellen could get to the bottom of Ellen's emotions.

Zach stood up, embraced Felicity and whispered in her ear, "I'll never forget you. My mind is moving too fast to process right now so I'm sorry I've been so quiet today. I've already learned the lesson not to blab all your feelings until you have a handle on them. I don't know if I'll ever see you again but right now I've never felt so alive and I have you to thank for that."

Felicity stared deeply into his watery brown eyes. "I understand. I have a new appreciation of all things New York, so maybe one day I'll see it for meself."

"You never know." Zach pondered.

Twenty-seven

7 June 1987

Dearest Zach,

It's been a week since we parted and I feel like I'm still in Greece with you. I find it very hard to think of anything else than your comforting smile and your broad shoulders riding majestically on the moped in Rhodes. Ellen keeps complaining to me that I frequently walk in a daze.

I have made the attached tape for you. Stanley Wells is the host of a radio programme I often listen to on Radio One. He plays the latest UK pop songs so you'll get a flavour of my entertainment tastes.

I attached a drawing of my room. I know I can't draw very well so there's no need to agree. I didn't realise I had so much clothes space. It's no wonder I can never find anything. The room is not as cluttered as it appears. The paper I used was the wrong shape, it wasn't wide enough. Bear in mind, I am prepared to pull some of my Donnie Osmond posters off the wall to give you space when you send me a picture of yourself. Don't accept that action nonchalantly.

I had all my pictures from Rhodes processed straight away so I could send you some. I especially liked the one we took at St. John's Bay after we met. I had my tank top back on so it should be suitable for sharing. I also included one of me you took when I was in the bubble bath.

Before I describe my typical week, I wanted to post this letter out to you.

Love and Kisses,
Felicity
xxxxx

June 26, 1987

Dearest Felicity,
I am overwhelmed with the tape and photos you sent in your previous package. I loved them. I was glad you were able to secure a picture of Marshall in his hospital bed (without his pecker showing, thank God) so I now have some proof of that unbelievable story.
I included the only large-size photo I had of me, my college graduation picture. I'm pretty happy with it as I'm looking smart, as you say, in my suit and tie. By the way, I will need your approval before I send the bubble bath picture to Playboy Magazine. It already has the approval of Duncan, my manager, and every other horny dude at the office.
Emotionally, I'm trying to get my head together. No doubt, I fell for you and we got so comfortably close in three days. I was glad that you were able to let yourself go and feel again since losing your mum.
I have to sign off now and deal with one of my father's nudging requests. I really can't wait to afford my own place. Please take care of yourself and write back soon!

Love,
Zach

22 August 1987

Dear Zach,
Yes, you've guessed it; in the enclosed blue envelope is your

birthday card.

Terrible luck will befall you if you open it before "the" day. It's an old superstition I just made up to keep you from opening it! I only posted it early to make sure it was there for your birthday, not three days after, like the card I received from a certain someone who shall remain nameless! But then again, when that certain someone rings me up and I'm out of the house, I should be ashamed of myself. I'm not only very sorry, I haven't stopped kicking myself yet.

You will have to write me as soon as the hangover wears off and tell me all about your birthday celebrations. I wish I could be there.

I keep thinking back when we were sitting at the Goodbye Lounge at the Rhodes airport. Marshall was reading his paper and you were telling me how much you both liked watching the Odd Couple TV show. I'm sorry but I have a confession to make. I wasn't really listening. I just kept on thinking that, in a few minutes, you'd be gone and maybe I'd never see you again. It had been a magical holiday and it all seemed to be ending too soon. Or maybe we'd only just begun? (The Carpenters' song is now in my head).

By the way, I just received an invitation for my Cousin Janice's wedding. She is planning to have it at Sheffield City Hall, which is a beautiful venue. I'd love for you to come and see it. I hope you'll consider it.

Write soon and have a nice time on you B-day. I hope you like your card and all the hidden extras! Remember, no peeping.

Love & Kisses,
Felicity
xxxxxxxxxxxx

Twenty-eight

Lower East Side, New York City

Zach and Marshall were sitting down at Seymour and Wilma's, each wolfing down a plate of meat loaf.

"You're going where?" said Wilma as if anywhere away from New York was alien territory.

"Sheffield," Zach replied curtly.

"Where the hell is Sheffield anyway?" Seymour asked wryly.

"Dad, it's in England, not Kamchatka. They speak English there."

Zach finally accepted Felicity's invitation to visit her in Sheffield. It was a pretty easy decision for him; he had over one hundred letters and packages from her over the past three months to persuade him. Since returning from Greece, letters, tapes, gifts sent in all kinds of fancy packaging became a constant reminder to Zach that he was inside Felicity's every thought. It was cute, but pretty overwhelming for him.

Zach felt he was definitely a changed man since returning from Greece. *I had an unforgettable time there. The way the two of us met was a great story to tell and I love sharing it with friends and family. Felicity is different from any girl I've ever met; but she is a million miles away from the New York force field.*

117

I can't afford to miss her but I really do.

When the guys got home from Greece, they really wanted to hide the intimate details of the nudist beach and the gay night club from his father and Wilma. But with their father's CIA-style interrogation techniques in full-throttle and Marshall's loud and boasting mouth, all the gory details came out, as it invariably did, at the dinner table.

Zach couldn't forget the whole scene. *Dad yelling at Marshall, "You could've killed yourself. Wilma, can you just imagine the discussion at the Men's Club at synagogue? Oh, your son's a doctor…mine's a lawyer. Now, I have to step up and say 'hey everybody, mine's a porn star'. That'll get me handshakes all around."*

"Dad, stop! You just wish it were you," Marshall said with a smile.

Zach was jolted to the present by his father. "Zach, what's with this girl?"

"What girl are you talking about?" Zach grumbled.

"What girl are you asking me? How about the one who has sent you so many packages; I now have the UPS guy on retainer."

"*Oh*, Felicity. I can't and won't control what she writes and sends. It was like we became best friends overnight and then someone zapped us three thousand miles away from each other. Apparently, these are the side effects," he mused.

Seymour saw that this relationship was really affecting his son. He ventured deeper, "Do you love her?"

Zach paused, ready to give a canned answer. Instead he shared, "I can't really answer that. Certainly what we had was intense but it was way too short to deal with. That's why I accepted her invitation to see her again in England. I just need to spend more time with her. I know I'm going to a wedding over there, but just remember Dad, it's not mine."

"When are you leaving?" Seymour asked.

"I'm traveling at the end of the month."

"When did you get the plane tickets? They must have cost you a fortune to buy them so close to the flight date."

"Not really. I bought them over a month ago."

"And you didn't tell me, why?" he said with a somewhat threatening tone.

"Dad, I know I'm still living at home and that gives you the perception that you can still run my life, but I am an adult. I didn't think I needed your permission."

Seymour frowned. "Where are you staying?" he asked.

"At Felicity's house."

"Who does she live with besides her sister, the circus performer?" Even after three months, their father still had not let Marshall live down his X-rated activities when they were in Greece.

"Her father."

"I bet he was thrilled hearing about Marshall's theatrics and your mental takeover of his daughter's brain."

"I don't know if he knows or cares."

"Zach I'm just looking out for you. This girl obviously saw something in you that she now has set her hooks into. She'll never let go until she extracts all of your nutrients and then what would I be left with? Just an ordinary Met fan." Seymour laughed to himself.

"Dad, it's not like that. The feelings we have are mutual. Now, if you continue to interrogate me, I will only give you my name, rank and serial number."

Seymour wrestled to let his son live life without his teachings. "Okay, enough for now. You are a big boy and I will have to trust you. Have a good trip and be safe."

After clearing the table, Zach remained there with Marshall.

"Well, that went well didn't it?" Marshall said

sarcastically.

"Did you see the steam come off my forehead?" Zach replied.

Marshall changed subjects. "You know, I didn't get an invitation to the wedding. I know why, but it would have been nice to get one."

"Have you communicated with Ellen since Greece?"

"Not really. She did send me a *foony* birthday card."

"Did you send her anything?"

"What? A thank you card for snapping my cock?"

"If I remember correctly, you thought it was a good idea at the time to try that little stunt, and besides, she did make up with you afterwards."

"Yes, she did very nicely at that; but her sweet personality had an alter ego. I'm telling you, it was as if she could impulsively switch between her Dr. Jekyll and Miss Hyde personae."

"Should I convey any sentiment when I'm there?"

"Tell her I mended completely!"

■■■

The next day on his commuter train, Zach reflected on his upcoming trip. He was alarmed with Felicity's overabundant writing habits. He thought Felicity was compelled to convey every single thought she had to him. He was amused and freaked at the same time. On his Sheffield trip, he committed to himself to find out what was driving that strange behavior.

Zach used the wedding invitation as a handy excuse to see Felicity again and explore whether the depth of their relationship was more than just a wild vacation encounter. He rearranged his schedule so he could stretch the trip to a week of his precious time-off from work. He calculated that it was more than double the time they had in Rhodes; he predicted that it would be enough time for him to assess the situation.

Zach returned from Greece a changed man; prior to the trip, he hadn't ever visited a foreign country, if one doesn't count Canada and some of the seedier sections of Brooklyn. Although Zach met a variety of foreigners living in New York, he never met anyone from Northern England like Felicity and Ellen. It made the world seem much smaller.

Zach had grown up as a typical New Yorker, one who felt that the world rotated around Times Square. Locations on the other side of the Hudson River, much less the entire Atlantic Ocean, were irrelevant. Felicity opened Zach to a new perspective where ideas and feelings were spoken with an alternative flavor; but core ideals and personal interplay were truly familiar. Zach knew he was vulnerable visiting Felicity on her turf, but he tingled with the exposure, acknowledging that he'd grow from the experience.

While Felicity intimated total devotion in her letters, Zach's commitment wasn't as exclusive. His father continued to set him up with blind dates, and he still allowed himself to act as Marshall's wingman. His defiance from Felicity's literary clutches barely satisfied him for a weekend but he upheld a bachelor's right to freely choose his relationships. He acknowledged these ladies lacked depth, but he justified the sex; he wasn't married or dead yet.

Zach's relationship with Felicity was just a lightning bolt; he couldn't describe it further. *Three blissful days and a file cabinet of letters cannot construe a relationship.* After committing to the trip, Zach held back analyzing his feelings for Felicity until he had her on visual.

Zach casually rolled into work mid-morning since tax season was over. While the tax season was brutal, he cruised through the off-season. When he reached his cubicle, Duncan approached him.

"Zach, my global rock star, how did your father take the news of your upcoming trip?"

"Not too well, Duncan. He hated that I kept my plans from him."

"What else could you do? You are your own man making your own decisions."

"Duncan, what do you make of all these letters and packages from Felicity?"

"She's in love with you, buddy. It's maybe the first time in her life. I've seen it many times after my conquests at Dartmouth."

"I know you're bullshitting me, Duncan. Give me one example."

He thought for a while as they walked over to the break room for a cup of coffee. They filled their cups and grabbed chairs around one of the small tables.

Duncan cleared his throat as he closed his eyes in memory retrieval. "Are you ready for one of my conquests?" Zach smiled. Duncan stood to recite. "Okay, here goes!"

"There once was a girl named Wendy,

Whose sex taste was always so spendy.

When she met Duncan A,

She found a great lay

Now she pays every day for his bendy."

Zach spewed out his coffee in hysterics. He grabbed a napkin to wipe the table. "Was there really a Wendy?"

"Yes," he laughed out loud. "*Oh* Wendy, she had the hots for me."

"Was the feeling mutual?"

"Not really. I found all that attention unsettling. I bet she would have paid me for the sex if I let her. It was freaky; she watched every move I made on campus which was a lot in those days."

"What did you eventually do about it?"

"I got my friend Denise to act as a jealous lover and call Wendy out. Afterwards, I thought Wendy was going to commit suicide or something."

"What did she do?"

"She had to leave school for a while. She had more affecting her judgment than just the psychotic attraction to me. It shouldn't give you an indication at what Felicity will do."

"Thanks buddy. I wouldn't put Felicity in Wendy's class but she certainly has a fixation, all right. My trip to England should be telling."

Twenty-nine

Boynton Road, Sheffield, England

Ellen, Felicity and their dad were sitting at the dinner table. "I know he's coming. It's only the four hundredth time you've said it," said Ellen.

Felicity was defensive. "Sis, allow me to be excited, okay?"

"Excited yes, but not like a demented groupie. By the way you're fussing all about, you'd think that Zach was the lead singer of Level 42! Ever since Zach left Rhodes, that's all I ever hear from you."

"Sis, stop!" She looked over to her father for support. "Dad, it's not like that."

"Kitten, I have to agree with your sister. It's like this bloke is Prince Charles and you're Princess Diana."

"Okay, Dad, I realise I'm infatuated, but, it's certainly better than grieving over Mum like some zombie."

"Amen to that."

Since Zach's plane left Rhodes, Felicity maintained her mental high. His departure didn't sadden her; she was crystal clear that she would see him again. She made sure of it. Through her letters to Zach, she released all her emotions as if he provided the spigot to bilge all those depressive feelings which had clogged up her brain. By freeing herself from this mental sewage, her writing hand flowed freely on the paper.

Felicity's fixation changed her daily routine. She mentally closed herself off from anything else. Although she remained Ellen's wingwoman for her sister's pub and club mating rituals, she personally had absolutely no interest in other lads anymore. It didn't stop the blokes from trying, but Felicity's icy stares kept them at bay.

Instead, she used her newly available discretionary time researching tourist facts about New York City. Meeting Zach introduced her to a new culture. She regularly visited the Sheffield Library after work, much to the chagrin of her sister and father who had to feed themselves.

Despite her writing prowess, Felicity hadn't received Zach's cherished invitation to visit his hometown. She felt cheated. She dreamed that Zach had given her the key to New York City without directions. Her frustration didn't derail her. She learned as much as she could wishing that someday he'd invite her over. Gauging from Zach's less emotional responses, she wondered how long it would take.

Her daily letters to Zach acted as a diary, more like insight into her daily trivialities. She thought there was greater reality in the mundane; anything to advance their relationship since they barely had any time together in Rhodes. In her letters, she described her daily routines, surroundings, people in her life, and personal tastes.

Felicity was surprised receiving the invitation for Cousin Janice's wedding. She assumed that there was a "muffin in the oven" causing the formal vows to be exchanged. *Janice is a good girl but sometimes the lads make you do things when your heart is all afire. Yeah, I'm one to talk.*

She buried the invitation to Zach within all of the banalities of her letters. She was confused when he accepted it, especially since he hadn't invited her to New

York. In subsequent letters, she interrogated him on his reasons to come to Sheffield instead of her visiting New York. He remained evasive. She expected a clear answer when he arrived.

George brought Felicity out of her daydream. "Now Kitten, I'd like to discuss the sleeping arrangements when the 'New York Yankee' shows up at our doorstep."

"Well," she said sheepishly. "I was expecting him to stay in me room."

"With you inside it? Remember, this is still me house."

"*Oh* Dad, I'm a grown woman and he's a grown man."

"It's that grown part of the man that concerns me."

"Dad, are you going to be putting up a glass to the wall to eavesdrop on us?"

He shifted up straight as if he were the Town Crier. "I'd rather not be knowing that me little girl is being violated under me roof. Therefore, I don't want you sleeping with him in me house."

Ellen interjected, "Hey Dad, you never showed this much care when I have one of me lads over."

He gave Ellen a frustrated look. "Because you always do what you want anyways. You know, sometimes I hear the goings on."

Ellen smiled. "I guess I do get meself a bit worked up sometimes."

George steamed. "Worked up? It's all I can do sometimes to keep me from calling the coppers on these buggers you bring home. But no, me Kitten is not like you. She still listens to her father. That's why I demand that he sleeps in Ellen's room."

"With me?" Ellen scrunched her face.

"No, I'm not daft. You can sleep in Felicity's room. Felicity, you can take the couch in the living room. I don't want him catching what you've been given off in your room. If he does, I pray for us all. Ellen's room should confuse his raging hormones."

"Dad, your overwhelming care about Zach is duly noted," Felicity said with a smile.

■■

Felicity readied plans for Zach's trip to Sheffield. She conjectured what he might enjoy on his short visit given what she was able to cull from his terse letters. She knew that the Sheffield Wednesday football season was in session. She found the schedule and polled her office for tickets. Her father's "Checkpoint Charlie" home restrictions inhibited intimacy, so she visited her travel agent during her lunch break. The agent suggested Blackpool, a family resort town on the West Coast. *The carnival atmosphere of the place should remind him of Coney Island.*

Back at work from the travel agent, Felicity decided to include her officemates, Carole and Lindsay, in her planning. The girls were dying to meet Zach and their playful chatter broke the humdrum routines of their work day.

"You going to take him around to the pubs?" Lindsay asked.

"I think so. To me knowledge, I don't think he's ever been in a proper pub before," Felicity replied.

Lindsay had an idea. "You could take him to me Cousin Howard's pub. Howard brews his own ale and could take him around on a cellar room tour."

"Where they keep the bodies?" Carole chimed in.

"Oh, come off it, Carole. He might like it," said Lindsay.

Carole mentally scanned her family tree for a fun experience for Zach and asked, "Felicity, has he ever been on a farm? I don't think there are any farms in Manhattan if I'm not mistaken."

Felicity challenged her. "I don't know, but Carole,

you don't live on a farm."

"But me Uncle Cecil does. He has a nice one in Barnsley."

"It's something to think about," concluded Felicity.

Lindsay asked, "Are you going to take him away on holiday?"

"Definitely. Me dad won't let him sleep in me room with me in it. My travel agent recommended Blackpool. He'll right like that, I suppose."

"Push him over to the games of chance so he can win you a prize," Carole suggested.

"He already has one. Me!" The girls snickered, then rolled their eyes.

■■■

Felicity worked feverishly to make the house tidy. George saw this and even helped out – by staying out of her way. George appeared sour on Zach's visit and Felicity couldn't understand why. She saw him, slowly but surely, recovering from her mum's death. He finally re-secured a steady second shift from the taxi service. His schedule allowed him to take his food break with the girls when they came home from work. But lately, whenever Felicity started talking about Zach, her dad froze up.

Felicity waited for Ellen to leave on a date so she could confront him about her concerns. They sat at the table eating dessert.

"Dad, I'm getting the feeling that you're not all aflutter in meeting me friend Zach."

"Not as much as you, Kitten," he replied without looking at her.

"I understand that but you've tried your best to be all grumbly about him."

"I have me reasons." It was clear that he was holding back something.

Felicity wasn't sure how to pry open the truth so she

purred like a little kitten. "Care to share any?"

He hesitated for a few seconds. *That kitten purr always puts me under her spell.* He blurted out, as if hypnotized, "There was this bloke in me day who had a fancy with your mum before we were a couple."

"I'm not surprised." She led him on. "She was beautiful."

"That she was! But this bloke had all the fast talking and the suave clothes going on."

Felicity eased him into his heroic tale. "What happened?"

"She fancied him right nice, got all googly-eyed towards him and then he dropped her like an anvil."

"I never heard about this." She lied. Her mother told her all about it and swore her to secrecy.

"She was pretty broken up about it." He paused and smiled. "I had to come in and save the day. It took some convincing to show her that I was a man who actually means what he says."

Felicity started to see the warped connection her father was making. "And you think Zach will do the same to me."

"You are your mum's daughter."

"Dad!" She didn't know whether to hug him or jokingly smack him. She eventually came around the table and hugged him. "I'm going into this whole thing with me eyes wide open."

"It's not your eyes that I'm worried about, Kitten."

Thirty

Sheffield, England

Zach arrived on the red-eye at nine A.M. at Heathrow Airport without fanfare. He was half-expecting a brass band and the key to the city of Sheffield, but the only one to meet him was Felicity. She was holding out a sign outside customs that read "Love of my life". Zach broke out a tear.

They held each other for two solid minutes while Felicity cried uncontrollably. She tried talking but kept making no sense. Through Zach's embrace and slow backrubs, she was finally able to compose herself. "It's just that there was a part of me that doubted if I ever was going to see you again," she explained.

They walked outside to the street and boarded the National bus to Sheffield. Mass transit would be their mode of transportation since Felicity didn't drive and Zach was petrified of driving on the wrong side of the road. The ride north gave them the chance to catch up and compare expectations of their time together.

"Felicity, I hope you know how much I appreciated all those letters…" he said with a smirk.

"But they were too much, I know," she interrupted.

"Good. Just so you know, my father thinks you are a

serial killer posing as a petite British spy seeking to destroy my heart," Zach declared.

"You haven't met me dad yet. Get your bullet-proof vest ready."

"Why? He hasn't been sharpening the Graham cutlery lately, has he?"

"He did sit me down for a bit-of-a-talk." Felicity reported.

'Oh God, he didn't order twenty-four hour police surveillance? About what?"

"You can't sleep with me in me own house."

"I was wondering about that. Okay, no police but no privacy either."

"We'll have to save our intimate time for Blackpool," she smiled. She gave him the travel agent's introduction to Blackpool.

"Fantabulous!" Zach raised his eyebrows in acknowledgement. "Sounds fun. Looks like we'll have to pick our spots for me to ravish your body."

Felicity looked around. "If this bus was empty, you could do it now." They kissed.

Felicity broke their embrace. "Me work friends, Lindsay and Carole, can't wait to meet you. They've reached out to their extended families to get you a personal tour of a pub and a farm."

"Good friends you have. You know I have been to both a pub and a farm before. They do let me out of *dubcity* sometimes."

"Well, I didn't know. By the way, did you bring your smart outfit for the wedding?"

"I brought the suit and tie that's on the picture I sent you. No tux; I didn't want to overdress."

"Suit will be just fine." She couldn't wait to parade him around to her family.

The bus ride flew by as they caught up on their lives after Rhodes. Zach hadn't even noticed the time or that he had missed an entire night's sleep. But as they reached the Williams' house, Zach's energy tank was only on fumes.

∎∎∎

Felicity opened the front door. "We're home. Dad, are you here?"

George was anxiously waiting in the living room. The two shots of Scotch he had earlier helped, but not much. It took all he had to get a first-hand look at the boy who had turned his daughter on her end.

George yelled back, "In the living room, Kitten."

Zach whispered to Felicity, "Kitten, huh?"

Felicity smiled proudly, "Me dad's pet name for me."

Zach chided her. "Okay Kitten, lead me to him."

She stopped him with a wry smile. "Only he gets to call me that. You'll have to think of your own pet name."

Felicity led Zach into the house, past the foyer and into the living room. There, Zach saw a large green fabric sofa flanked by two matching chairs. George, in black reading glasses extended out to the tip of his nose, sat in one chair reading the newspaper. George put down his glasses and the paper; he sized up Zach for the first time.

Zach's first impression of Felicity's dad focused on George's round red face. George appeared to be rather imposing and Zach mentally searched his hands for a ring to kiss.

George's coolness compelled Felicity to make a formal introduction. "Dad, this is Zach. Zach, this is me dad."

Zach came over to the chair and reached out his hand. "Very nice to finally meet you in person, Mr. Williams. Felicity has talked and written so much to me about you."

George was puzzled about what Felicity could have conveyed in her letters, so he just accepted the hand and shook it firmly. "It's George. Come sit down around here for a chat."

Zach inspected George more closely. *He looks older than his fifty years. The red nose, the slow movements in the chair, and the subtle protectiveness in his voice are all signs of the vestiges of despair. I guess that losing a loved-one to cancer could do that to a person.*

George studied Zach. *He's a good-looking boy but not like anyone around here. I wondered how he'll get along with the local folks.*

George motioned Zach to the corner of the sofa facing him. "I bet you're a bit knackered from your trip."

"Sorry sir, I'm what? I beg your pardon. Did you just say naked?"

"Knackered," he said more slowly. George seemed puzzled. "You know..." He simulated a stretch and a yawn. "Hey Kitten, I thought he knew how to speak English."

Zach finally figured it out. "*Oh...* You mean...sleepy,"

"Sleepy...knackered...All the same."

Felicity shifted the subject. "I already told Zach about the sleeping arrangements."

"Mr. Will...sorry, George. I want to tell you that it's perfectly fine with me."

"It better be."

Zach turned away from George and rolled his eyes at Felicity, who was sitting beside him on the couch.

George didn't know what else to say, so he abruptly got up from his chair. "Okay Zach, we'll finish this little chat later. Felicity, why don't you take Zach up to Ellen's room so he can recover a bit from his journey?"

"Good idea, Dad."

Zach went upstairs, dropped his bag, and checked out all the weird posters in Ellen's room. Exhausted, he dove onto the bed and crashed.

Waking up four hours later, Zach felt refreshed and started downstairs to check in on Felicity. As he slowly descended the staircase, he detected all kinds of noises in the kitchen, from snips, to plops, to sizzles. When he walked into the kitchen, she was busy peeling carrots.

"Look who's being 'Miss Domestic'?" he remarked.

"Welcome to me world," she said while nodding.

"What are you making?"

"Me world-famous shepherd's pie. Want to help?"

"Sure. What do you need? I'm great at boiling water."

"That'll help–little," Felicity joked.

"What can I say? I'm spoiled. I have all my meals cooked for me."

"Yes, 'Mr. Spoiled'. Relax, and I'll cook you a feast. Tonight, I plan to feed you dinner, and then feed you to me girlfriends at a nightclub."

Felicity knew that the way to a man's heart is through his stomach, so she worked feverishly to wow him with the meal.

"So you plan to fatten me up for the slaughter?"

"Your words, not mine."

At that time, Ellen came home from work. She saw a smiling Zach in the kitchen and gave him a massive hug. They danced around the kitchen while Felicity laughed.

"My brother wanted to let you know that he has healed completely, and he is a better man, in every sense, since he met you," reported Zach.

"Let him know that I had the memory of that popping sound I heard from him surgically erased from me brain." Ellen replied.

Not to be outdone, Zach quipped, "By the way, Andy Gibb called. He wants his complete poster and *Teen Beat* magazine collection back."

Ellen bantered back with a smile looking at her sister, "As soon as Felicity gives back her Donnie Osmond one."

"Never!" said Felicity in deathly defiance. "Now the two of you stop making fun of me idol and help set the table. Dinner is now ready."

Ellen looked around. "Is Dad here?"

Felicity looked down. "He made an excuse not to be home for dinner. He seemed agitated."

Zach defended him. "I'm sure my arrival was tough on him. You're his kitten, you know? *Meow.*"

Felicity started serving the shepherd's pie. "He didn't look too good, Ellen. He barely spoke to Zach."

"Zach is an obvious threat to him. I'll work on him," Ellen promised.

Zach completely devoured his dinner. Even though he was famished, he could still see that Felicity's cooking was truly marvelous. He had heard about the lack of culinary skills in England. It must've missed Felicity's kitchen.

After dinner, Zach got into his nightclub attire and waited by the door. Shortly thereafter, Felicity came down wearing her best clubbing outfit: a tight-fitting, satin black cocktail dress with tiny straps and three frilly white polka dot swirling ribbons at the bottom. Her appearance jolted Zach like dose of caffeine, immediately getting him in the mood for excitement at the club.

"Wow, you look gorgeous. I'm now ready and raring to go," he remarked.

They took the bus downtown to the Lunatic Laura Nightclub and met up with Carole and Lindsay outside the entrance. Felicity introduced them to Zach. The place was pretty packed, but they were able to find a booth. That night, the club had a deejay instead of a live band since it was Disco Night. As they were shifting into their booth, "Sledgehammer" by Peter Gabriel was booming through the speakers and spinning mirrored balls created a kaleidoscope of lights.

Zach knew that the way to a woman's heart was through her friends, so he turned on his charm for Lindsay and Carole.

Zach sized them up. Lindsay and Carole were both

cute and dolled up for the club. Lindsay had her dirty brown hair in a ponytail. She wore a silver, oversized shirt that acted as a skirt tied up with a thick black belt, complementing matching black leggings and boots. Carole had dark brown hair tied up in a wide band purple headscarf. Her attractive globe-sized brown eyes seem to pop out of her head. She wore a teal tank top under a shiny purple shirt open on one shoulder, along with teal leggings and purple shoes.

Carole said. "I heard that you're the next John Travolta. Want to dance?"

"Sure," Zach replied and got up.

Zach and Carole made their way on the dance floor as the deejay put on, "Don't You Want Me" by the Human League. Since the Lunatic Laura was the band's debut concert location, practically everyone in the club made their way onto the dance floor except Lindsay and Felicity, who preferred to stay back and gossip about Zach.

Lindsay complimented Felicity on her choice of man. "Zach's dreamy. He seems everything you said about him."

"Thanks, it's so great to finally see him here. It's almost surreal."

"Just so you know, me Cousin Howard is ready for the pub visit tomorrow evening. Will that work?"

"Yes, we're going over to the farm in the afternoon and will head on over to the pub later."

Out in the center of the nightclub, Zach put on some dance moves for Carole. The crowd opened up a circle so they had more room for him to display his stuff.

"Look over on the dance floor! Zach's channeling Michael Jackson." Lindsay motioned to Felicity.

"I expect to see more of those moves personal-like in Blackpool."

"Beat it." said Lindsay as they both giggled at the joke.

■■■

Carole's Uncle Cecil lived an hour's drive from the city. Carole took the afternoon off from work, picked up Zach and Felicity at noon, and drove them out of Sheffield into the quiet countryside. On the way, Zach remarked that the scenery resembled a giant golf course with its rolling hills in varying shades of green.

They arrived at Cecil's farm in Barnsley, a small town north of Sheffield. The farm was on eight acres and included an outcropping of old brick and metal buildings on a sloping footprint. The ivy-covered main house was weathered, dating back almost a hundred years. Its interior remained unchanged since the sixties. Outside the house was a barn for horses, and a metal-rusted building where Cecil raised chickens.

Cecil jogged to the driveway to meet them when they arrived. He was wearing a cream-colored short sleeved work shirt with a khaki-colored pocketed vest. He had short brown hair and weathered pasty skin. When he introduced himself, Zach couldn't understand a word he was saying. He looked at Carole and Felicity at times to help him decipher his heavy Yorkshire accent.

Zach hadn't spent much time on a farm, yet didn't want Felicity to recognize it. So, when Cecil declared that one of his cows was breeching, Zach offered to help.

They all strode out to the barn to check on the cow. The bovine was lying down on its side, and Zach felt its pain. He tried to mask his reaction to Felicity, solely due to his male pride. He wanted to shield Felicity from the truth, that he lived a sheltered life at home in New York City where things were planned and predictable. Seeing the cow writhing in pain, Zach was energized with the spontaneity of the event.

Cecil went up to the cow and called Zach over.

"She's ready to birth but the calf is in a breech

position with her hind legs first. She needs to be adjusted so her hind legs come through the birth canal. Can you push the cow here on her abdomen so the calf's legs have a clearer path with its mother?"

Zach looked at Carole for help in translating. "Sure, I've seen this problem a few times before," he lied.

Zach elbowed the cow's stomach while Cecil kneaded other parts to adjust the calf's position. Finally, when the hind hooves appeared out the birth canal, the cow let out a soothing groan then immediately stood up. Zach nervously hopped out of the way.

Cecil smiled at Zach's trepidations and was ready to test his visitor. "Okay, me new friend, the cow's in a better state but we're going to have to reach in and adjust the calf's position so she'll slide out better. Put this on." Cecil handed Zach a shoulder-length plastic bag with fingers at one end.

Zach examined the bag. *Does he want me to put this on and stick my hand in there? That's totally gross! Man, does it smell in here! Felicity is loving this but how can I keep my disgust from her? I could be her hero. Looking at her anticipation, there's no turning back now...*He put his arm through the bag and into the finger slots.

He turned to Cecil. "What do I gotta do?"

Cecil calmly schooled him. "Reach in and feel for the calf's head. We can't pull her out until she's completely right."

Zach looked to Carole and Felicity for a translation.

"Feel for the head!" they cried out.

It took some silent self-coaxing, but with Felicity looking on, Zach smiled as if he'd done it a thousand times. He cringed a bit as he put his hand into the cow's behind all the way up to his shoulder. The cow was warm and gooey inside and he could feel the outline of the calf's body. "I feel the head!" Zach announced.

Cecil smiled. "Good. Slowly pull your arm out and grab the hind legs. Zach obeyed and grabbed the calf's legs. "They're stuck!" he squawked.

Cecil motioned an astonished Felicity over to the calf. "Zach needs help pulling." Cecil put a set of chains around the hind hooves and directed them to the back of the cow. "Okay, so I can count on you both to pull slowly and steady when I count to three?"

Felicity nodded and checked Zach's understanding. "We'll be ready," he said with a slight hesitancy.

When Cecil yelled "three", Zach and Felicity pulled firmly on the chains. With Felicity's added strength, the calf's legs started to emerge from the cow. The cow's birth canal ballooned as its torso made its way through. After they saw the calf's ribcage, the resistance slackened. The calf, no longer obstructed, plopped out easily onto Zach, who slipped onto the hay-strewn floor. The cow roared its relief and expelled her sticky afterbirth onto Zach and Felicity.

The calf appeared lifeless with a bluish tinge. Felicity was horrified. Cecil hurriedly jumped over Zach and searched for a heartbeat. Zach quickly shuffled out of the way as Cecil put a clean piece of straw up one of the calf's nostrils and tilted its neck to create a clear airway. He then closed its mouth and one nostril while blowing gently in the other. In response, Zach saw the calf's chest wall rise. Cecil kept breathing into the calf until it started breathing on its own. He then splashed a bucket of cold water on the calf to startle it into movement.

"It's alive!" Zach screamed in delight. Cecil smiled and helped Zach and Felicity stand up. They stood dripping, somehow managing to wear a simultaneous pleased and disgusted smile.

As Zach stood in the barn trying to clean himself off, Felicity said, "Looks like we're not going dancing right now, unless it's with the pigs in the sty outside the barn."

Zach walked up to her and gave her a slobbery hug. "Not bad for a city slicker, *huh*?"

■■■ ı

Cecil lent Zach and Felicity clothes they could change into and give back to Carole. After separate showers back at Felicity's house, they felt more human than bovine. Shortly thereafter, Lindsay picked them up and drove them to her Cousin Howard's pub, The Fertile Cow. The pub was in Norton, a small town forty-five minute drive southeast of Sheffield. As they arrived, Zach thought the building came right out of the movie, *An American Werewolf in London.*

The Fertile Cow had been a drinking establishment for over two hundred years. The building's exterior had a medieval appearance. It was a simple structure made of stone with Tudor-style white and dark wood styling along the top half. Its entrance door was comprised of heavy wood and rounded at the top as if pictured in *The Hobbit.*

Upon entering, Zach detected an acute aroma combination of shoe leather, fireplace ash and dank beer. They noticed an 1800s-style hearth on one side of the eating area surrounded by twelve tables with old wooden high-back chairs. To the left was a freshly re-varnished bar in a U-shaped configuration.

Cousin Howard met the three of them at the bar wearing an apron and a wide smile. Howard was a roly-poly sort with big features and a permanent red nose. His uncombed black hair and matching full beard gave him the appearance of Bluto in the *Popeye* comics.

"So, this is the American, here to taste true English ale, are you? Howard's me name. Pleasure to meet you." Howard also had a heavy Yorkshire accent; Zach found it barely more decipherable than Cecil's.

"Same. I'm Zach." He reached out his hand for Howard to shake.

"Want a *tooer?*" Howard asked.

"What?" Zach said puzzled.

"A *too-er*," Howard said slowly.

Zach scratched his head. "I don't need a two-pence coin."

Howard guffawed. "No, you bloody wanker, where I makes me beer."

A light switch clicked on in his brain. "Oh, a tour!"

Howard held his hands up in wonder. "That's what I said, a *too-er.*"

After showing Zach the restaurant and kitchen, Howard led Zach, Felicity and Lindsay down narrow stairs to a dimly lit cellar. On one side, there were stacks of beer kegs, and on the other, was a small working area with a large vat attached by water hoses. Howard waved the group over to smell the contents of the vat.

"This vat is brewing an Irish stout." Howard lifted the lid for them to see and smell.

"It smells like tea," Felicity remarked.

"That's essentially what it is before it ferments, a tea brewed with hops, malt and flavorings. I just tapped a new ale. It has notes of coffee and vanilla." Howard asked Zach, "Do you want to try it?"

"Sounds delicious," said Zach. "Sure, I'll take some."

They walked back upstairs and Howard pointed to a booth he reserved for them. "All right then. Three pints, coming right up. Can I serve you up some bangers and mash to go with it?"

Zach was hesitant. "As long as they won't kill me," he replied.

"Haven't killed anyone yet...this year, Howard retorted.

When Howard brought out the pints, bangers and mash for the table, he sat down with the three of them.

"Hey Howard, I was thinking, what's the economy like out here? I heard that Chinese steel and cutlery makers are giving the city a run for its money."

"Yes it's bad. I see it every day as a pub owner. The lads come in and pour their hearts out to me. Many have left town because there was no longer work for them here. These are desperate times."

"Where did they go?" Zach asked.

"Wherever they can find work or attach themselves to a better life. Mostly London and Europe, but there are stories about people relocating all around the world."

"If you don't mind my asking, how's business here?" Zach looked around the pub. "Seems fine for a Thursday night."

Howard nodded. "In these parts, going to pubs is the last thing people will stop doing. Business is okay but I do worry now and again."

Zach paused to consider Howard's comments. "Thanks, Howard."

On the ride home, Zach and Felicity continued the topic.

"It seems that many people are getting laid off in this region," Zach remarked.

Felicity agreed. "Most companies are really working the redundancy issue."

"What is that?" asked Zach.

Felicity thought of Claire and gritted her teeth in frustration. "That's when the company lets people go because others can do their same jobs with more overtime and less pay."

"Sounds rough," Zach empathized.

Lindsay chimed in, "This year, we lost our dear friend Claire at the office. She did a fine job but the Company laid her off to cut expenses."

Zach turned his attention more personally at Felicity. "What would you do if you got laid off?"

"Don't rightly know. Guess I'll have to find other work."

"And if you couldn't?"

Felicity felt she was back on her heels. "Why are you asking?"

"I'm starting to get worried about you."

"I'll be fine. Me guardian angel will look out for me."
She closed the distance between their faces.

"Who is that?" Zach smiled.

"Some fairy prince wearing a New York Mets cap."
She kissed him. Lindsay smiled widely at the wheel.

Zach gathered his thoughts. *I hope you don't rely on me. I can barely take care of myself.*

Thirty-one

Town Hall, Sheffield, England

Cousin Janice's big wedding was the next afternoon. Zach dressed up in his best charcoal gray suit and sported a crimson paisley tie. Felicity wore a conservative navy blue sequined gown with simple matching pumps.

Her father drove Zach, Felicity and Ellen downtown for the wedding at Sheffield City Hall in his cab. The site was a popular wedding venue due to its distinct charm and classic architecture. It was an immense four-story structure with multiple steeples including one containing a clock that resembled Big Ben.

The highlight of the interior was the expansive, rectangular stairway with high ceilings that was the ideal backdrop for formal photographs. Felicity asked Ellen to take photos of her and Zach descending the stairs. After the formal shot, Ellen insisted that Zach take a seductive one of her to give to Marshall for a laugh.

The ceremony room was massive, able to hold double the expected two hundred attendees. The maroon carpet matched the rows of velvet and gold metal chairs emblazoned on the back with Sheffield's city crest.

Felicity found seats closest to the aisle so she had a direct view of the bridal path and the altar. The wedding service was nondenominational. A local judge wearing a long flowing black robe officiated the event.

During the ceremony, Felicity kept glancing over to Zach to gauge his interest. He appeared casual with it all, but she couldn't read any more into it from his body language.

After the ceremony, the guests were led to an adjoining room, set with circular dining tables. Zach, Felicity, Ellen and George were seated at a table with George's younger brother, Robert, his wife Ginger and their four children. George introduced Robert to Zach and they chatted about the Williams family. To Zach's delight, Robert spoke only with a slight accent.

"How many generations of the Williams clan go back in Sheffield?" asked Zach.

Robert looked up as if the answer was written in the ceiling and replied, "As far back as anyone can remember. Things get clearer in our family's history when our ancestor, Randall Williams, built a fastener business back in 1870."

"What happened to it?" Zach asked.

"The Fastener Building was a major fixture in Sheffield until it was bombed in World War II. The business never survived after that." Robert shook his head.

Zach waved his hand. "But this family is huge. Did all of the family stay close to Sheffield? What did they do to find work?"

"Most hung around here. The family is pretty tightknit, although you do get the odd bird that flies the coop. These people, you see, are pretty inventive. They retrained themselves just to stay here in the Sheffield area," Robert replied.

Zach pondered about how the Williams' desire to stay close to Sheffield mirrored his own family's invisible force field around New Your City. *It would be a struggle for either Felicity or me to be the one to relocate.*

■■

Felicity had a grand time showing off Zach in his smart suit to her family. His dark complexion made him stick out like a foreigner from the mostly pasty-faced crowd. Having Zach's arm around her waist made Felicity feel special, as if he had personally picked her out of the global population.

After dessert, all the unmarried women attendees came out to the base of the regal stairway for the bouquet toss. Given her small frame, when the bouquet was about to be thrown, Felicity sneaked her way up to the front. When Janice tossed the bouquet out of Felicity's reach, she made a beeline towards it, flattening two teenagers in her path, then dove for the flowers before they hit the floor. The crowd was aghast at her aggressive play. She ignored the startled cries as she dusted herself off.

Zach, moving center stage, broke the tension by announcing, "Hey everyone, Felicity was just practicing her header move for the Sheffield Wednesday Ladies Club. Remember, tryouts are next week!"

That garnered a smattering of laughs that appeared to have slightly diffused the tension. Zach walked up to her as she stood with flowers tightly gripped in her hand.

Zach put his arm around her and whispered in her ear, "What happened out there?"

Shaking her head, Felicity whispered back, "I don't rightly know. I just reacted without thinking."

Zach peeled his eyes towards the exit. "Okay, go get your dad. I think we should make a clean getaway."

Thirty-two

The Blackpool FC Hotel and Conference Center - Blackpool, England

One of Zach's specific requests on the trip was to attend a soccer match. He had heard about the English fanaticism for 'football' and was eager to see how that passion compared to his feelings for baseball. One of the fortunate timing coincidences for this trip was that the local Sheffield team, Sheffield Wednesday, was playing an away game in Blackpool that Monday while they were there.

Felicity was fortunate; not only did she get tickets from a work connection, but also secured a room at the Blackpool FC Hotel and Conference Center that overlooked the soccer pitch.

After a three hour, northwesterly bus ride, they checked into their room in the late evening. Zach pulled the curtains back to reveal a full view of the stadium. It was such a unique vista, Zach felt like one of the team's owners. The room was otherwise ordinary except the décor was in team colors: white, black and tangerine.

As soon as Zach finished tipping the bellhop and closed the door, Felicity embraced him and pulled him to the bed. She seemed much more sexually hungry than he had ever seen her in Rhodes. She quickly took off all her clothes and helped Zach with his. Their bed became a frenzied array of garments. Felicity, with her petite strength, pushed Zach down on the bed facing her, and quickly jumped on top of him with urgency. She rhythmically lifted herself up and down on him until she came explosively. Zach was confused, both marveling at her actions, but speechless about his surprise. As they lay motionless next to each other, Zach confronted her.

"What just happened? Who is this person? Did you just channel your sister?" Zach quipped. "You know you didn't even give me any time to put on a rubber?"

Felicity finished catching her breath. "I don't know what just happened there. I guess it had been building up inside of me for three months now."

"I'll say! I wonder what would have happened if I visited six months later. Would you have brought the whips and chains?"

She sat up and declared, "Long before then I probably would've spontaneously combusted, and me heart would've been expelled to you all the way across the Atlantic Ocean."

Zach pulled her back down. "My turn now," Zach growled, flipping her and reaching for a rubber in the wallet in his trouser pocket. The two of them danced the horizontal bop one more time before crashing for the night.

Thirty-three

Blackpool Tower - Blackpool, England

Blackpool was predominantly a seaside resort, much like Zach's memory of the Jersey shore. It had games of chance, a boardwalk, and rides. Its feature attraction was the historic Blackpool Tower.

The Tower was a forty floor steel structure, resembling the Eiffel Tower, with a viewing platform. Fortunately for them, it was a rare cloudless day for October. Felicity signaled it as fate. From the top, Zach could see clear across the Irish Sea to the Isle of Man on one side, and down the coast to Liverpool on another. Gazing out, Zach further broached into Felicity's seemingly odd behavior on the trip.

Felicity paused to connect her mental dots. "It's something I'm having difficulty explaining to meself," Felicity shared.

Zach put his arm around her shoulder. "But don't you see that your behavior is starting to show a pattern." He listed: "The volume of letters, the diving for the bouquet, and the aggressive sex is alarming. I didn't expect this mania after your laid-back attitude in Rhodes."

She looked up to think. "I guess I had more time to

149

reflect after meeting you in Greece and got a little scared. I've never met anyone like you before. I know it was fate how we met that day. I just don't want us to be a holiday fling."

Zach stared into her tearing eyes. "I don't either, but I thought we could take it emotionally slower with each other. We've really only just met and I'm a bit of a basket case myself."

Felicity looked away, then turned back, pleadingly. "With all those letters I wrote you, I thought if you read them, it would bring us closer." Her face fell in frustration.

Seeing her expression, Zach's heart fluttered, so he adjusted his tone, "Maybe so, but just exchanging letters is much different than spending actual time together." He made a T shape with his open flat palms. "Okay, let's call a timeout and see if we can recapture the vibe we had in Rhodes."

She relaxed and smiled at him. "Okay then, we'll have to stop at the gift shop to buy a whole bunch of candles."

■■■

They descended down from the Tower platform. Their conversation brightened their moods which carried over the rest of the day in Blackpool. Zach won a stuffed frog at the milk can ball toss and they shared rock candy and floss along the boardwalk.

Felicity took Zach over to Stanley Park so he could try his hand at lawn bowls. The local players were delighted to show Zach their favorite game. The game reminded Zach more of curling than bowling back home. Players had to roll their three and one-half pound dimpled *bowls* along the green lawn square, in turn, trying to finish closest to a smaller white ball called the *jack*. The dimples on the bowls were familiar to the fingertip holes on his bowling ball back home, allowing Zach to impress Felicity with his ability to hook the bowl near the jack. He had so much fun, they barely had time to return to their hotel for a quick shower before the evening's football match.

While Zach was staring out the window at the Stadium, Felicity silently sidled behind him wearing only a blue and white striped soccer uniform shirt and panties. She grabbed at Zach's crotch.

Zach smiled widely as she announced, "I'm all ready for the football match!"

"I'm ready to skip the football match," Zach countered.

"I have a surprise for you" Felicity directed him to hold out his hands.

Zach complied and said, "More than just the lovely creature standing in front of me?"

From behind her back, Felicity grabbed a matching Sheffield Wednesday uniform shirt for Zach and held it out proudly for him.

"I'm an instant fan." Zach appreciated the thought but remembered episodes in New York whenever people wore visitor's uniforms to Met games. He had researched the British fervor towards soccer. It was worse than in America. He hesitated, "Since we are sitting in the visitor's stadium, aren't we going to get razzed? I've heard some crude things about partisan crowds at English soccer matches. For example, I read that one time, the Blackpool fans peed down on the visitor's section."

"I've never had a problem at a match. We'll only have an issue if we antagonize the crowd, or if Sheffield beats Blackpool."

"That sounds promising," Zach sneered.

■■

The Bloomfield Road Stadium that hosted that evening's game between the Blackpool FC Tangerines and the Sheffield Wednesday Football Club seated seventeen thousand spectators. The stadium had been in operation since 1901, and it looked it. It was a simple structure with long rows of orange covered metal seats covering the four sides of the field. The north side stands, called the Kop, had "B F C" spelled out in white seats. The Kop was the location for Blackpool's most rabid fans.

Felicity didn't realize until they were already inside the stadium that the tickets she acquired from her office connection were located in the heart of the Kop. When Felicity and Zach walked out to their seats in the middle of a center row, they became the only people dressed in white and blue amongst a sea of the bright orange field jerseys of the Tangerine fans. As they sat down, they were met with grunts and raspberries from their viewing neighbors. Although the rest of the Stadium's seating was sparse, the Kop was filled to capacity.

Zach looked around and felt like a rabbi crashing the Führer's dinner party. He looked over at Felicity who, with bulging eyes, signaled him to be perfectly quiet.

After the match started, it was hard to hear anything other than the indecipherable singing chants of the Tangerine faithful. Zach strained to decipher the words, but relented quickly, remaining stoic in his seat.

The game's pace started slowly with both teams only getting a few opportunities for shots on goal. Then, with five minutes left before halftime, a Tangerine player passed up to his teammate in the penalty area whose over-the-head kick drove the ball into the Sheffield Wednesday goal. The crowd in the Kop went delirious; many made a point to directly scream juicily at Zach and Felicity. Zach remained passive but wild eyed as he soaked it all in.

The second half was as boring as the first, until a long punt, as Zach called it, from Sheffield Wednesday's goalkeeper led an attack down the field, culminating in a carefully choreographed two-pass quick kick in on the far side of the Blackpool goal to tie it up.

With five minutes left in the match, the tension in the Kop had built to a boisterous frenzy. Zach's seat neighbor, a brawny sort who Zach thought resembled a boxer, screamed beer-laden Blackpool cheers directly at Zach, prompting Felicity to wipe his face. The building tension had drawn Zach into his natural competitive spirit; he needed a conscious effort to keep himself in check. However, when a Sheffield Wednesday player scored with a header off a corner kick with two minutes remaining, he jumped uncontrollably out of his seat erupting "*Yay,* Sheffield!"

After realizing what he had done, he quickly and quietly cowered. As Zach began to sit down but before he was settled in his seat, his frustrated boxer neighbor slugged him in the right eye socket with an upper cut. Zach reeled back from the impact and fell to the row below.

"Zach!" Felicity screamed.

The grumbly fans seated by Zach's now crumpled body pulled him up quickly as though he was diseased. As Zach held his eye in pain, Felicity quickly led him across the aisle to the exit, as Kop spectators pelted them with beer swill and snack packaging.

They skirted the angry crowd, avoiding further injury until they reached their hotel room. There, Felicity more closely and calmly inspected Zach's black and blue eye.

"You'll live, thank God. Looks like your eye is now your souvenir tattoo of your trip."

"I'm sure my dad will give me the third degree."

Sensing the opportunity, Felicity asked, "Speaking of which, will I ever meet your dad?"

Zach thought how the two would interact. "We'll see. Dad needs a lot of buttering."

"I'll charm the pants off him." Felicity said defiantly.

Zach concluded it would be a battle worthy of a coliseum. "No doubt," he said to end the topic.

While Zach eased his throbbing eye with an ice pack procured from the front desk, they planned out their next moves. They kicked around ideas, but soon the conversation waned as realization of where their relationship was headed dawned on both of them.

"Where do we go from here?" Felicity said with a hint of sadness edging her voice.

Zach took a huge breath. He knew the next chapter of their relationship involved a trip to New York but couldn't see past the family issues. "Let's just take it day by day!"

Felicity stared at him. "I don't know if I'm that patient."

Thirty-four

Liverpool, England

The next morning, after checking out of their hotel, Felicity and Zach found a local chemist shop and purchased a soothing eye patch for Zach. Then, on whimsy, they took a bus detour to the town of Liverpool. The prospect of touring the birthplace of the Beatles brightened Zach's spirits, and Felicity was delighted to be his companion.

When they arrived, the buzz by the record stores indicated a special event. The town was celebrating the Beatles' release of their *Magic Mystery Tour* album on stereo compact disc. Zach and Felicity didn't have a CD player with them, so they lingered in one of the stores to hear the rich clear sound of digital audio on a Beatles album for the first time.

In conjunction with the event, the store was selling a "Beatles Tour" to the famous places included in their songs such as Strawberry Fields, Penny Lane and the Cavern Club. Felicity signed them both up. For the tour, they rode on the top of a double-decker bus.

The tour's first stop was Strawberry Field. It was a Salvation Army children's home out in the suburbs. As a child, John Lennon lived nearby and used to go there to a

155

summer garden party with his Aunt Mimi. The tour guide indicated that this place inspired John to become a musician. Zach made sure that a passerby could take a picture of him and Felicity next to the famous replica gates.

The next stop was Penny Lane. Zach was surprised that it was only just a bus terminal; its significance was derived as the name was displayed on many buses during Lennon and McCartney's childhood. Later, the tour guide pointed out the original Bioletti's barber shop mentioned in the song as the "barber showing photographs of every head he had the pleasure to have known". Felicity treated him to a trim before the bus shuffled off to its final stop.

The Cavern Club was the venue for 292 performances of the Beatles in the early sixties. In 1961, The Beatles soon established themselves as the Cavern Club's signature act. It became the place where their musical identity was forged and many of their fans maintained that the band was its best during those lunchtime gigs, learning stagecraft through the exchanges with the audience only inches away. Zach felt he was on a pilgrimage to the spiritual center of music. The low rounded ceiling added to its distinctiveness.

At the end of the tour, Zach and Felicity were pretty tired. They found a direct bus back to downtown Sheffield and slept most of the way. When they arrived home, they found both Ellen and George waiting up for them. They had laid out a Monopoly board on the dining table for them all to play. Zach was psyched since, as a kid, he used to play the game all the time with Marshall.

The Monopoly game they used was basically the same except the currency and properties were all different than the U.S. version. During play, Zach was able to secure the game's highest valued properties, Park Lane and Mayfair, but lost out to Ellen who eventually had hotels spread across the board.

When Felicity and Zach shut the lights out after talking until three am, they started to fully regret when they had to separate.

■■■

Their final full day together was quiet. Zach sensed Felicity's growing dread about never seeing him again. They took a walk around the tree-lined suburban streets, and Zach pictured living there with Felicity. Could the love they were building for each other sustain such a radical change in lifestyle? Zach pictured his relocation. *Where would I work? Is there even one synagogue here? How many New Yorkers live in Sheffield? How can I keep up with the Mets? My family…could you see my dad visiting this place? They'd treat him like a UFO!*

Felicity broke Zach out of his trance. "A shilling for your thoughts."

"I'm trying to see myself living here"

"Would you even consider it?"

"Yes, just to be with you," he reflected.

"We do need chartered accountants here. I'm sure you could find work."

"It would be a stretch for me. I have so much to learn in order to fit in: the culture, the sports, and the slang. I don't know if I want to give up who I am just yet."

"I understand. But those things are only on the surface. I don't want you to change the man inside."

Felicity imagined the changes Zach would undergo to live in her small city. Sheffield was a great place to grow up but it lacked the excitement, sophistication and worldliness she craved for the next chapter of her life. She took the helm of the conversation.

"What about my visiting New York."

"I need to pave the way for that."

"You had the chance to live my life for a week. I

need to see yours."

He knew she was right. He relented. "Fair enough. Give me a chance to work out a way where you'll feel welcome."

"I can hardly wait!" Felicity beamed.

Thirty-five

Lower East Side - New York City

Seymour popped his eyes a bit out of their sockets. "Now are you gonna tell me how you got that black eye?"

"Okay, from a crazy fan whose hometown team just lost to the team I was supporting on my shirt," Zach related.

"Son, you have to be careful at sporting events."

"He got aggressive with me. If he didn't have twenty-five hundred other rock-chewing people standing right behind him, I would've torn him to pieces."

Zach was sitting alone at the dinner table with Seymour and Wilma. He made it back home without further physical incident, but the mental weight of paving the way with his parents for Felicity's promised visit hung heavily. In the meantime, it seemed that while Zach's relationship with Felicity had been advancing in Sheffield, Seymour and Wilma were brainstorming concerns about it. Zach wanted to have Felicity come and visit New York, but now had the challenge of securing support from his opinionated father.

"Zach, where are you going with this girl? I know I've asked this question before, but that was before you spent a week in her lair."

Zach gave his father a disgusted face and moved on, saying, "Dad, it seems that when I'm physically with her, time stops and we have such a memorable time. However, we're so different. Do you know that I'm the first Jew she's ever met?"

Seymour was taken aback. "Does she think we all have horns?"

Zach put his hands up to deflect the racist thread. "No, it's not like that. It's just that she hasn't a clue about things I take for granted: Jewish culture; baseball; and living in a great city like New York. That's why I want her to visit here. I need better clarity on these things while she's on my turf."

"Are you serious with this girl?" He stared at Zach's eyes for more non-verbal clues.

"Her name is Felicity."

"Okay, are you serious with Felicity?"

"I think so."

Seymour thought through the possible progression of events. "Do you think she'd ever convert to Judaism?"

Zach was expecting this guilt play from his father but didn't have a clear answer. "We never really talked about it. I don't think I'm ready to discuss it either. That just seems like a down-the-line issue. You do need to know that when we went to the old city of Rhodes, she was fascinated by the synagogue there."

Seymour was turned off. "*Aaaah*, that was the Sephardim," Seymour responded. He thought for a second for a way Felicity might be able to get some exposure to his sect of Judaism, the Ashkenazim way. "Maybe you should invite her to come to Wilma's nephew Jacob's Bar Mitzvah in December," he said both to Zach and Wilma.

Wilma nodded her approval. "I did hear it was going to be a sprauncy event!"

The opening Zach had been waiting for was in place! "You know, that's a great idea, Dad. December in New

York would be a great experience for her."

"At least you can get some of your questions answered."

Wilma thought about hosting two uninhibited twenty-somethings in heat. She interjected, "Where would she stay?"

"In my room." Zach said flatly.

Wilma couldn't deal with that as she felt she would lose control of her house. "Seymour, I'm very uncomfortable about that. A *shiksa* under my roof doing..."

Seymour immediately turned to Zach. "Zach, you'll sleep on the couch!"

"Daaaaad!" Zach shrilled. "I'm a grown man. I'm only sleeping here now to save money. I can do what I please."

Seymour looked and received confirmation from Wilma. "Not in my house. My house, my rules."

Zach thought quickly about that. Since he already had his father's agreement to have Felicity visit, he conceded to his terms. Hopefully, he could work out a deal with his brother to borrow his apartment during Felicity's stay. "Okay, I'll sleep on the couch."

Seymour got up from his chair. "Fine. It's decided, she'll visit. Anyway, I need to meet this undercover British spy who's been subverting your mind."

After dinner, Zach pulled out the calendar and started planning for Felicity's trip. Jacob's Bar Mitzvah was scheduled for Saturday, December 26, a perfect time to visit, sandwiched between Christmas and New Year's.

Felicity would probably love Christmastime in New York City. Maybe we could go to a fun place for New Year's Eve. I definitely want to take her down to my office building at the World Trade Center to visit the observation deck. I know Ma wants to meet her, so we'll plan to go over there for some of her famous Sephardic appetizers—burekas and yaprakes. I'll figure out the rest as time gets close, but I should call Felicity with the news as soon as possible.

■■

Felicity had her own issues to deal with as her father was also becoming concerned about his daughter's tightening relationship with "The American". They were sitting down at the table after one of Felicity's gourmet meals.

"Dad, you're barely eating your Yorkshire pudding."

"Not hungry. I keep thinking about the boy."

"Not Zach again?"

"Kitten, he looked so out of place here. It was like he came here to shoot a foreign film. He got everybody all excited, and then he left with a *poof!*

"I think he had a grand time…except for the black eye."

"It just shows that he doesn't understand the rules. I could see it in his eyes that he'd never live here and that means you'd likely go there to live. Then, I'd lose you forever." He started tearing up.

Felicity struggled to handle her father's delicate emotions. "Dad, you will never lose me. I'm staying right here. Besides, he hasn't even invited me to New York."

George quickly turned defiant. "What, you're not good enough for him?"

"It's not that. He has a father who's as grumbly as you are."

George envisioned a kindred spirit across the pond. "Amen to that. Maybe I should have a chat with Zach's father. We can both discuss how ridiculous this situation is."

"*Daaaaad!* I'm not ten years old anymore."

The truth was that Felicity had started having her own concerns about her relationship with Zach. Seeing him in Sheffield was certainly an eye-opener to how different they both were; but it seemed unimportant when the two of them were together alone.

■■

Zach called Felicity after dinner in Sheffield, when he knew that she would be home. He couldn't wait to break the news about the invitation to visit him in New York. Felicity was both taken aback and thrilled to hear the words she had waited for months. She asserted that she was especially looking forward to visiting New York during Christmastime, when all the lights were on display. She had never been to a bar mitzvah and thought the experience would be entertaining, and give her more insight into Zach's religious customs. By the end of the conversation, she was determined to show Zach's parents that she was a proper girlfriend, despite their cultural and geographic differences.

On the phone, Zach conceded, "One thing though, my dad also won't let you sleep in my room with me. I'll talk to Marshall and see if I can pull a favor from him. He's now seeing some girl more regularly and I hope he can stay with her while we borrow his apartment in Riverdale."

Felicity started to put the thoughts in motion. "Sounds like a plan. I'll make me flight reservations. I can hardly wait to see you and your family. Christmas in New York, how utterly romantic!" She danced downstairs to share the news with her dad.

George tried to block her raging excitement by asking "So, you going to miss Christmas here?"

"Dad, this is a once-in-a-lifetime chance."

George envisioned a Christmas without his youngest. "Kitten, I know, but last year was really hard without your mum. I don't know how I'll hold up without you too."

"Maybe you can stay with Percy or Robert for a bit?"

George pondered this idea for a minute, his face

thoughtful. *She's going to go regardless of my actions.* "Percy, no. But maybe I could join Robert and his family on his holiday in Majorca."

"That sounds like a great idea."

He paused to set a condition. "I'll have to ask Robert if it'll be all right."

Felicity knew she'd plead to Robert if she had to. "Good, then it's settled."

George took in a huge breath and blew it out. "Kitten, you better know what you're doing. I'm worried sick about you."

Thirty-six

Riverdale, Bronx, New York City

The days passed quickly ahead of Felicity's visit as Zach finalized her itinerary. He worked out staying at Marshall's apartment in exchange for his prized Willie Mays autographed baseball he got when he and his dad went to a Mets game back in 1973. It was a highlight of his baseball memorabilia collection, but well worth it so he could spend more quality time with Felicity.

Zach was delighted to have his own apartment for Felicity's trip. Riverdale was a calm contrast to the manic pace of Manhattan. Although it still remained in the confines of one the boroughs, Riverdale featured a local shopping area on Johnson Avenue, fifties style apartment buildings and more parks and greenery than the urban grid of Manhattan.

Wilma's brother Isaac was happy to host Felicity at the Bar Mitzvah, and even said he'd talk to the Assistant Rabbi to schedule a brief time with her so Felicity could be more comfortable with the unfamiliar Jewish rituals.

Zach was both eager and panicky about Felicity's visit. He was eager to show her his hometown, an introduction into his religion, and was curious how she would interact with his family. He worried that their

165

relationship couldn't move forward after this trip without some kind of promise from him. The onus of commitment gnawed at his brain as he and Marshall checked the arrivals board at JFK looking for Felicity's British Airways flight.

Marshall sensed something was bothering his brother. "What's up bro?"

"I'm a bit overcome with emotion right now. I feel that after this visit, my life will change forever."

"Are you ready to commit to her?"

"No…Yes…well, no-ish?

"What's no-ish?"

"No-ish means that I no longer have complete control of my senses and my vocabulary. Thanks for the apartment. I'm excited to see her again but a piece of me just wants to have an out of body experience and see how I play it out."

"I get it. Here's a little brotherly advice; she's a cute girl who loves you more than I love you. I could joke but that says a lot. Enjoy yourself and let things play out. Don't let Dad get into your head. It's your life."

"Thanks Marsh, I officially love you less than Ellen does. She'll never find a better stud than you."

"Ellen is a distant memory. I'm making beautiful music with Melody."

"I'm glad it's working out."

"Good enough to pluck your Willie Mays signed baseball in exchange to have an excuse to crash with her."

Zach saw Felicity walking towards them. She resembled a mob daughter under witness protection, wearing an indistinct sweatshirt, blue jeans and dark sunglasses. She saw the sign Zach prepared for her reading "Luv of me life" and burst into his arms. Zach smiled. *I hope I know what I'm doing.*

Marshall drove them back to his apartment in Riverdale and gave Zach the house keys. "Okay, little brother, do whatever I would do," he said with a laugh.

When they were alone in the apartment, they frantically tore off their clothes and jumped each other's bones with a fever they couldn't explain. It was if both their bodies were incommunicado since the last time they made love and they were in a frenzy to catch up. It was only until their session was over that he could calm himself enough to think rationally. Afterwards, lying quietly in a bath together, Felicity broke the silence.

"I'm so glad Marshall put himself out to give us his apartment for the week"

"I had to part with my prized Willie Mays autographed baseball."

"Who's Willie Mays?"

Zach covered his face and sighed.

She continued, "It's Christmas Eve; can we go to midnight mass? Since I'm away from home for Christmas, I want to say a prayer for me mum and dad. He didn't take my leaving so well."

Zach considered it. He stared at the ceiling and remembered passing an old church along Henry Hudson Parkway on his trips with his brother to Yonkers. "Maybe we can go to this local church I know nearby." Zach stepped out of the bath and walked over near the phone. He pulled out the Yellow Pages and confirmed that the church was only walking distance away. He was fortunate that someone answered his call and he was able to secure seats for that night's service.

∎∎ı

The Riverdale Presbyterian Church was architected by James Renwick, the same man who designed the famous St. Patrick's Cathedral. It was built in 1863 and was one of the oldest buildings still standing in Riverdale. The A-frame stone structure, with its heavy wooden door, reminded Felicity of her local church back in

Sheffield. Inside, attached to the high ceiling, hung a row of chandeliers along the aisle-way of the sanctuary. The inside wood roof paneling and the antique pews strongly reminded Zach of a synagogue, except for the large cross displayed at the front, which put him on edge.

Zach had only been to a Christian service for the occasional wedding, so he felt pretty uncomfortable as soon as he walked in. Felicity, however, smiled calmly and remained in deep thought for her parents as they waited for the service to start. The place was completely filled and they sat near the back.

When they started the service with "Come, All Ye Faithful," Felicity sang loudly while Zach pretended to know the words so he wouldn't be called out by the other parishioners. When communion and wine was offered, Felicity raced out into the aisle leaving Zach alone and feeling like "The Antichrist". Sensing his discomfort, Felicity beckoned him to keep her company in line. Zach scooted over into her safe protection.

Zach wasn't paying much attention on line so when the Minister directed him to open his mouth, Zach hypnotically obliged.

"...the body of Christ," the Minister announced as he slipped a wafer into Zach's gaping hole. Zach choked a bit, perceiving he was instantly baptized. Felicity hit his back as he went into a coughing fit and she led him down the aisle of puzzled congregants out the door so they'd be out of earshot. They stood in the cold as Zach finally regained his composure.

Felicity broke their silence. "I saw your face back there. It looked like you were going to pass out. Are you okay?"

Zach was still recounting the experience in his head. "Felicity, that was the first time I ever attended a formal Christian service. It seemed so foreign to me."

Felicity empathized. "Wait until the Bar Mitzvah. I haven't a clue of what to expect."

"Yeah, I was meaning to tell you about that. Isaac, the bar mitzvah boy's father, arranged for us to meet with the assistant rabbi down at the Park Avenue Synagogue tomorrow to explain the event rituals to you."

Felicity remembered how quiet Sheffield got on Christmas. "On Christmas Day? Wouldn't it be closed?"

It was clear to Zach that Felicity was clueless about a non-observant Christmas existence. "Earth to Felicity—this is Shimon Peres speaking. The synagogue is open during the day on Friday, even if it's Christmas. It's just another weekday to Jews."

Thirty-seven

Riverdale, Bronx, New York City

After Zach woke up at seven AM on Christmas morning to announce evidence of Santa's overnight visit, he gave Felicity a diamond lettered ankle bracelet with her name in script. Felicity pulled out Zach's gift from her luggage–a set of steak knives from Graham Cutlery. Zach took one knife out and they carefully cut both their pinkies rubbing their blood together in a ritual bond.

"Now only the Mafia can break us apart," said Zach.

Zach called the synagogue and finalized the timeslot with the assistant rabbi who was orchestrating the Bar Mitzvah ceremony the next day. That afternoon, they took the train down to mid-Manhattan to the synagogue.

The Park Avenue Synagogue was established in 1882, after renovating a church that was located on the Upper East Side of Manhattan. Given its upscale location, the synagogue was considered one of the most prestigious temples in Manhattan. Zach and Felicity peeked inside the main sanctuary before heading up to meet the rabbi; they saw a huge ornate room that could seat two thousand people. It reminded Felicity of the synagogue in Rhodes, but on a much grander scale. They walked down a long hallway on the first floor to the back where the clergy offices were. Off to the side of the huge senior rabbi's office, was a much smaller office for Assistant Rabbi Leah Friedman. She was on the phone so Zach and Felicity waited outside the door.

Leah was animated on the phone. "Yes, Mom, the head rabbi put me in charge of the next Purim Show. It's a parody of the Beatles I'm calling, 'I Want to Hold Your Yad'." When she was able to reach a pause in the conversation, she beckoned her visitors in.

"Mom, I'm going to have to call you back…Yes, I have visitors."

When Zach walked in, he was immediately struck by the rabbi's beauty. She had black shoulder length hair, sparkling blue eyes and high cheekbones like a model. She was dressed conservatively in a gray wool knitted sweater and matching yarmulke. When she moved around from her desk, Zach noticed shapely legs, heavily covered with black leggings and a knee length gray skirt. *This is a woman of my father's dreams.* Felicity noticed Zach perk up and kept a watchful eye on him.

"Pleased to meet you both. My name is Rabbi Leah Friedman. Please sit down."

After they settled around the desk, Felicity broke an uncomfortable silence. "I never knew you could have a woman rabbi."

Leah had heard this question countless times before from both Jews and non-Jews so she was ever ready for the answer. "In our Conservative Jewish denomination, we believe in equal rights for women. Our sect is more liberal than the Orthodox that separate men and women in prayer. I perform all the duties of the senior rabbi, but I'm still fairly new here since I've just completed my studies at the Jewish Theological Seminary last June. Women rabbis are fairly new to the Conservative movement, so I often have to provide extra assurance to my congregants."

"You mean I can sit next to me sweetheart and not

in the balcony" Felicity smiled up to Zach as he mildly blushed.

"Absolutely." She continued, "Conservatism is considered a middle ground between the Orthodox and Reform movements. We are tied more directly to our Jewish laws and the Bible than the Reform denomination. Reform Jews take a more modern view on the Jewish religion in that they more frequently adapt current ideas into the religious rituals. It can get very confusing for people.

Zach was mesmerized with Leah during her explanation, then sparked up when there was a pregnant pause. "Thank you for your time, Rabbi. As I explained on the phone, Felicity is attending Jacob's Bar Mitzvah tomorrow and wanted an introduction of what she'll see."

Felicity interjected, "Yes, I don't know what to wear, what to say, when to stand. I don't want to embarrass meself like Zach did last night at Christmas mass."

Zach blushed and glared over at her.

Leah sensed the tension in the room and tried to calmly press on. "I certainly understand and want to take this opportunity to welcome you to our synagogue, Felicity. You'll find that the congregants and door greeters are very helpful to guests. Jacob's Bar Mitzvah service will be part of our normal Sabbath morning service. On Shabbat, people usually dress up more formally in suits and dresses. The service progresses as follows: After some preliminary prayers said in Hebrew, we open the religious cabinet on the dais called an ark. We then take out religious scrolls containing the Old Testament and read preselected passages assigned to that day's service."

Felicity tried to equate it to her own church's Sunday service. "Does everyone read together?"

"There are times when people read prayers and the congregation reads responsively. Other times, such as when the Old Testament is read, the reader chants alone," Leah said while checking Felicity's non-verbal understanding.

"Is it read in English?"

"In our service, most prayers are chanted in Hebrew. The Old Testament is also chanted in Hebrew according to its *trope* which are notes displayed with the words." Leah pulled out a passage of text to show her.

"Fascinating!" Felicity remarked with genuine interest.

Leah went on, "It has taken Jacob a year to prepare for this event. Kids Jacob's age are dealing with puberty issues and it often shows with their cracking voices. Jacob, like many great kids, deals with it as part of the ritual. I'm confident he's ready, and you'll get a chance to see a good example of a traditional bar mitzvah." Leah went on to answer all of Felicity's remaining questions.

As they stood up to leave Zach blurted, "Why did you become a rabbi?" He moved closer to her and whispered, "You could've been a model…"

Leah blushed but tensed up sensing Felicity's rising jealousy. She maintained an objective posture. "Thanks. It's really the difference I feel I can make with the students and their parents."

"My parents fought over their Jewish faith. It has left me with permanent guilt and confusion," Zach confessed.

"If you like, we can discuss this further. You'll need to make an appointment with me with the secretary down the hall."

Zach smiled and turned towards the door. "Thank you so much for your time. I look forward to seeing the service tomorrow."

Leah smiled at the two of them. "No, it was my sincere pleasure. I hope you enjoy yourselves."

As they walked out of the synagogue into the cold crisp air, Felicity pulled Zach close. "What was that in there? If you kept staring at each other, I was afraid I was going to break one of the Ten Commandments."

"I was only trying to be nice. She did take the time to answer your questions, didn't she?"

"What was that comment about permanent guilt and confusion?

"Just wait. Tonight you'll get a chance to meet my father and Wilma."

■■

Seymour and Wilma invited Zach and Felicity over to their apartment for dinner. Walking down the hallway to the front door, Felicity was stunned to see the hall absent of any Christmas decorations and music. When Zach unlocked the door, she peeked in to confirm no presents under any tree. It was as if Santa Claus had the Stillman apartment on his "naughty" list.

Recovering herself quickly, Felicity readjusted her expectations and focused on charming Zach's dad and stepmother. She readied herself to speak clearly and slowly without her accent getting in the way. Seymour ran out into the foyer to greet them.

"Here she is! The girl that has my sonny boy in a tizzy. Come here sweetheart so I can get a piece of ya."

He reached out and gave Felicity a crushing hug until her eyes bugged out a little. As they moved towards the kitchen, they could smell the mouth-watering aroma of oven roasted chicken.

Seymour led Felicity into the kitchen. "Wilma can use some help getting the meal ready. Zach has told us many times that you are a gourmet."

With Wilma directing Felicity on cutting vegetables for the salad, Seymour pulled Zach away from earshot over in the den.

"She's very pretty in a gentile sort of way," Seymour judged.

Zach was happy that his dad chose his words more carefully than he expected. "She is who she is."

Seymour decided to probe a bit. "I heard you had a nice chat with the assistant rabbi today. Isn't she something to look at?"

"Wow, news sure travels fast! Did you and the rabbi both beam over to Mount Sinai for a chat?"

"Well, she did call Wilma's brother after your visit to confirm that you guys met. She slyly remarked to Isaac how handsome you were. Did you think she was pretty?"

"Dad! She was very helpful." He then stopped close to Seymour's ear and whispered, "I never saw a more stunning woman wearing *kipot*."

"And very available, I have on good authority," Seymour whispered back.

"Dad!"

Seymour continued in hushed tones, "Zach, just be careful with Felicity. Now that I've seen her in person. I can see the way she looks at you."

"And…"

"And now that you're on her line, she'll want to reel you in and take you away from all that you are." He stood up and faced his son. "There, I said it. At least you can recognize an alternative hook if it dangles by your swimming lane."

"Dad, I can handle myself. You have to let me figure this out on my own."

Plating noises came from the kitchen. Seymour nodded his head at his son. "Well, I hear them rumbling inside ready to come out. Let's enjoy dinner but I want to follow up on this conversation after Felicity leaves."

Dinner was delectable. Wilma made chicken with *kugel,* an Eastern European bread pudding. The kugel reminded Felicity of traditional Yorkshire bread pudding. But as they ate, it was clearly apparent that Wilma and Seymour were tag-teaming their interrogation of her, spoiling her enjoyment of the mouth-watering feast.

Wilma started in. "Did you know Zach, I just found out that Felicity doesn't even know what a bagel is. I didn't know there was such a person in this entire world who didn't know what a bagel was."

Zach rolled his eyes. "Apparently two Himalayan Buddhist sects and Felicity."

"You better make sure you pick some up for her for breakfast tomorrow," said Seymour.

"Yes, with lox and cream cheese. It's on my list," Zach responded.

Seymour directed his attention to Felicity. "Are you ready for the Jewish extravaganza of the year? I heard that Wilma's brother mortgaged one of his buildings just to pay for this bar mitzvah." He looked over to Wilma and then frowned. "Oh, I probably shouldn't have said that."

"Anyway, we can't wait for the event," Felicity slowly concluded, clearly uncomfortable with the way the conversation turned, but willing to soldier through it. "I'm looking forward to it. I've never been to a bar-mitzvah before. Matter-of-fact, it's the first time I'm not eating dinner at home on Christmas Day."

"What do you think, child?" Wilma asked.

"I find it very strange; like I'm on a different planet."

Zach tried to diffuse the tension. "Most people think New York City is on a different planet,"

Felicity went for her large handbag. "To mark the occasion, I've brought a present for all of us to have fun with. It's a Christmas tradition that my family has always observed. It's called Christmas crackers."

Seymour objected, "If it has anything to do with a communion wafer, you can count me out."

Felicity laughed "No, it doesn't have anything to do with that." She defiantly stared at Seymour and said, "But Zach did take one for the team last night at Midnight Mass." Zach glared at her in response. She smiled and explained further. "The 'cracker' in the name is for the sound it makes." Felicity then pulled out of her handbag a set of six brightly colored tubes in blue crepe paper with a snowman scene. "The object is to hold the tube at both ends and pull. Why don't you try it Mr. Stillman?" She handed him a tube to pull.

"It's Seymour. Okay, here goes." Seymour pulled from both ends gently and they all heard an audible *pop!* The contents of the middle fell into his lap. He jumped from the surprise.

Felicity smiled at Zach's father's first attempt at cracking. "Seymour, it's okay. There's some kind of chemical that causes the noise when the ends are pulled. That's the fun. We typically read the jokes they put in the cracker while wearing the silly paper hats they include."

Seymour looked down on his lap and floor to see a tiny plastic car, a note and a small tightly wrapped paper package.

Felicity stood up and led the process by directing, "Wilma, your turn!"

Wilma picked up her cracker and popped it with a startle and a laugh. Zach, then Felicity did the same. "Okay, it's time to put on our hats!" Felicity announced.

All four of them unraveled the blue tissue hats from the plastic package. One side was straight and the other had triangles like a crown. Zach rushed into his bedroom to grab his camera to try to capture the comical scene of them wearing their outlandish hats at the table.

"What do we do now, Felicity?" asked Seymour.

"Now you have to read your joke aloud," Felicity answered with a smile.

"Okay." Seymour picked up his joke from his lap and read it aloud. "What is a skeleton called when it doesn't get up in the morning?" He waited a second before continuing. "Lazy bones. Well, these joke writers are certainly not Mel Brooks. Wilma, you're next."

Wilma opened her piece of paper from her cracker. "Where can you find health, wealth and happiness? In a dictionary. I like that one. Go ahead, Zach."

Zach took his turn. "What do you call a monster with no luck? A luck-ness monster. That's pretty lame."

Felicity smiled at Zach. "The jokes are always silly. They're funnier when we've been drinking the eggnog for a while."

The crackers, jokes and silly hats further dispersed the building tension at the table. Felicity charmed Seymour by taking a sincere interest in ideas about cultural differences and bar mitzvah rituals. When Seymour and Wilma went into the kitchen to make coffee, Zach looked lovingly over at Felicity and gave her a thumbs-up. Felicity's heart jumped like she had just done a proper curtsey for the queen.

When they had put on their coats to leave, Seymour came over to Felicity to give her a peck on the cheek. "Go home, get some rest. Tomorrow's a big day for you."

Thirty-eight

Park Avenue Synagogue, New York City

Zach and Felicity arrived at the synagogue for Jacob's Bar Mitzvah with Marshall and his girlfriend Melody, a tall redhead with a sweet smile. As they arrived, Zach noticed that the lower sanctuary was crowding fast. Wilma had told Felicity that her brother Isaac, not only was a well-established real estate manager in the Upper East Side, but was heavily involved on the synagogue's Board of Directors. The Manhattan Jewish royalty were there in force.

They found seats towards the back third of the ground floor. The service had already started so Zach found his place in the service siddur. Zach showed Felicity how to find her place in the service so she could participate when they read responsively in English. As the service progressed, Zach often glanced over to Felicity who was smiling widely and trying to follow when to stand and when to follow a prayer with an "amen".

Zach thought Felicity stuck out, especially with her V-necked dress sporting a sizable gold and sparkly cross. It discomforted Zach, like he was a double agent for the Mossad, the Israeli intelligence agency.

While the prayers and readings pressed on, Zach

179

fantasized a bit about Leah. His thoughts alternated between excitement and humility. Rabbis were not placed on this earth for their physical attractiveness. Zach recalled the rabbi who taught him his bar mitzvah lessons, a man in his sixties with a long gray beard who occasionally let out an audible fart during his lessons and services. He and Marshall used to take bets whether he would do it, and when, during a service.

The room had a different vibe with Leah guiding the service. Her words sounded sweet, almost angelic. The ritual prayers sounded fresh like they were synthesized through a mystical machine ordained by God. Even Jacob, the bar mitzvah boy, was touched gently by Leah's guidance. His initial cracking voice gained confidence as she helped him through his Torah portion.

After the service, there was a small Kiddush lunch in a social hall behind the sanctuary. While walking about, Zach saw Leah and decided to share some of his thoughts.

He nervously fumbled with his composure. "Rabbi, I was really impressed with the way you managed Jacob. You know, I find that the service sounds so much more digestible for me with you at the helm. Your voice made me feel that God was communicating to me on a whole separate channel," he flirted unconsciously. "Look, I usually get really uncomfortable listening to rabbis, but today you took the time to make everything seem so easily understandable."

"Thank you, Zach. Please call me Leah. Did Felicity enjoy the services as well?"

"I think so. It was her first bar mitzvah, so I think it was a lot for her to take in."

"Well, if you have any more questions, you know how to reach me. How much longer is Felicity staying?"

"She's planning to leave just after New Year's."

"Well, if you ever have any religious questions or need someone to talk to, maybe we can have a coffee or something sometime if you're interested."

"Thanks, Leah. Maybe you could see it when we visited yesterday, but it's the first time I ever had serious feelings about a girl who isn't Jewish. It has left me a bit confused." *Especially now looking at you.*

"I work with many interfaith couples so let me know if you want to schedule some time."

"Sure, thanks."

■■■

That night, the reception was at the Plaza Hotel, one of the most opulent venues in the city. The Plaza's Grand Ballroom was a most sought-after location for the upper class of New York. It seated five hundred people and had two rows of vaulted marble columns outlining its sides retaining its neoclassical decor. Jacob's reception had a circus theme; tables were dressed in white and red stripes appointed with cotton candy, balloons, Cracker Jacks and the traditional Jordan Almonds. In the center of the tables was a rectangular dance floor. On one side of the room, they erected a stage that included three trapeze bars hanging from the ceiling above a catch net.

During the cocktail hour, hired clowns and jugglers entertained the guests. Zach and Felicity had a chance to mill about. Felicity was awed by the spectacle and glad she had packed her nicest dress, a satin black gown with gold trim lace with high-heeled black slip-ons. However, she still felt it paled in comparison to the designer dresses she saw amongst the crowd.

The lights dimmed as the Master of Ceremonies introduced the bar mitzvah boy. Zach expected Jacob just to walk out from the cocktail area to the dance floor, but was surprised to see him swinging back and forth from the trapeze like a circus performer, then fall to the net in a somersault below. The crowd exploded with cheers and applause while Jacob's parents were heralded as the "Jewish Parents of the Year".

The hired five-piece band struck up Jewish music right away causing all the guests to create a melee inside the dance floor. Felicity was caught up in the stampede and almost went down. She steadied herself and stepped back towards the stage to observe the action. In doing so, she noticed one of the hired performers coming toward her. He walked right up to her and whispered something to her in her ear. Felicity laughed, nodded, and went back with him behind the stage area while a bemused Zach stared at her in puzzlement as she walked away from him.

The crowd danced the *hora*, a line dance, similar to the Greek dancing they had watched in Rhodes. The guests made rotating concentric circles around the bar mitzvah boy and his family. People grabbed chairs and promptly hoisted the star of the evening and his hosts raising them up and down in tune to the music.

To add to the theatrics, the trapeze performers were swinging a young petite lady dressed in a leotard back and forth between the three bars. No one was really noticing them until Marshall, standing next to Zach, shouted "Hey, there's Felicity!"

Zach looked back to see Felicity swinging by her arms and legs wearing a circus performer leotard and a permanent smile. The crowd followed Zach's gaze and gave her a round of applause as Zach doubled over with laughter.

When Felicity got down, she walked away from an open-mouthed Zach into the bathroom and changed back into her gown. When she got out and walked back to Zach, he remarked, "Why on earth did you do that?"

"Well, with your eyes peeled on 'Lady Rabbi' over there, I thought I might grab your attention for a minute," said Felicity, with jealous amusement in her voice.

Zach blushed a deep crimson. *Busted.*

She went on, "Look, they didn't have their regular

girl with them; they saw that I was a perfect fit for her petite outfit so they coaxed me up there. Besides, circus stunts run in me family," she said with a bright smile.

Thirty-nine

The World Trade Center, New York City

On Sunday, Zach and Felicity scheduled time to see some New York City tourist sites. Zach was proud to take Felicity downtown and go up to the top of his office building at the World Trade Center. They took the *Seventh Avenue* train down from Riverdale. The graffiti disgusted Felicity as well as the smell of urine and body odor of the transients they met on the train. She was surprised that Zach just treated it as normal.

After the hour-long trip, they arrived at the base of the Twin Towers shortly before opening. Zach's tenancy of Two World Trade Center gave him free access to the observation deck. He also used some pull to make sure he was at the front of the line when it opened.

After obtaining their tickets, they headed up the dedicated observation tower elevator to the 107th floor. There, they entered the Top of the World Exhibition where they took a virtual helicopter tour of New York, including sites like the Verrazano Bridge, Central Park and Times Square. After the six minute ride, they jumped on an escalator to the 110th floor observation deck. It was a clear but bitterly cold day. With the wind howling outside, they decided not to risk freezing themselves and stayed behind the protective windows.

Felicity gaped at the skylines in wonder. In that moment she felt a million miles away from Sheffield. She reflected on how her life had changed so quickly since meeting Zach to allow her the unique opportunity to view this majestic scenery. It moved her so much that she needed some time alone by the window overlooking the Statue of Liberty to reflect. *I wish Mum were alive so I could share this with her. She'd love New York and all the new experiences. I wish she could help me deal with my feelings for Zach and the guilt from Dad.*

Zach saw that she was deep in thought and gave her some space and then slowly walked up to her.

"What's the matter, Felicity? You look like Moses on Mount Sinai, without the gray wild hair, long beard, tall frame, and biblical music in the background..."

Felicity smiled, "Let me people go," she laughed quietly. "I was thinking about how quickly things have progressed during the last few months. Starting with us meeting on the nudist beach to the top of the world right here. I often had considered me life so ordinary until then. Now being up here with you, I couldn't feel more special." She reached out to Zach. He met her and they tongue wrestled, causing a mini spectacle for the other tourists.

After leaving the towers, they aimlessly walked north, jointly enjoying the comparably quiet splendor of a crisp Sunday in New York City. By the time their legs told their brains that they were tired, they had reached Zach's favorite eating spot in Manhattan.

■■■

New York City had so many "original" Ray's pizza parlors that the competition between them for their authenticity resembled many a New York rivalry. Zach took Felicity to his favorite Ray's in the West Village on

Sixth Avenue.

Zach ordered just one cheese slice each for both of them. Felicity marveled at the plate-sized slice in front of her oozing with thick mozzarella cheese sliding off onto the paper plate below as she ate.

Felicity was electrified from the sensory overload. Zach could only get about every third word she said. Given her petite stomach, Felicity couldn't even finish her one slice. Zach was more than happy to take it off her hands.

From Ray's, they walked north to Herald Square so Zach could proudly show Felicity Macy's Department Store and the site of the Thanksgiving Day Parade. From there they walked to Times Square and up to the Carnegie Deli, where Zach pointed out the colossal size of the sandwiches. From there, they headed east to Rockefeller Center. Although the scene was less maddening than before Christmas, it still took them over an hour's wait to skate on its ice rink.

Zach and Felicity weren't very adept skaters so they gingerly worked their way around the crowded rink mainly just trying to avoid bumping into folks. After an hour of holding themselves up on the ice, they grew tired and decided to call it a day. They rode the Riverdale Express bus back up to Marshall's apartment, picked up some Chinese take-out and watched *Educating Rita*, a video Zach reserved for Felicity's visit.

Even though both of them had seen this movie about a working-class Yorkshire woman seeking a path to self-discovery, Zach wanted to see it together with Felicity. As they watched Rita radically transform herself from a heavily accented Yorkshire hairdresser to an educated Englishwoman, Zach thought about how their own story would transpire. They talked at length about the similarities and differences of Rita and Felicity, and both thought there were poignant comparisons.

After the movie, and after enough time to fully

critique its double meanings into their lives, Felicity grabbed Zach and in her most refined English accent announced, "I think it is time for us to retire to the bedroom, Sir Charles."

Zach matched her accent. "With pleasure, Diana, my sweet!"

Forty

Riverdale, Bronx, New York City

Zach got up early and let Felicity sleep in. He walked over to Johnson Avenue to pick up the required bagels, cream cheese and lox. Felicity was now a bagel convert and wanted it every morning. Upon his return, he noticed that she was awake and dressed in only a bra and panties in mid-cleaning mode. Sheets had been changed, dirty clothes had been picked up and dishes were out of the sink and on dish racks.

"*Wow!* You got busy in a hurry. I think that if Alice, the maid on *The Brady Bunch*, looked as hot as you, then older brother Greg certainly would've had '*A Very Brady Christmas*'." Felicity chuckled even though she didn't have an idea who *The Brady Bunch* were.

"I keep a very tidy house, whether it's me Sheffield home or this little sparkle of paradise here."

Zach thought she looked captivating. "Will you come over here and tidy me up?"

Felicity smiled. "With pleasure," she said then jumped up and crossed her legs around him as he carried her to the bedroom.

In the afternoon, Marshall came by, picked up Felicity and Zach, and then drove them out to Queens to his mom's apartment near the New York City-Long Island border. She lived in an upper class apartment complex, called the North Shore Towers comprised of three buildings protected by a guard gate.

Helen's apartment was on the fifth floor and when she opened the door, a gush of spiced aromas charged out into the hallway.

"*Kalimera,* Felicity. Hi, I'm Helen. So good to finally meet you," she said with a grin. Felicity thought that Helen was regal with brown eyes, dark hair and complexion giving her a pronounced Mediterranean look. She wore a long flowing black jumpsuit and large-rimmed matching glasses. It made Felicity pause momentarily; memories of her mum suddenly sprang to her mind as she walked into the apartment and settled in at the kitchen table. There, Helen was busy finishing up the *yeprakes* by rolling marinated grape leaves around the rice stuffing she had previously cooked.

Helen shooed Zach and Marshall away from the kitchen so the guys went into the living room to catch up. The living room motif was comprised of Greek and Sephardic themed pictures of rabbis and weddings. Zach and Marshall sat down on the tiger-striped long curved sofa to share notes.

"Zach, how did Felicity take Dad and Wilma's grilling?"

Zach stood up and faced him. "You heard something?"

"They do talk about you behind your back, you know." Marshall reflected. "God only knows what they're telling you about me."

Zach sat back down and collected the intel. "Are they plotting against Felicity?"

"They clearly don't like that she's not Jewish. They had a deep discussion over Felicity's cross, like they never saw one before."

"It did stick out…"

"They feel that the only way the relationship will progress is if you move away or invite her to stay."

Zach popped the thought of Felicity moving to New York in his mind for a second. "Felicity sure loves everything I've shown her but I don't know if it's real to her yet. She'd have to sacrifice a lot of things and people she holds dear. At a minimum, I would definitely have to find a new place."

"Yeah, you can't take my place forever," he chided from the side of his mouth.

With the analysis complete, Zach was still puzzled. "I know, right now I'm pretty confused. Life was so free and easy in Rhodes..."

"...when you didn't have other feelings to consider," Marshall added.

"...like the minor practicalities of life, such as job, religion and citizenship," Zach completed the thought.

Meanwhile in the kitchen, Felicity helped Helen take the *burekas* out of the stove. The phyllo-covered spinach and feta appetizer smelled delectable. Felicity was calm but remained on guard to speak clearly and humbly to Zach's mother. The casual pace of their actions was interrupted when Helen called over the counter and said to her directly, "So, are you in love with my son?"

Felicity was somewhat prepared with Zach's New York cultural directness, but Helen's comment took her aback. She acknowledged, "Wow! Let me get back on me two feet from that question." She put the tray of appetizers down on a trivet before she answered giving her more time to consider the severity of the question. "I don't rightly know. I care an awful lot about him, but life is a lot more complex than when we first met in Rhodes."

Helen subtly shifted the conversation to see how Felicity's arrival was being interpreted by her ex-husband. "How do Zach's father and stepmother feel about it?"

Zach had previously debriefed Felicity on his divorced parents' lifetime spats, so she sensed an empathetic ear. "I only know what I can sense. Frankly, I fear that I'm a cancer to them. Wilma even made a joke in my face that I wasn't suitable for Zach because I didn't know what a bagel was."

Felicity's revelation spurred Helen. "Typical... *Al diablo con ella!* To hell with her," Helen said, gesturing widely. "To think that Seymour left me for that whore!" She shook her head and tried her best to focus on Felicity's feelings. "What are you and Zach going to do now?"

"I need to talk to him about my feelings. I'm getting the same pressure from me father. Me sister Ellen and I are all me dad has since me mum passed away..." Felicity hesitated and started to sob through her words.

Helen touched her arm. "You must miss her."

"Terribly. Meeting you has made think of her...She..." Felicity started to cry more steadily. She had reached a steady wail on Helen's shoulders when Zach walked into the kitchen.

Zach was shocked at the immediate connection made between Felicity and his mom. He said with a crack of a smile on his face, "Ma! What are you doing to her? First, Dad starts grilling her like she's veal chops, and then you bring her to tears!"

Felicity stopped crying and defended her. "It's really okay. We were...talking...woman stuff."

Zach conceded, "Ma has a shoulder as big as a king bed to cry on."

"She sure has."

After wolfing down their appetizers in the kitchen, they sat down to eat the rest of the meal in the dining room. The dinner started with Greek salad. The diced vegetables looked straight out of a gourmet restaurant in Rhodes. The main course was steak kebabs complemented with mushroom orzo. Felicity couldn't eat enough and she especially enjoyed the comedic banter that Zach had with his brother and mother.

After they finished their meal and while Helen cleaned up and readied dessert, the guys tried to teach Felicity about American football while watching the Monday night game on television. Felicity remained completely confused and declared that English football would be the only football for her. The guys screamed at the TV until their mother called them back to the table for coffee and baklava.

They were just finishing their coffee when the phone rang. Helen hesitated answering it, but Felicity insisted. Helen grabbed the phone and started listening with immediate focus. Felicity only heard Helen's end of the conversation.

"*Uh huh...wow! Oh* my God! Tell me everything and I'll relay it to her." Helen then stared at Felicity with a sincere frown before she returned her attention to the phone and listened for two solid minutes repeating "okay" in a frenzy before thanking the caller. She hung up slowly.

Helen turned away from the phone and carefully approached Felicity. Zach, who was watching his mother, cried out, "What was that all about?"

Helen looked somberly, first down at the floor, then directly at Felicity and shared, "It was Zach's father. He received a call from Felicity's Uncle Robert. Felicity honey, I'm sorry to tell you that your father had a stroke and he's now in a hospital in Majorca, Spain."

Felicity gasped. "What? He seemed perfectly fine when I left for the States. What happened to him?" she asked anxiously.

"Apparently, he was having shortness of breath and dizziness issues while on his vacation. Then, he collapsed on the beach. They all went to a local hospital and the doctors did a battery of tests..."

Felicity interrupted. "Is he okay?"

"Robert doesn't know right now, Sugar. But he said that the doctors think he may have damage on his right side."

"*Oh*, Dad!" She started weeping uncontrollably. Zach tried to hold her but she became inconsolable. "I thought…if he could just get away…for a few days…he'd be okay," she said through her sobs.

Zach stood up and faced Felicity. "I'll help get travel arrangements set up as soon as we get back to Riverdale. Hopefully, we can rearrange your return flight to get you to Majorca right away."

Marshall drove Zach and Felicity quickly back to his apartment. Felicity remained completely silent. Her memories over her mum immediately took center stage, which caused her to shake her head repeatedly.

When they got back to the apartment, Zach took control of the situation and quickly called British Airways to reroute her return flight through Majorca. The next available flight wasn't until the following day, so they had one more night together.

After Felicity had gained some control over her emotions, Zach joined her on the couch in the living room. She broke her silence.

"I blame meself. I was too selfish coming here knowing that me dad has been a bit round the twist lately."

Zach figured she was saying he was feeling ill and didn't want to stop her train of thought. "The stroke could have been caused by anything."

She stared at him and raised her voice. "You met him. He's putting a lot of stress on himself and me."

"Why?"

"He doesn't want me to leave him."

"You want to move here?"

"If we are to be anything more than just pen pals and holiday lovers…"

Zach didn't know how to ebb the cyclonic rapids forming inside her head so he tried, "It's been a blast so far," Zach interrupted.

Felicity raised her voice at him. "But that's not how life works! It can't always be just a holiday!" She got up from the couch, went into the bedroom and started crying again.

He followed her. "Felicity." No response. "Felicity!" Still no response. "Kitten!" She looked up.

He imitated her accent. "*Coom'ere.*" She walked over and melted in his arms while sobbing quietly. "This last week has been too much for me to process. Can we just stay in the moment for a while?"

They decided to give themselves a mental holiday and tried to shut out everything else in their heads but themselves. They spent the night in wordless camaraderie, letting their bodies do all the talking. They made love like it was the last night they'd ever see each other again. Afterwards, while Zach was silently catching his breath, Felicity started sobbing again with bodily jerks and wails.

Zach moved up on the bed and held her. "What is it, Felicity?" Zach said tenderly.

She stared almost through him. "Zach Stillman, I love you with all me heart, but I don't know how we can ever be together!"

Forty-one

Hospital son Llatzer, Majorca, Spain

After leaving New York and flying all night over the Atlantic, Felicity walked into the hospital where her dad was in intensive care. It was midmorning and she found her sister in the waiting area outside the ICU. She ran to her and they hugged while blurting out nonsensical half words to each other. It took them a full five minutes to settle themselves down before Ellen led Felicity to one of the couches. She reached out to her at an arms-length to study her emotions. "You need to sit down before you see him."

"Why? What am I going to see?" Felicity started to whimper again.

Ellen made her voice strong and clear. "Nothing. He's resting comfortably."

Felicity was a mess again. "Are there still signs of paralysis?"

"Please sit down." Ellen took a deep breath to control her own depressive emotions and pulled her over to sit on one of the couches.

After they were seated, she continued, "He's still showing signs of lost use of his right side. You can see it in his mouth, arm and leg. The doctor induced him into a coma so he can try to heal himself."

"Do they know what caused all this?"

"Since he arrived in Majorca, he was feeling off. He was complaining of short bouts of memory loss and dizziness. They eventually would go away, so Robert decided just to keep an eye on him."

"What happened the day he got the stroke?"

"Dad went with Robert's family to the beach. While he was walking back to their rental car, he collapsed on the sand. Robert got help straight away."

"What did the doctor say is his prognosis?"

"A lot depends on his progress in the next couple of days. He said it's likely not to be life-threatening, but many people like him need constant care."

"How will we do that?" Felicity wailed.

Ellen looked lovingly at her younger sister. "I don't know. Me mind's a jumble, just like yours. Let's just see how things go today."

"Can I see him?" Felicity pleaded.

"Yes. Let's go on in to see him. Remember, he's still in a coma."

They made their way over to George's semiprivate room in the ICU. As Ellen pulled back the curtain surrounding her father's bed, Felicity was stunned.

"He looks… dead." She started sobbing again. Ellen grabbed her and hugged her while swaying a bit.

"But he's not, you twit. He's still is in an induced coma and hopefully healing. Once they bring him out of it, we'll see what we're dealing with."

"Oh Dad!" Felicity went over to the bed and knelt down. "It's me fault. I knew you weren't feeling right about me trip, but I went anyway. I hope and pray you'll forgive me."

"Sis, stop blaming yourself. I don't."

"I can't lose him now."

"Me neither."

They walked out of the room and grabbed a tea with milk in the hospital cafeteria. Ellen brought Felicity to a small circular table and caught up with her about her trip to New York.

"How did you leave things with Zach?" she asked.

Felicity was upset at hearing the word "leave". "What's to leave? I said goodbye and left. I was not in the mental state for a rational discussion. We left much unanswered. I figured I needed to see Dad straight away and then try to unscramble me feelings about Zach some other time."

Later that afternoon, Robert and his family returned to the hospital and met Ellen and Felicity in the ICU waiting room. Felicity was very interested in Robert's perspective of her dad's behavior before his stroke. She pulled Robert aside and they sat down in corner chairs in the waiting room.

Robert was unsteady. "I'm glad you made it here, Felicity. Until Ellen flew down, we've been here at hospital every second since your dad's stroke. We would've been here to greet you, but we needed a break to…"

Felicity politely cut him off. "Robert, I understand. Please tell me what happened."

Robert gained his composure. "As I told your sister, your dad was out of sorts straight away, experiencing some dizzy spells. I figured it was on account of your trip."

"He talked about it?"

"Yes. He felt that you'd eventually move to the States to live with Zach. He was happy for you but you could've certainly read the sadness in his face."

"*Oh*, Dad…" She started tearing.

Robert put his arm around Felicity. "Now child,

please don't blame yourself. I don't and he didn't." He gently pulled his arm away and continued the story. "We felt we all needed some sun, so we packed lunches and made it out to the beach. Your father was sleeping much of the day under an umbrella. While we were walking back to the car, he staggered and then fell into the sand. He was twitching a bit and we called for an ambulance straight away. Felicity, they came immediately. It probably saved his life. Once we arrived at hospital, he was put directly into the ICU where the doctors did a battery of tests. As soon as I was able to get a free moment, I called Ellen and then the number you gave me as a contact in the States."

"That was Zach's father. I eventually got the message and then came here as soon as I could." She paused, "What are your plans?"

"Ginger and the kids are flying back tomorrow. I'm staying on here until we know more about his condition."

That evening, George's doctor, Dr. Rafael Mendez, used medication to get him out of his comatose state. Once his condition stabilized, the doctor came out of the ICU to chat with the family. He wore a white medical jacket with his name printed over the pocket. His Spanish-tinted English showed the sign of many years speaking the language.

Ellen met him even before he reached the waiting room. "Is he okay?"

The doctor waited to respond until he reached the waiting room where the rest of the family anxiously faced him. He announced, "We were able to successfully pull him out of a coma. His condition has improved since we first admitted him, but he still suffers residual effects of a stroke."

Felicity frantically jumped in, "What effects?"

"He has slurred speech from the stroke's impact to his right side. He can move his right arm but will need therapy to fully regain functionality. Unfortunately…"

His voice trailed off.

Felicity interrupted, "Unfortunately what?"

Dr. Mendez gently took hold of Felicity's arm and tried to comfort her as he said, "Unfortunately, he still cannot move his right leg. He has some feeling there, but does not have motor function."

Ellen pulled the doctor along. "Meaning..."

"If his condition doesn't improve soon, he will likely need a wheelchair for the foreseeable future," the doctor confessed.

Felicity became hysterical. "Oh God!"

The doctor added, "The good news is that he is now awake and I encourage you both to see him to help raise his spirits."

The girls simultaneously charged out of the waiting room and walked purposefully to their father's room. George shared a room with another patient separated by curtains. When Felicity pulled back on the curtain surrounding George's bed, she saw him awake and attempting to grin.

Felicity tried to heal him completely with just her smile. "Hi, Daddy, Kitten here."

Ellen snuck over to the other side of the bed. "Dad, Ellen's here too."

He raised his eyes and slowly uttered in recognition, "Good. You're both here." He seemed to relax a bit. "Having...trouble...speaking."

Felicity rubbed his left arm. "Just take your time. You're doing fine."

"Can't...move...leg."

"It'll be fine."

"Don't...want...to trouble...you."

To keep busy, Ellen straighten his sheets. "You're never a trouble," she smiled widely.

George tried a smile. "Yes, I'm...perfect...angel."

"Well, I wouldn't go that far," Ellen joked.

Felicity interrupted the banter. "Sis! Dad, we're here

now and we'll make sure you're okay. We'll..." she started sobbing, "get you through this."

George was laboring a bit. "What...about...Zach?"

It was clear to Felicity that Zach and their relationship caused her dad's stroke. She wanted to be firm with him so he could heal again. "Zach's in the States; you're here. End of story."

"Kitten, no!" He painfully tried to shift his body up on the bed with his left hand. "I know...you...love him."

Felicity's eyes were deep pink by now. "But I love you too, Dad. Now, I'm going to take care of you."

"Can...take care...of meself."

Ellen butted in, "Dad, you know you can't. But now that you're awake, why don't you try taking it easy, okay?" She motioned Felicity to the end of the bed.

"Okay...Ellen...me sweet."

"I know you're' in a bad way if you call me 'Ellen, me sweet'," Ellen said aloud.

The girls quietly huddled at the end of the bed silently contemplating the situation. After a pause, Felicity quietly said to her sister. "We're going to have to change the house around since he won't be walking up any stairs no more."

Ellen was shaking her head trying to make sense of it all. She finally replied, "Yes, lots to think about." She pulled away from Felicity while starting to cry. "Right now, I need some air."

Forty-two

Dearest Zach,
This is the hardest letter I've ever had to write. I feel so torn. It's as if my heart's been ripped in two.

My father suffered a major stroke. He lost function on his right side, including all use of his right leg. He has trouble with his right hand and speech, but the doctors here in Sheffield think he can be rehabilitated over time.

Where does that leave us? I've thought this question over time and again trying to make our relationship work, but I can't see through it. Maybe you have some ideas I hadn't thought of. I feel dead inside knowing that you and I can't be together. It's clear to me that I need to take care of my dad. I cannot ask you to come here, so I won't invite you, much as it pains me.

I am resolving myself to realise that what we had was incredibly special but that was all there was to it. It was an intense relationship that was blocked by fate. It was as if God was telling me that my relationship with you was over before I could accept it myself.

Please write back so that I know you are okay and we can start getting on with our lives.

Love always,
Felicity

January 20, 1988

Dearest Felicity,
I'm still numb from the sequence of events. I truly didn't know how things would turn out for us, but never expected your dad would have a stroke. Please give him my love as I am dealing with my own guilt about his condition.
 Ending our relationship makes logical sense for many reasons, but my heart tells me otherwise. I cannot, and will not, end my love for you, now, or in the future. However, I do need to figure out how I can now get on with my life.
 Doing so means that I don't know if I can go on writing you while I'm in this state of mind.
 My whole family wants to express their love and support for your father, even though they've never met him. I hope you received the flower arrangement we sent. Your dad is a tough old bugger; I'm confident he'll make the best of it, especially with your beautiful face to look at.
 I'm sorry that we didn't have enough time together for me to create a pet name for you. Take care of yourself, your sis and your dad. What we had was incredibly special; I wouldn't have changed any second of it.

Zach

THREE

Forty-three

Sheffield, England

Felicity was interrupted from her busy day at the office by a phone call from Ellen, who was now watching the day's events at home.

"Sis, did you hear what just happened at the World Trade Centre?" Ellen shrieked on the phone.

"No. I've been in closed-door meetings all day. What happened?"

Ellen tried to gain her composure. "Passenger planes have crashed into both towers and the buildings are on fire."

"Oh, please Sis, don't be daft. I'm having a crazy day already."

"No, Felicity! You need to get to a telly straight away; it's happening now!"

"Okay, okay."

Felicity was now the Office Manager at Graham Cutlery holding the position that used to be occupied by, now retired, Titus Graham. Felicity scurried as fast as she could hampered by a business skirt and high heels over to the factory break room where all the staff had stopped work and crowded over to watch as the events on BBC-1 unfolded.

205

Felicity's mind was racing as she uncontrollably retrieved deeply recessed memories of her past.

"The tower is collapsing!" one worker screamed as the rest of the crowd gasped in horror. Felicity struggled to keep her balance as she thought, *Oh God, please tell me Zach's not in there.*

Lindsay was watching Felicity as she almost fell down, so she quickly grabbed her and led her to a chair in the far side of the break room.

Felicity looked up at her friend in gratitude. "Lindsay, I can't watch anymore. It hurts too much."

"It's Zach, huh?"

"He could be in there...We stopped writing..."

Lindsay grabbed a cup of water as she vainly tried to help Felicity confront the fragmented images of her past. But Felicity was lost in a turbulent time warp between her memories of New York and the horror unfolding before her. For her, time played out in slow motion...

Twenty minutes passed. "There goes the other tower!" a worker announced to the shocked audience.

Felicity looked up, then held her face in her hands. "I can't believe this is really happening. All those people..."

"They said it was a terrorist plot. Another plane went into the Pentagon," Lindsay reported.

"I feel like I'm watching some sick summer blockbuster. This can't be real?"

"Lindsay asked, "Do you really think Zach was in there?"

"The last time I heard from him, me dad just had his stroke, may he now rest in peace. At that time, Zach had an office in one of those towers. There was no more we could say that didn't cause us deep pain. We had to go on with our lives..." She started crying uncontrollably.

Lindsay put her arm around her friend. "Fel, it's okay. You did what you had to do."

"Lindsay, I'm resolved with it. It's just that I hadn't

thought about Zach in such a long time. Did you know I went to the top of one of those towers?"

"Yes, you told me. That's why I rushed to find you. I knew that you would be more effected by all of this than anyone here."

"What will I tell Lance?" she asked aloud.

"You never told him about Zach?"

"I couldn't. First of all, Lance is a bit of the jealous type. Plus, Zach is buried deep in me past... Did I just say buried?" She started crying again.

"Fel, get a grip. You're no good anymore for working today, so let me drive you home.

"You are a true friend Lindsay. I'll explain things to Lance over time."

■■■

Lindsay drove Felicity home to her house in the west Sheffield countryside. Since her marriage and job promotion, Felicity had lived a much higher class lifestyle. Her house was a stately, three-bedroom stone cottage built in 1706 rumored to be owned at one time by the Duke of Norfolk.

As she raced through the front door through the stone entrance, she made her way into a charming sitting room, where its tall natural stone fireplace was highlighted. A television set was situated in the corner facing cream-colored sofas. Felicity turned on the set and caught up with the events of the bombings.

She walked over to one of the floor-to-ceiling bookcases where she reached high for a photo album. She wiped off the dust of the album and sat down at the coffee table revisiting pictures of her and Zach. *I was so young and naïve but the world seemed such a better place when we were together.*

Felicity wondered how much she was now willing to tell Lance about her romance with Zach almost fifteen years ago. Her life was now stable and happy, albeit humdrum. Lance had been a reliable husband, but she did suspect he had affairs over the years with his students at the University of Sheffield where he taught business management. She should know since his infidelity brought the two of them together.

She recalled that day since it so contrasted with her first encounter with Zach. Lance taught an evening creative writing class at the Institute of Lifelong Learning at the University. She enrolled shortly after losing her father to a massive heart attack in 1994. Ellen pushed her to enroll in the night class, given her enjoyment of writing and so she could stop brooding about the house in grief.

She signed up for the introductory writing class and Lance was the teacher. He was an associate professor in the business school, but had a passion for creative writing in his spare time. She didn't know that Lance had also developed a fondness for the appeal and sexual talent of the mostly female students found in creative writing classes.

When she first met Lance, the scene reminded her of the movie, *Educating Rita*, since she was so unrefined back then in her speaking and writing skills.

She clearly remembered that day; Lance was academically captivating wearing a Burberry bowtie and brown wool blazer. She appreciated how it augmented his brown curly hair and full brown beard enough to raise her pulse a few beats. He had broad shoulders over his five foot ten inch frame, and spoke with a warm, deep, and sophisticated voice contributing to his masculine charm. He was seventeen years her senior, but it never really mattered to her. He represented the strength and maturity in her life she sorely needed.

She heard Lance's Saab driving into the garage so she abruptly returned the photo album to the bookshelf and turned off the television. He walked in, casually carrying the mail when he saw her standing in the kitchen.

She said evenly, "Did you hear the news?"

Lance looked lovingly at her. "City, it's all over the radio and television." He still spoke with an aristocratic air befitting his upper class education in London. "What is the world coming to? The terrorist's target could just as well have been Westminster Abby or the London Bridge."

"Do you think there will be war?" She walked over and hugged him for comfort.

He kissed her cheek. "I don't rightly know. There will definitely be changes in how we live. The University has already suspended all business travel."

"Shirt, what about our planned holiday to Greece?" She liked using the Cockney slang nickname she made up for her husband—from "shirt and pants, rhymes with Lance".

"Looks like we may have to delay that, City."

She pulled him over to the couch and cried on his warm chest. Despite his drifting eyes and suspected wandering hands, he was a reliable and loving husband. He had taken comforting care of her for the last seven years. When she first met him, she was still a basket case of unsettled emotions. Now, she felt mentally tougher, more socially refined, and fiercely independent. She gave him much credit for her transformation.

Felicity remained quiet for the rest of the evening; she pawed through her dinner, then caught the last bit of the somber news report before retiring to bed. They went upstairs and Lance held her in his arms. That night she needed his masculine comfort without the anxiety of unrequited sexual desire. Lately, there were more hugs and cuddles between them than sexual pleasure. While her yearning flame ran on, his pilot light seemed to be out, causing her to stifle her own longings.

She had trouble sleeping. Lance was snoring noisily

next to her. He wasn't a pretty sleeper and most nights his locomotive imitation tended to screw up her sleeping patterns. That night, her consciousness was enveloped with the images of the falling towers circling her brain like caffeine. She sneaked out of bed and walked downstairs into the kitchen to make herself a cup of warm milk. Her alertness at three o'clock in the morning was an omen that she needed to resolve her feelings of that day by finally inking a letter to Zach. It frequently seemed that she could get more in touch with her feelings by scrawling a letter instead of sending an email. Handwriting gave her the chance to see the words as she wrote them, allowing her feelings to sharpen as it appeared on the page.

She went into the den, sat down at the desk and looked around the room searching for the words to start her letter. The den's warm crème walls accented by dark brown support beams evoked a safe mental place for her writing mood.

Felicity turned on the desk light and took out a writing tablet. The letter didn't take long once her heart started speaking; the words pumped through her blood into her hands.

11 September 2001

Dearest Zach,

Today I watched with horror as the Twin Towers went down. I never had such a sharp feeling of dread in my life. When I saw the buildings crashing down, I could only hope that you weren't inside. I still don't know if you were.

I'm not writing this letter because I've resurrected a need to get back together. I'm now a happily married woman sharing custody of two of my husband's children. It's just that this tragedy unlocked the key to a special part of my life and I'm not willing to give that up right now, despite any terrorist wanting any different.

Over the years, my radioactive love for you has been properly quarantined like underground nuclear waste. Did you like that sentence? I took a creative writing class. That's where I met my husband, Lance, who has taught me proper etiquette and writing skills. I hope you have found someone to share your life with.

Reflecting back, I know I couldn't change my decision to break up our relationship after seeing my father in intensive care. Unfortunately, life lessons don't always make their choices easy. After his stroke, he was able to regain his speech and reasonable use of his right arm. Tragically, he was never able to walk again. We had to rearrange the house for him, which frustrated him to no end. It drove me to spend more time out of there. I was especially grateful when I could finally afford a visiting nurse for him. Dreadfully, he died from a massive heart attack in 1994.

You can tell Marshall that Ellen is fine and plump for the sixth time. Yes, you read that right. Shortly after you visited here, she met this great lad who worked at the local television station. Apparently, they have matching libidos. Now she is the typical stay-at-home mother. I do love it when she comes over with all her little rug rats. It is sheer bedlam.

Zach, I truly hope and pray this letter reaches you. If so, I've included a mailing address for you to respond. I don't think I can handle a phone call, so I didn't include my phone number.

Always and forever,
Felicity

The next day, even though mail to the States was being held up, she posted the letter anyway, happy just to get the thoughts down on paper and allow them to slowly drift from her system.

Forty-four

Riverdale, Bronx, New York City

Seymour boasted, "Zach, you can sure cook up a storm!" He was famished.

Seymour was just sitting down with Zach and his wife Leah while breaking the Yom Kippur fast at Zach's seventies' era three-bedroom apartment in Riverdale. Seymour and his gorgeous daughter-in-law had just returned from Leah's *shul*, the Beth Tikvah Synagogue, a block away from their first floor apartment. Zach had stayed back home to plate their feast so he could avoid all the uncomfortable comments he'd typically get being the obscure husband of a prominent woman rabbi.

Walking back from synagogue with Seymour gave Leah pause to reflect on her own life and her relationship with Zach. She clearly remembered the day they met, Zach accompanying his gentile girlfriend for some ritual education on the bar mitzvah service. She rarely broke character while working, but there was something about Zach, aside from his striking appearance, that made her so forward with him. He responded to her invitations to talk and through their regular conversations, found a lost soul.

In their sessions, she helped him become at peace

212

with his faith and his guilt of dating out of it. Their relationship stayed mostly professional until during one of their sessions, Zach's macho exterior broke down, and his deep-seeded feelings over the loss of his relationship with Felicity came out. He was intentionally sketchy on the details but she connected the dots and realized that the events changed him. He had admitted that he strayed from his faith because he never felt committed to Judaism, as it was given to him as a birthright. She shifted the conversations by helping him "choose" Judiasm as a faith.

As she educated him to embrace the religion, he changed his countenance towards her. She became swept up in his excitement, which challenged her ability to objectively counsel him. The underlying torrent between them became increasing difficult to insulate. After some soul-searching, she finally asked him to dinner to air out her personal feelings.

That night, they shared their mutual attraction and agreed to change their relationship to regular dating. She started to confide in him about her inner faith and passion to make a difference in people's lives. He was a good listener and allowed her to expose her frailties. She could just be herself with him, without the layers of self-protection she applied as a clergywoman. Their relationship flourished, both satisfying each other's needs.

They married, feeling a happiness she never thought was possible. But soon after, their troubles conceiving a child irreparably tainted their lovemaking. They quietly tried for years and were left feeling damaged. They both couldn't see past the issue and kept it hidden from their families and congregants. Leah eventually filled the void by putting all her energies into her work.

The ten High Holy Days between Rosh Hashanah and Yom Kippur were the most grueling for any practicing rabbi. According to the Jewish faithful, God inscribed each person's fate for the coming year into a book, the Book of Life, on Rosh Hashanah, and waited until Yom Kippur to "seal" the verdict. Leah's synagogue had surveyed the congregation and found that about half of all congregants only attended services during the High Holy Days or a life-cycle event such as a wedding or bar mitzvah. Therefore, she put inconceivable stress on herself during Yom Kippur's long sequence of services since she concluded it was her best opportunity throughout the entire religious calendar to influence her congregants' spiritual lives.

That effort was taxing on her stamina and her availability to Zach. Even though traditional work was prohibited during the solemn day, Yom Kippur was not only a "work" day for her; the additional debilitating effects of the required twenty-five hour fast put her near delirium.

Zach was intimately familiar with seeing Leah in this state and tried his best to get her through the break-fast until she could stabilize her anxiety. "Leah honey, how were services?"

Leah was barely listening to Zach as the food smelled so heavenly. She reached out and stabbed a few of Zach's world famous kosher beef short-ribs and put them on her plate, "Same as usual, except Zev Cohen came to *daven* with us."

Zach was so proud that Leah was catching the attention of the rabbinical elite. "Why would a famous Orthodox rabbi come to your synagogue on Yom Kippur?"

Leah scolded him while eating, "Remember? It was an exchange thing. I went over to his Hebrew Academy on Rosh Hashanah."

Zach placated, "Oh, that's right. It's hard to remember all you've got going on." Zach bit his lip.

Indeed, it was challenging for Zach to track the details of an up-and-coming rabbi serving a thousand family congregation. Leah barely had time anymore for Zach. These days, all the lectures, sermons, weddings, funerals and bar mitzvahs took up every moment of her shrinking calendar. Most of the time he felt like her secretary–and her cook. It was especially grim after September 11, since two of Leah's congregants perished in the towers. In the week following the event, she spent all of her available time consoling their distraught families.

He recalled the many times that he cherished being married to her. Their outdoor wedding by the Dead Sea in Israel was awe-inspiring and it gave him opportunity to connect with his father's Israeli history.

They shared their Jewish bonds both intellectually and spiritually. Even though Zach wasn't Seminary-trained, he and Leah had common family beliefs and about *tikkun olam*, the Jewish people's shared responsibility to heal, repair and transform the world. Through their socially prominent position, Zach was thrilled with the positive result that Leah, and he in his own way, had on people's lives. When Zach first met Leah, he was an immature, rudderless and naïve guy. His relationship with Leah matured and grounded him, giving him purpose with his life.

Over the years, they managed to squeeze in some alone time in their busy schedules. Their recent Caribbean cruise they took on their twelfth wedding anniversary was another of a series of escapes they carefully carved for themselves through microscopic planning amongst her brimming schedule.

Zach's unease in the relationship was attributed to his restrained lifestyle. He felt he repeatedly had to be properly presentable; Leah discouraged him to even have two days of growth on his face, since at any minute a congregant could stop by.

He had also gained over twenty-five pounds in the last five years. Maybe it was the tens of congregant

NATHAN JEWELL

weddings and bar mitzvahs he had to attend each year or the permanent head chef duties he acquired so she could work more hours.

Although Leah sustained her love for Zach, she eventually lost time and interest in sex. Leah had to physically block out personal time in her schedule in-between common rabbi work events, such overseeing a circumcision and a senior home visit so they could have any quality time when she actually had energy for him. However, most of the time these forced encounters kept her feigning through the motions and Zach's middle leg at a shrivel. On Sundays, Leah used her only scheduled day off to catch up on sleep trying to refuel her stamina, leaving Zach to wonder if this level of commitment was all she was capable.

Fortunately, Zach still had Marshall and Duncan in his life. But Marshall had only limited available time for him as well; he eventually married his girlfriend Melody and they made beautiful babies together. His eleven year-old twin nephews, Joseph and Wayne, were a large part of Zach's life since they only lived two blocks away.

He finally partnered up with Duncan to create Arpad and Stillman, CPAs when Zach rejected the stifling partner track of his prior accounting firm. Working with Duncan was a great fit; Duncan did most of the marketing, while Zach managed the operation. It was a good business marriage and they had built up an inseparable trust.

Zach was ready to drive Seymour back to his Lower East Side apartment. It was the first time since the tragedy that the police let his dad back into his apartment. The aftermath of September 11 made it virtually impossible to live within a five-mile radius of the World Trade Center; his dad was humbled when Zach and Leah invited him to stay with them for the past month.

Zach asked with annoyance, "Dad, are you packed

216

and ready to go yet?"

"Give me five more minutes, for chris'sakes!"

Zach loaded Seymour's multiple suitcases into his SUV and drove south into Manhattan. They were both quiet until Seymour chimed in, "You know, Leah is pretty exceptional. The way she commanded the pulpit tonight, I felt like I was attending a Broadway play."

"What should it be called, *My Son Married a Rabbi?*"

Seymour snickered, "That does have a lovely ring to it." He changed subjects, "Hey, I kept thinking during the service, when are you two gonna finally produce me some grandkids? You know I love Joseph and Wayne, but I still need some numbers from your team to fill out the roster."

Zach was all too familiar with his father's attempts to get inside his personal issues. "Dad, I've told you we've tried. Either it's the stress or the lack of skill of my one-armed swimmers."

Seymour, a business consultant by trade, loved to problem-solve his son's challenges. "Have you received any medical counseling?"

"Yes, Dad, I don't always tell you things. Leah is a very busy woman. It's best if we don't discuss it anymore." He shifted to the offensive. "Frankly, I've noticed that you've been even more into my personal issues since Wilma died." Wilma was the most sensitive topic in Zach's arsenal against his buttinski father.

Seymour quieted hearing Wilma's name. He zoned out and stated flatly, "Yeah, I can never use my Fred Flintstone impression any longer. Please let's keep Wilma out of it. It's been five years now."

Zach felt better being in control of the conversation. "Five years, and you're still a real crankypuss."

"Wilma was really something though."

Zach thought, "*Really something? Just ask Ma what she was.* He decided yet again for his dad to resolve himself to Wilma's premature demise to leukemia, and let him see who she was to his living family. "Yes, she was something–a home wrecker."

"Zach, don't get into that again."

Zach positioned himself as his mother's publicity agent. "I just see Mom so disheartened without any meaningful man in her life. Your divorce killed her spirit."

"Enough with passing the guilt; though I now believe you have officially broken the NFL record for pass attempts."

"Would it hurt for you to call Mom from time to time just to say hello?"

"Did she finally remove her witch's spell over me?" Seymour swore Helen put a hex on him after he embarrassed her by having three rabbis come to her lobby, incognito, for the ceremony of the *get*, the Jewish religious divorce.

"Yes, especially now that Wilma has passed. I also wish that you can finally move on with your life without her. "Share a cup of coffee with Ma or some other Jewish yenta. You need to think about your future," Zach encouraged.

"Future, *smoocher.*" At that point, Seymour just wanted to be left alone.

They arrived at Seymour's apartment building and Zach took his father's bags upstairs.

"Zach wait, I'll walk back down with you; I want to get all the mail that was held up."

"Okay, Dad."

In the lobby, Seymour kissed his son on the cheek and waved goodbye. He then moved to the rows of mailbox slots for the apartment's tenants. His small slot was completely stuffed. It took him three hard tugs to unclog it. Then, letters fluttered to the ground. One of the pieces included a manila envelope with an airmail stamp. He brought it up closer for inspection and saw that it was addressed to Zach with an address in Sheffield and a return name of Felicity Gordon. He paused. *So, Felicity got married. Why in the hell is she writing my boychik?*

On the way back up to his apartment, Seymour thought about Zach's life with Leah. *The two of them seem blissfully happy together. Leah is a prominent and loving daughter-in-law who sincerely cares about me and makes me feel blessed. She is that angel of mercy that got me through losing my beloved Wilma. In shul, it's clear that she deeply uplifts people's lives. Whatever Felicity wants with this letter, it cannot be more important than my son's happiness and Leah's life mission.*

Seymour opened his apartment door and walked slowly over to his desk. He opened up a drawer and took out the fire safe box where he kept his will. He opened the box, stuffed the envelope under some papers and waved goodbye to it as he shut it closed.

Forty-five

Lower East Side, New York City

"Dad, you know you're not getting any younger. It's critical to have all your final wishes settled," Zach counseled his father.

"You may be forty-two years old and think you've become my parent, but I'm not dead yet!" Seymour announced.

"Unfortunately, you will be at some point. They haven't developed a cure for death, yet."

Zach, Marshall and their wives were sitting at the round dinner table in Seymour's apartment. They were there to celebrate Seymour's seventy-fifth birthday. Seymour lived defiantly alone in his apartment since the September 11 tragedy. He still looked healthy, smiling whitely with new dentures contrasting with the dark complexion of his now fully bald and tanned head.

Seymour thought for a minute. "Wait, I think that I have a will." He searched his failing memory. "Yeah, I remember. Wilma and I created simple ones shortly after we got married leaving everything to each other."

"Dad that was twenty-five years ago! Everything about your life has changed so dramatically since then."

Seymour started to drift off into the past. "Time sure

passes in a flash," he acknowledged.

"Let me and Duncan look it over for you. We've had tons of estate clients pass through our practice. The least we can do is to make sure you are on firm financial footing."

"Yes, I've got plenty in my retirement accounts, so don't worry about me. But if you are so hell-bent on helping me organize my finances, go ahead."

"Where is this mythical will?" Zach kidded.

He paused. "I think I left it in a metal lockbox I keep unlocked in my desk."

"Great safety technique, Dad," he chided.

Seymour smiled. "It's safe from fire. Who's going to snoop?"

"No one. I'll be right back."

Zach went into his dad's office and searched through his desk. He found the lockbox and opened it. The box was filled with a variety of papers and envelopes. While he searched through the box's contents for the will, Zach noticed a manila envelope addressed to him.

Zach called into the other room, "Dad, what's this unopened letter addressed to me doing in your box?"

"*Er...ah...*I don't know what you're talking about."

"Can you come in here, please?"

Seymour walked over to his office, searching in his aging mind for what Zach was talking about. He came into his office and Zach held the envelope up to him.

"What's this?" He angrily tossed it over to his father.

Seymour inspected it; his faced flushed with a jolt of recognition. "You were never supposed to see that."

"Dad, how long have you been keeping this letter from me?" He pulled back the letter and slowly inspected the post office mark. "2001? That's almost four years! How could you do that?"

Seymour struggled to justify his actions. "Son, you are a happily married man. Felicity is no longer part of your life."

Zach had become completely fed up with his father's meddling. "Let me be the judge of that."

"What does that mean?"

"It means that I am responsible for whomever I choose to have in my life, not you!" he scolded.

"Are you going to read it?"

He lowered his tone. "Not now, and I'd appreciate it if we kept your little crime here to ourselves."

Seymour pondered that. He was resigned that Felicity's letter was now out of his control. He couldn't see anything else for him to do. He looked dejectedly down at the floor and murmured, "Okay. Please don't condemn me."

"We'll see after I read it."

■■ι

Driving home to Riverdale, Zach silently scanned his Felicity memory files. After their breakup, he never imagined that he would ever hear from her again. He had moved on in a totally different direction with Leah, one that was comfortable and safe with no objections from his prodding father.

It was past midnight when Leah was finally sound asleep. Zach got up and walked into one of the bedrooms they used as a study. He quietly closed the door, sat down at the desk and slowly opened the manila envelope.

He pulled out the letter and read its contents. Tears welled up as he thought how Felicity must've felt the day she wrote it. *She must still think I'm dead. I could just kill Dad for holding onto this letter for so long.* The thought motivated him to immediately get out a pad and start writing a reply.

May 13, 2005

Dearest Felicity,

I write this letter while very much alive. I know it's been almost four years since you sent your letter just after the September 11 attack, but please understand that I only just read it tonight. My loving, but slightly deranged father felt he was protecting my current life by keeping it from me all these years.

It's been almost a generation since I've written to you and this writing process brings back a part of my memory that was so alive back then. It made me want to reach out to you with this letter. I hope you can forgive me and my dad for the pain you must've felt when you did not hear back from me.

I married Leah, the rabbi. I'm sure you are not surprised as you clearly noticed that we had a connection when you and I met with her before Jacob's Bar Mitzvah way back when. Despite her incredibly busy schedule, she cleared some time for our relationship to flourish. I'm working on my "mensch" (means truly good man in Yiddish) degree and even manage a kosher home. We do not have kids for a variety of reasons, but I do have Marshall's sons Joseph and Wayne in my life whenever I need a fatherly fix. Yes, Marshall is married. He lives two blocks away and we're as close as we were when we came to Greece.

I'm now a partner in a CPA firm and live a comfortable lifestyle as a rabbi's husband. It wasn't the path I necessarily chose, but I think God had his own plan for me and I'm reminded of it whenever congregants call me Mr. Friedman.

I hope that you are still at the address you supplied in your letter. Nowadays, if you are so inclined, please contact me at zachstillman@zmail.com.

I look forward to hearing from you.

Love,
Zach

■■■

From: felicityg@boohoo.co.uk
To: zachstillman@zmail.com
Date: 28 May 2005

Subject: Your letter

Hi Zach,

I hope this email finds you well. I can't tell you how relieved I was to receive your letter. My mind quickly raced back to that time when I was hoping to hear back from you after September 11 and I remembered how much I grieved for you.

Things haven't changed much for me since that day. I'm still working at Graham, which has gone through cutbacks over the years. I am now the Controller having gone back to University to get a business management degree. I am still married, yet Lance and my relationship has been tested more than once, as I have caught him in our house with students in inappropriate states of dress. I may not have the figure of my twenties to compare with these young lasses, but I'm still proud of how I look these days now that I've just turned forty.

You now have my email address and I'm fine with the correspondence. You've been a guardian angel in my life, one whom I can reflect with when I can't talk to anyone else. I hope you feel the same.

Bye for now,
Felicity

Forty-six

Grand Central Station - New York City

"Did you know I just published a novel?"

Zach was sitting with his financial advisor and good friend Sheldon Harris in the food court of Grand Central Station, across the street from his office on Forty-Second Street in Midtown Manhattan's Lincoln Building. Zach and Sheldon met there once a quarter for the past two years since Sheldon put together Zach's financial plan.

Zach was completely shocked. Sheldon had never mentioned it before. "*Wow*, a novel. What's it called?" Zach asked.

"It's a book of anecdotes from a Jewish comedic perspective entitled, *My Grandmother Sued the City*" Sheldon said proudly.

The title seemed odd to Zach. "What kind of title is that?"

"Haven't you heard the joke, 'My grandmother was so short that she sued the city for building the sidewalk too close to her ass'?"

Zach chuckled. "I guess I missed that one. How did you get your book published?"

"I did it myself with this new website, iGalaxy. You work with the site on the book formatting and iGalaxy makes the book available to print on-demand.

It didn't even dawn on Zach that this was a trend in book publishing. "What a cool idea!"

"Better yet, I actually got one of the Bohemian bookstores in Chelsea to hold a book reading for me."

A book reading sounded very impressive. "Really?"

"Yes, the event is this Friday night. Think you can come?"

"*Uh*," he pulled out his daily planner, "It is the start of the Sabbath. I don't know if Leah will let me have a play date."

Sheldon had heard this cry a mountain of times before, especially during their financial planning process. It took three months to find an available hour on both their calendars just to interview them on their life goals. It remained a frustration point between them. "Zach, you have to stop letting her treat you like a child."

"You're right. She does get dictatorial when it comes to Jewish law."

"Look, I'll pick you up and bring you down myself so you won't have to drive on Shabbat. All you have to do is sit there and listen to me blabber on to a bunch of Jewish grandmothers."

It sounded like fun. "Okay, I'll work it out with Leah."

■■

Rebellion Books was an alternative bookstore on West Twenty-Sixth Street in Manhattan. It catered to new talent, and ran a book reading series for first novelists. Sheldon had some challenges in marketing his book reading event, so they were only about fifteen people sitting in chairs when he started introducing himself.

Sheldon greeted his audience of mostly elderly Jewish grandmothers and started to read excerpts from his book. Zach laughed out loud with the others. *This book is pretty good. I'll have to read it cover to cover.* He purchased a copy and Sheldon proudly dedicated it for him.

When the event was over and Sheldon was driving Zach back up to Riverdale, Zach questioned him on the book writing process.

"How long did it take to write your book?"

"Only three months. The Internet cut down a lot of the time I needed to physically check out all the facts."

Zach envisioned a room filled with books in Sheldon's house. "How did you get it printed?"

"iGalaxy does it all for you once you load up its template. When people order the book, it prints it, and then sends it directly to them. It automatically cuts a royalty check out of the purchase price and sends it to you."

Zach's negative vision was busted and he started getting very interested in the publishing process. "How much have you sold?"

"I didn't do it for the money. I found that I really liked the writing process."

He thought about Leah and her potential support for this moonlighting career. "What do your wife and family think of the book?"

"The book pretty much consumed me for six solid weeks. Lisa was very understanding. While I was writing, I read her excerpts in bed before we went to sleep. Her laughter kept me motivated for the next day's writing."

They reached Zach's building. His head started working through an idea. "Sheldon, thank you for an eye-opening experience. I do plan to read your book and will give you feedback."

"Thank you so much for attending tonight. It's unnerving to put one's self out like this in print, so having friends support me keeps me sane."

He walked into his apartment. Leah was still at Shabbat dinner with the Synagogue President and his family. Zach moved into the office and sat down at his desk rehashing the experience at the book reading.

He started visioning through the idea he germinated earlier. *You know, I bet I could write a book, but what should it be about? Maybe a book about the comedic episodes of a henpecked rabbi's husband. Ah, who'd read that? Maybe that sci-fi thriller that I can't get out of my head. What was the name I called it again—Superwomen from Zeldar? And how did it go again? Right, the planet Zeldar was inhabited with women of super strength and the ability to shoot laser beams from their chesticles.... Ah, only Duncan and Marshall would ever read that.*

He finally pulled an idea from the deep recesses of his brain that just was waiting his whole life to be plucked. *Wait...nah...too personal...But it was such a great story.... Maybe...I'll ask her opinion.*

Forty-seven

From: Zach Stillman, CPA
To: Felicity G
Date: August 5, 2005
Subject: Crazy idea

Hi Felicity,
Tonight, I went to a book reading given by my friend and financial advisor Sheldon Harris. He self-published a book and it triggered a thought that I felt I needed to discuss with you.
I'm thinking about writing a romantic comedy about how you and I met. I'd change the names to protect the guilty, and thought it would be therapeutic for me to go through the novel writing process.
Let me know if you are comfortable with me dredging up our past experiences for all to see. I think there is a story to tell there that we could laugh about in our old age.

Love,
Zach

She answered the next morning.

■■

From: Felicity G
To: Zach Stillman, CPA

Date: 6 August 2005
Subject: Re: Crazy idea

Hi Zach,

Go for it! Sounds like a fun idea. When I took my creative writing class, I felt it was quite freeing to be able to imagine things and express myself on paper.

Let me know how I can help.

Love,
Felicity

■■

From: Zach Stillman, CPA
To: Felicity G
Date: September 1, 2005
Subject: I'm stuck

Hi Felicity,

I was ready to send you a rough first draft of my new novel, As the Grecian Turns, but the more I self-edit the text, the more I'm thinking that it lacks imagery. I want the reader to feel totally immersed in Greece: to smell the sooty air, to feel the Mediterranean sunshine and to taste the sweet honey of the baklava. So, in Leah's downtime after the High Holidays, I've planned a trip to Athens and Rhodes with her, masking it as a re-return to my roots. Only Marshall and Duncan know that I'm still in touch with you. It's just better that way.

You last wrote me that you wanted to know how you could help. Please meet me in Rhodes and help me get this book right. You won't even have to go topless. I have already booked the Hotel Fontana (yes, it's still there) for November 1-3.

I hope you don't think I'm crazy. You used to be very understanding of my wild ideas.

Love,
Zach

●●●

From: Felicity G
To: Zach Stillman, CPA
Date: 6 October 2005
Subject: Booking is complete

Zach,
    It has taken me a while for me to think through your request to meet you in Greece. I thought a lot about whether I could handle seeing you and rehashing our special moments together. Those memories have been so neatly packed away in my mind. However, as I think through my current life, it becomes all too apparent to me that it lacks passion and excitement. The more I think of seeing you again, the hairs on the back of my neck rise up. It's a sign to me I can't ignore. So I approached it as a holiday idea to Lance, presenting a vision of an oasis for the two of us and working on our relationship. He agreed, although reluctantly. I have shielded him from you or your book idea.
    I'm unclear how you wanted to work the logistics of actually getting together. I will feel pretty awkward if we were suddenly to meet with our spouses by chance by the hotel pool. Please advise me on your ideas.
    Regardless, I'm committed to checking into the hotel on Tuesday, November 1 and departing Sunday, November 6.
    I look forward to seeing you again and learning how I will deal with it.

    Love,
    Felicity

●●●

From: Zach Stillman, CPA
To: Felicity G
Date: October 11, 2005

Subject: Re: *Booking is complete*

Hi Felicity,

I'm so excited that you have accepted my invitation to meet me at the Fontana Hotel. I perfectly understand your concerns. I have not told Leah about the book as well. I am concerned about how she would handle it, though it's not like we have anything to worry about anyway, right?

I have been getting up at four AM every day to write sections of the book. I've told Leah it is insomnia whenever she questions me.

My suggestion is for us to meet at four AM on November 2&3. I figure we can have four hours to discuss the book each of those days before we have to return our respective rooms. At that point, we can look all sweaty like we just worked out in the fitness room. Let me know if you can work with that scenario.

Based on your response, we'll plan on meeting at four AM by the Fontana Hotel bar on Wednesday, November 2. If I see you at the pool beforehand, please ignore me and try to keep away from any of Leah's penetrating scanners.

I look forward to seeing you again!

Love,
Zach

Forty-eight

Fontana Hotel, Rhodes, Greece

"City, this is a really a posh place," said Lance as they checked into the newly renovated Fontana Hotel.

After they arrived in their room, Lance immediately dragged Felicity downstairs with him. *For someone who is reluctant to come here, he sure seems raring to go. It must be all those nubile lasses working on their golden tans by the pool.*

"Look at that breathtaking vision of the Mediterranean Sea," Lance declared as they arrived at the pool area.

"Yes, Shirt." Felicity wasn't really listening to Lance. She was eye-patrolling the pool and chaises for Zach and Leah. "It is spectacular." She stopped her scans to see Zach's familiar brown eyes in the distance. Zach caught her glance and hand-motioned that Leah was asleep and that she should try to move to the other side of the pool area.

Felicity directed Lance to the far corner of the pool area as far away from Zach and Leah as she could.

"This is a nice quiet spot," she encouraged Lance.

"City, I may need to purchase a shuttle bus ticket to get to the pool!"

"I confess, I needs me privacy with you," she teased.

"Okay, that's encouraging. All right then," Lance conceded with a sigh.

They made it over to two chaise lounges, stripped down to their swim suits, and laid down. The weather was warm enough in the sun for a comfortable laze. Then, when Lance closed his eyes for a nap, Felicity slowly got up, and then motioned Zach to meet her in the hotel lobby.

Felicity found two sofa chairs and watched as Zach came over. He remained strikingly handsome; age certainly agreed with him in his early forties. He looked much like before, except with some wrinkles on his face and salt in his peppery hair. He grew husky, but it only added to his masculine attraction.

He sauntered over and inspected her. "You look stunning." He quickly pecked her on the cheek. "Why did you call me over? I thought we had a no-contact policy until four AM tomorrow morning."

Felicity was impressed that the heaviness in Zach's New York accent was gone. "I didn't think you'd be actually laying out at the pool since you wrote me that you did not want Leah to know that I was here. Your words not mine," Felicity slowly explained.

Zach took notice of Felicity's more refined accent. "I know I was acting a bit paranoid in my letters. I shouldn't have because I've been busy subtly checking Leah's long-term memory of you for the past week."

"Okay, 'Mr. E-S-P', how'd you do that?"

"By checking what she actually knows that far back in her memory. The thing is, with so many people in and out of her rabbi life, she's developed this strange memory system."

"Let me guess, the aliens put implants in her?"

"Very funny. That's rather good." He pulled out a pen and small pad he now invariably had with him "I need to put that in the book." He shifted back, "Anyway, she does these mental exercises to make sure she remembers people's names, especially during the time she's being with them."

Zach's odd behavior was new to her. "How about when that's over?"

"That's the thing; afterwards, she tosses the memory away or pushes it in the mental garbage can for permanent erase."

"So, you think her memory of our little session together with her eighteen years ago is completely erased?"

He hesitated. "Exactly. I'm not too worried, but we should tread lightly, just in case. It's not like we have anything to worry about, right? Just old friends rehashing old times…" He started walking back to the pool. After twenty feet, he looked back and said, "By the way, you still look hot!"

Felicity and Zach carefully kept their distance from each other for the rest of the day and through the evening. They both went out separately with their spouses for dinner and made sure they turned in early.

Felicity didn't expect the rush of raw feeling she experienced seeing Zach again. It was if she entered a time warp where almost half of her life was erased and she was back in Zach's mother's house having baklava. Rationally, she was in love with Lance but the connection with Zach was on a totally different emotional level. She never cheated on Lance but the memory of him sleeping around with his students made her defiant.

Zach felt the same emotional surge. It was as if his feelings spoke a separate language that only Felicity could decipher, one that came without the strict protocol driving his interactions with Leah. He was programmed never to cheat on Leah. In thinking ahead to the next morning's encounter with Felicity, the only thing holding him back was Jewish guilt.

They independently schemed their spouses so they could ensure more alone time for the two of them; both encouraged them to stay up late and read a book so they would be tired when they sneaked out of their rooms early in the morning.

Felicity set a rather quiet alarm on her mobile phone to go off at a quarter to four, and placed it under her pillow. She then laid out all her workout clothes near the bathroom so she could just jump in them and leave in ten minutes time.

Zach woke up at three-thirty with an excited tingling he hadn't felt in almost a decade. It was as if his life had represented a car trip slowly plodding along cornfield-filled plains for a thousand miles. He desperately needed a life spark; being so compliant under Leah's restrictions had blanched his personality. In just the quick moment he had with Felicity, he felt unleashed in more than one sense.

Zach tiptoed out the door and down to the lobby. Within his 360° scan of the area, he only saw the night manager, moving away from the front desk.

A few minutes later, Felicity met him downstairs and they agreed to find a quiet place by the pool. It was a chilly night, but they both wore warm sweatshirts to protect their cover story. Zach examined her closely. She still looked striking now with darker hair and a rounder face. Her smile still penetrated him like a Taser.

The realization of his diabolical plan finally hit Zach. "Wow, I can't believe we carried out this crazy plan! Now that I'm actually seeing you in the flesh again, I totally forgot about what I was going to ask you about for the novel."

Felicity couldn't believe it either. "The way we're sneaking about, I feel like we're in high school cutting class to smoke fags." Felicity came back to his question. "Remember, you said you needed help with imagery."

"Looking at you, my image is clear. A growing part of me wants to go back to 1987."

"Well, put that growing part back in your pants and

let's try to get this book proper."

Zach did bring a list of questions that helped both of them remember their prior experiences in Rhodes. He asked questions such as, "Can you remember what it smelled like on the dance floor during Greek dancing?" or, "What were you thinking when you first saw me?"

Felicity handled the first questions pretty easily, and then Zach asked the one that changed the tone of their session. "I've been sadly aching to recall all the details of the 'black-negligee-in-the-candlelight' scene. Can you walk me through it again?"

Felicity did her best to give Zach as many details as she could remember. Recalling every motion and emotion got both of them perspiring, even in the cold morning. Zach, feeling competitive, set out to turn on Felicity with just his voice. "I often fantasize about that signature swirl you used to do with your tongue. *Ohhhhhhhhhhhh.*"

She started to breathe perceptibly faster and returned his serve in her old dialect. "O', t'at was b'fore I smot'ered yer face wit' me molt'n lava."

The vision was making Zach's one-eyed monster spring into life. He finished with a backhand along the baseline. "And when they exploded perfectly in unison, Roman candles lit up the sky." *Game, set, match.*

Felicity's breathing had become labored. "Hey, we're getting pretty good here. I now need a cigarette and a cold shower. I believe we now have the making of the world's worst-selling, trashy novel."

Catching her breath, Felicity moved on top of Zach while he was laying on the lounge chair. "I think that there is only one way that we're really ever going to recapture the imagery," she said philosophically.

"How's that? Zach smiled back."

Felicity grabbed Zach face, closed her eyes, and gave him a deep tongue-filled kiss that practically had them levitating off the chair. "How's that for imagery?"

Zach kissed her back and they started moving hands. He then felt one of Leah's guilt spears stabbing him in his eye socket so he pulled off and said in a Yorkshire accent, "Okay, enoof fer one session, me euro has just run out," he sighed.

Felicity got up and straightened her sweatshirt. "Brilliant, it looks like those feelings didn't go away permanently. Maybe it's a good idea if we don't see each other until tomorrow morning."

"Okay, we better get into our cover story right now."

"Let the sweat begin."

The workout ruse functioned perfectly and they both made it back into their rooms without issue. Lance remained snoring soundly and Leah was finishing some morning prayers when he returned to his room.

They both reconnected at the same time the next morning, and immediately sought the far side of the pool for privacy.

Zach opened the conversation, "I've been tingly since last night. I forgot how that felt. I feel like a kid again. Ma'am, I think I have a crush on you."

"Well then, are you going to take me to the school dance?"

"Only if you let me feel you up later." Zach made circular hand motions in front of his chest.

"I used to have a real thing for you, you know."

"Yes, I had a ten pound box of letters to prove it."

She reached back in her mind to her writing days. "Back then, I felt that I needed to be your Sheffield news correspondent, so I recorded all me thoughts for you."

"By the way, I often wanted to tell you that your letters got me through some really difficult times."

They chatted for a long while about their current lives and how decisions they made years ago affected their current routines. Felicity told Zach that she had stress attacks after her dad had his stroke from the guilt she felt. She acknowledged Lance for getting her through his death and the subsequent grieving period.

Zach confessed that Felicity's Christianity drove him to the safe confines of his birthright religion and into Leah's loving embrace. Leah was great to look at but he admitted that her needs often outweighed his.

They both agreed that Ellen and Marshall's outlandish behavior in their twenties pulled them like an ethical rubber band to a more conventional middle age.

As the morning sun started to rise, Zach pulled Felicity closely into him and kissed her passionately. She kissed him back and they started the accelerating train of kisses, then gropes. Zach made sure that Leah's guilt spear was properly locked up. *I deserve these feelings.* With nothing holding him back, Zach wedged his body tightly against Felicity, grinding…

"City! Now I understand the workout you were getting. Who is this bloody cretin?" Lance demanded.

Felicity fell off the lounge chair in surprise.

Zach tried to think quickly. *This man must be Lance!* He had no patience for a full confession at seven AM, so he decided just to wing it. In his best Spanish accent he said *"Mi señor,* it is I who is to blame. A thousand apologies. I was just sitting here looking at the spectacular sunrise and this beautiful creature sat down next to me. It must have been the breeze of the Mediterranean that got over me." He turned to Felicity. *"Lo siento* lovely lady, what was your name again? Maybe another time?" Zach got up quickly and ran away to the lobby.

Lance didn't buy the contrived story. He had never seen Felicity with another man despite his own infidelities. While he raged to follow this man, he gaped in shock at his wife. He stared down at her cowering on the chair and demanded, "What was that tonsil inspection all about?"

Felicity got up abruptly. She was caught red-handed

without a good explanation. She decided her best defense was some kind of offense. "Give it a rest, Lance. If you need some relief, go on and find some college-age floozy to bang." She then trotted off.

Forty-nine

From: Zach Stillman, CPA
To: Felicity G
Date: November 23, 2005
Subject: The novel is done!

Hi Felicity,
    The book is now complete and has been submitted to the iGalaxy bookstore available for purchase. You can see it on their e-bookstore with the title, As the Grecian Turns by Duncan Marshall. I decided to use my two closest friends' names for my pseudonym. Tell family and friends (you can skip Lance) that you have heard of this great book. I've put a fair amount of money on advertising and promotion so we'll roll the dice and see how it goes.
    I still can't believe that our tryst worked out like it did. I had such an indescribable time. I cannot stop thinking of you...Okay, back to the humdrum life of a servant of God's servant.

    Love Always,
    Zach

■■■

From: Felicity G
To: Zach Stillman, CPA
Date: 24 November 2005
Subject: Re: The novel is done!

Zach,

My heart is still racing from the time we spent together. I have to say you are masterful in playing the overzealous Spaniard (I hope that was whom you were imitating). It allowed me to diffuse the situation down to a mutual ignore. Now, at least, Lance knows I can play around too.

I will be your UK agent for your book and will promote it to everyone that I know. The book is an eternal gift. Just being able to see you again and let me feel my heart beat again made the project worth it for me.

See you on the bestseller's list!

Love,
Felicity

■■■

From: Zach Stillman, CPA
To: Felicity G
Date: November 30, 2005
Subject: I received a favorable review!

Hi Felicity,

The editors at iGalaxy read my book and named me their Shooting Star for November! This acknowledgment comes with additional promotional support that it provides free of charge. The editors said the book was "a hysterical roller coaster romantic romp". They also added that "it is mainstream worthy". I cannot tell you how excited I'm getting.

Love,
Zach

■■■

From: Zach Stillman, CPA
To: Felicity G

Date: December 6, 2005
Subject: Book sales

Hi *Felicity*,

   Book sales are starting to take off since one of the staffers at iGalaxy got the book into one of Cindy Perkins' staffer's hands. Her national broadcast TV talk show is the most popular one in the States for my target audience! I got feedback that the staffer was absolutely thrilled by the book and made a point to show it to Cindy. Felicity, can you believe that Cindy Perkins may be reading my book?

   I just got word that Cindy did read her staffer's review of my book and plans to mention it on the air! I will record it and send a copy out to you. Oh God, these events are incredibly exciting! The big question now is, how can I keep this story from Leah any longer?

   Update: Cindy mentioned my book on the air; she called it "a man's fresh and hysterical take on the dime store romance novel." She also called it "creative and a unique chance for men to read a romance book with their ladies". Felicity, get this! She's including it in her famous Book Club List!

   I'm sorry that I couldn't send this email off yet, but things are happening so quickly, that I've been holding back sending it to you until these incredible sequence of events quiet down. Today, I was informed that the Barnes & Noble bookstore in the Chelsea section of New York City has invited me to do a book reading on Saturday, December 17. I would love you to be there since I couldn't have written the book without you. I would perfectly understand if you couldn't make it. Life has just gotten so crazy by now, so I'm going to just hit send.

   Love Always,
   Zach

Fifty

Sheffield, England

Felicity stared at the computer screen in the den of her Sheffield cottage and finished reading Zach's latest email. The early morning light trickled in from the large window highlighting another foggy morning.

I can't believe that Zach's book has gone viral! Felicity personally loved it, but she was much too connected to the main character, Annie, to feel objective. Carole and Lindsay thought the book was a total laugh. The description of the sex acrobatics scene turned them into giggling schoolgirls. Ellen was more embarrassed than amused as the book highlighted a time in her life she'd rather forget.

Since returning from Greece, things between Felicity and Lance were awkward at best. They argued more about petty things, ignoring the real issues that lay just under the surface. Lately, she had seen an angry, jealous and bullying side of him that had never previously raised its head. It made her question whether, going forward, her marriage stood on firm footing.

She considered whether she should travel alone across the Atlantic to go to Zach's book reading. Confronting Lance openly about going would certainly

244

escalate the arms race in their wobbly marriage. But she was getting sick and tired of playing games with him. In the end, she couldn't see past the aftermath of going without him. She needed to talk it through with her most trusted confidants.

Quickly logging off her email, Felicity rushed upstairs to get ready for the work day. Done with her morning preparations, she pecked Lance on the cheek while he was in bed and rushed out of the house. Thankfully, she beat the early morning rush hour and was able to get there an hour earlier than normal. Walking into the wing reserved for middle management, she found her office and closed the door. She fervently hoped that her sister had a calm minute within her typical manic morning to help her work through her trip issues. It was so reassuring to talk plainly to her sis in times of need without putting up an aristocratic front, as Lance taught her over the years.

"Hey Sis, are you in the middle of mother-of-the-year duties?"

On the other side of the phone line, Ellen was in Army General-mode. She directed her two oldest in heating servings of Weetabix for all her children while simultaneously breast feeding her youngest and pushing two others to brush their teeth. "Hey Sis, always, but what's wrong? You sound troubled," Ellen replied.

"Well, I need some sisterly advice."

"Okay, can you call me back at ten o'clock when I can focus more? If I don't push these kids along, they'll never get to school."

Felicity was relieved that she could reserve some of her sister's precious time. "Okay, I'll also see if Carole and Lindsay are available, so don't be surprised if they're on the phone."

She then texted Carole and Lindsay to join her in her office at ten o'clock for a call. Her work day was regimented into a series of business meetings. The good ones got right to the point and helped to solve knotty problems. In her University studies, she learned team problem-solving skills that elevated her ability to the cream of the crop at Graham. Her personal thoughts were twisted like spaghetti; Felicity decided to detangle them using a systematic business approach. She blocked out the time on her calendar and busied herself with work.

Carole and Lindsay arrived promptly at ten and Felicity closed the door.

"Felicity what is this all about? I thought we just discussed November's financial numbers?" Carole asked.

Felicity moved toward both of them and talked quietly, "Carole, this is completely different. I need some guidance on a personal decision. Wait, I'm going to conference Ellen in."

She called Ellen and put her on speaker. "Now that I'm here with me three closest friends, let's start the meeting. The first and only agenda item involves me attending a book reading event in New York City on December 17."

Ellen screeched into the phone. "Zach's book!"

Felicity confirmed it. "Yes, apparently the book is a massive hit in the States, and also has a small, but growing following in a South Yorkshire city that'll remain nameless. This means that our Zach is now a minor celebrity and I'm officially his muse."

Carole chimed in, "How do you feel about that?"

She considered her answer. "That's the point. I'm so confused."

Lindsay peppered, "Do you want to go?"

"Yes, but I don't know how to handle it with Lance."

"You got a point there," Ellen concluded. Ellen could never break Lance's hardcore shell since Felicity started dating him. She regarded his flippant weekend-and-vacation custody of his children as a lack of commitment, which denied her sister her birthright opportunity to nurture children.

Carole continued, "Did you already commit to going?"

"I just got the formal invite today," Felicity confessed. "Apparently, in the last month, Zach's life has turned upside down. He did write that he wants me there. He said he'd understand if I couldn't make it."

Ellen interjected, "What is your heart telling you?"

Felicity knew the answer as soon she heard Ellen's question. "What it has told me since the day I met him." She stared at Carole while stifling a cry.

Carole also had a tear in her eye. "Then you have to go."

"Wait, what will she do about Lance?" Lindsay asked.

Ellen put up a protective front around her sister. "I've seen Lance's jealousy before. If she flies all that way without him, he'll go ballistic. She needs to maintain control of the situation."

Felicity had seen Lance's jealous streak. "I remember one time I was at a club and some bloke tried to chat me up. Lance saw this from a distance, charged up to him and wrenched him away from his bar stool like we were *bonking* right in front of him. It has bothered me to this day."

Lindsay tried her best to figure out a solution. She probed, "Does he have holiday time coming?"

Felicity reported, "The University shuts down the last two weeks of December. Usually, we get his kids and go on a 'family' vacation. What are you thinking, Lin?"

Lindsay followed, "Here's an idea! I know Graham has a sales office in New York City. Tell him it's a business trip."

She considered it. "He may want to come anyway; I know he's never been. He'd have to figure out kids' custody, but I'll let him do that." She thought of a stumbling block. "He'd expect the business to pay for me. How'd I explain that?"

"I'll lend you the money," Ellen announced.

"I can't let you do that, Sis"

Carole interjected, "I'll contribute!"

Lindsay followed, "Me too!"

Felicity was humbled. "I'll pay you back in cash when I return."

"If you take him, you still have to figure out the book reading attendance part," Ellen reminded.

She polled her brain trust, "Any ideas?"

Carole had an idea. "Has he read the book?"

"Blast it, I wouldn't let him get near the book. Besides, his literature taste does not…" she imitated a highbrow stance, "…include pulp fiction. What are you getting at?"

Carole explained. "Just tell him you've read this book and you just wanted to meet the author."

Felicity put her hand up. "No good. He's already met Zach; remember, we were dry humping each other in Rhodes?"

They all said in unison. "Yes, we all heard the story."

Lindsay suggested, "At least you can decide what to do when that time comes."

She didn't think it was her top option, but she didn't even know if Lance would accompany her to New York. "And let me feelings play out then?"

"Probably your best bet for now," Lindsay concluded.

"Okay, let's put our plan in action"

There was quiet amongst the three of them. Ellen finally spoke up. "It's your life, Sis. Follow your heart."

Fifty-one

Riverdale, Bronx, New York City

Zach couldn't sleep. It was a nightly occurrence, especially since he germinated the book idea into action. He spent his early morning hours brainstorming how to address his new fame to Leah.

Ah, Leah. She is two completely separate people. One, who is jumbled into the empathetic personae she displays to her congregants and two, the personal side that only few in her tight circle are allowed to see. That side was fragile, determined and hot-blooded. That side came out rarely, but formed the foundation of her psyche. I know she holds her emotions in check from me. She wants more from life that I can give. But she is so protective of her image, if the man behind the curtain somehow shows himself with a bestseller about his ex-lover, God will certainly strike me down as if I just published a novel blessing the Golden Calf. There is just no way in Hell I can tell her about this book.

He urgently needed counsel from his blood brother Duncan and his real brother Marshall to strategize his attendance at the book reading.

His pseudonym, Duncan Marshall, successfully deflected much of the buzz from the book away from him. He even published the book without his dad's knowledge so he could discuss it with him on his own timetable and terms. Nevertheless, the disclosure wasn't easy.

As soon as book sales started taking off, he arranged a casual lunch with his dad at Noah's Ark, a local kosher deli in his father's neighborhood. He assumed that meeting in public place would control his dad's theatrics. They were both munching on pastrami sandwiches with Dr. Brown's sodas when he decided to confront him with his news.

"Dad, I have something I want to talk to you about?"

"What's up?"

"I wrote a novel," Zach blurted out.

Seymour stopped mid-bite, almost choking. "You wrote what? When did you find the time to write a novel?" he declared with food in his mouth.

Zach knew it was a rhetorical question, so he played along. He countered with mother's favorite expressions. "Between four AM and seven AM every day since God was teenager."

Seymour contemplated how it suddenly explained his son's recent, odd behavior. "No wonder you've been acting so *meshugah*. Why didn't you tell me about it?"

"I needed to get it down on paper first. The subject matter is pretty sensitive to me."

"What classified material could an accountant write?"

"Not that kind of sensitive, personally sensitive."

"About you and Leah?" *Maybe that's why I don't have any grandchildren from them.*

"Noooooo," he said slowly with a lilt in his voice. "Felicity and me."

Seymour was dumbfounded. "Felicity?" his voice rang loudly in the deli. "What does she have to do with you anymore?"

Zach took a deep breath and waited until he had his father's complete attention. "Dad, I wrote a novel about how Felicity and I met in Rhodes."

Seymour put his sandwich down and just stared at his son. "Why would you do such a thing?"

"My friend Sheldon wrote a book and I thought I could do the same. I thought about all the topics that I could write and this story kept singing out to me. I found that the writing process really cleared my head about things."

"What clearing do you need? You are married to an amazing woman who has God on speed dial."

"Dad, I know you are Leah's personal publicity agent, but please don't overdramatize."

Seymour couldn't see Leah agreeing to this latest folly by his son. "Does Leah know anything about this literary work of yours?"

Zach's frustration was building. "That's the thing I wanted to discuss with you. She doesn't know yet and I really think it would be wise if she never does. That was one of the main reasons I used a pseudonym."

He nodded. "Good thinking. What name did you use, Ian Idiot?"

Zach half-chuckled, the other half wanting to grab his father's throat. "Dad, stop. Please! The thing is…"

"What? There's another thing? I don't know if my system can handle it." *And I thought Zach's family situation was the stable one of my two kids.*

"It's a significant thing. Much to my surprise, my book's sales have gone through the roof. It's now on Cindy Perkins' Book Club List."

"What?" Seymour took a minute to visualize books flying off bookcases. He was proud of his son's past successes, but these happenings were so unexpected. He readjusted his chair. "*Who-da-known?* My son, the best-selling author. I'm *kvelling.*"

Zach was now at the boiling point. Controlling his father's actions was a near impossibility. Zach moved his hands together and apart. "That's the point of this conversation. Don't be kvelling around Leah!"

Seymour clearly saw the only logical path his son's marriage could absorb. "You have to tell her, you know."

Zach calmed down. "I'm having trouble there. She's the jealous type. I don't know if this specific situation is covered in Jewish law.

"Yes it is. I think it is Commandment number seven – 'Thou Shalt Not Commit Adultery'!"

Zach compared this conversational thread to a Catholic confessional he saw in the movies. "Dad, I only wrote a book. I'm not having an affair."

"However, Rabbi Leah may interpret that you did considering that cockamamie imagination of yours." Seymour had spent hours with Leah coming to terms with the loss of his wife. Leah guided Seymour through his guilt over his divorce and his spark-infested battles with his children. Seymour considered her more deserving than his son did.

"Yes. That's the rub."

Seymour touched Zach's arm. "So how'd it feel bringing back all these images of Felicity?"

Zach moved closer to his father and said just above a whisper, "Recently, I saw her in the flesh."

Seymour almost fell off the chair. He screamed out "Where?" The other deli patrons were startled.

"In Rhodes when Leah and I went there last month."

So he's been deceiving my precious daughter-in law for months now. "Oh my God! I'm gonna collapse right here on the table."

"Dad, it was perfectly innocent. I needed Felicity's help on the book."

"What? Did you reenact *shtupping* her?" *Might as well since he's screwing up his marriage anyway.*

"Dad!" The deli's owner took a step towards their table. Zach shushed him away promising they'd be quieter. He then lowered his voice. "No, but we did recapture a little bit of our chemistry together."

"I knew it!" he yelled. Zach stood up to reassure the deli owner. Seymour lowered his voice. "That's why I held that letter from you. I knew it would only cause harm in your life!"

Zach had resolved his dad's reasons for quite a while now. "I knew that you were only trying to protect me."

"That's right! So what are you going to do now that you've caused such a commotion?" Seymour said with a cynical frustration.

Zach found it close to impossible to tell his father what to do. "First of all, I need you to be quiet about our conversation. I didn't like it when you got personally involved and held back that letter from me. I plan to handle it in whatever way it transpires."

Seymour bit his lip. *I knew I was right holding that letter back. Now he's got the gag order on me. I hate it when he forces me to choose sides. But he has given me no other choice.* He let out a big breath. "Okay, I don't like it, but I guess I should finally treat you like a grown-up. Mum's the word," he said moving his thumb and forefinger across his closed lips.

"Good. Now that that's done, do you want to come to the book reading?"

"Seymour thought quietly about it for a few seconds and smiled, "I wouldn't miss it for the world."

Zach shifted subjects. "How about taking Ma? You know she always talks about you. Since Wilma died, I think she'd be open to rekindling an old flame."

Seymour gave it some thought and felt it was finally something to pursue with Helen on his own. "Smart idea. I do get lonely without a woman in my life. I'll call her. Now look who's being the parent," he said with a smile.

■■

Zach next needed Duncan and Marshall's inspiration on

alibis for his time at the book reading. He scheduled lunch with Duncan at Tom Seaver's restaurant in the balcony overlooking Grand Central Station.

Duncan was impressed with the atmosphere. "Lunch at Tom Seaver's? What big fish did you reel in?" Duncan was typically the partner who brought in the business.

"This is not a business meeting," Zach said flatly.

Duncan loved to tease his partner, especially when he was now so vulnerable. "Oh, what then? You need help keeping away all the forty year old women that are now so in love with Duncan Marshall?"

"Something like that. I need your help in keeping Leah in the dark about the book reading."

"Why don't you just tell her?"

"Because even though she is so empathetic to all of her congregants, she can be so judgmental with me. She wishes I was perfect."

"I know that's not the case."

"Thanks."

"You said she's constantly busy. I'm sure that works in your favor."

Zach leaned over the table. "It does but lately we've kept Saturday nights free. The Sabbath ends early this time of the year so she'll plan to go out. I need an excuse to free me from her loving, but overprotective grasp."

Duncan rhythmically bowed his head up and down. "Gotcha. Let's see...we could invent a client dinner?"

"Not on a Saturday night; think again."

Duncan let his eyes roam around the impressive view of the station below. When his head got back to Zach, he exclaimed, "Got it! My birthday poker game!"

Zach mentally walked through the idea and then exclaimed, "Great idea!" Zach started owning the thought. "We'll pretend it's at Marshall's house so I can leave clothes there. We'll all meet there and take one car downtown. After the event, we'll come back to Marshall's place and smoke cigars. The odor will cement the ruse of our poker game. Duncan, you now have earned the honor of my pseudonym."

Duncan was thrilled to help his buddy out. "That's what partners are for!"

■■

Zach invited Marshall over for dinner the next night. He knew Leah had previously scheduled a condolence call and a Shiva service for a long-standing congregant who just died. To solicit Marshall's help, Zach prepared him his favorite menu: Lungen Stew, Stuffed Derma, Hot Pastrami and Lokshun Pudding.

When Marshall arrived, Zach made sweeping motions with his hands to encourage Marshall to come into the kitchen and smell his feast. Marshall nodded and smiled as he opened up each of the pots and the oven to see what awaited his appetite.

Marshall was suspect of his brother's obvious attempt to bribe him. "Zach, this must be a pretty big ask. You have many of my artery-clogging favorites here.

"Well, sort of."

Marshall couldn't understand what issues Zach could be having. "What's happening, bro? Book sales are through the roof, right? Your business is thriving. Why the long face?"

"I'm struggling with my feelings about this upcoming book reading."

Marshall hadn't heard any story of Zach telling his wife about the event. "Leah?"

"Yes. She still doesn't know about the book and how its popularity has gotten out of hand. Do you know congregants are now blogging about it? Even though I substituted Leah's character for a woman cantor in Scarsdale, people will start to figure things out and make the connection to Leah. She's very protective of her reputation."

"How can I help?" Marshall filled his plate and made it over to the dining table.

Zach followed suit and looked directly at Marshall from the dining table. "I need your help on the cover plot."

Marshall frowned and uttered, "You mean we're not going to the book reading? I'll swear Melody to secrecy from Leah."

Zach reassured him, "No, I really want you and Melody there. I'm planning to tell Leah that I'm celebrating Duncan's birthday by playing cards at your house with our regular poker guys. The guys were planning to come to the book reading anyway so this ploy also gives them an excuse to come."

Marshall was puzzled. "Why do they need an excuse to go to a book reading?" He slurped up his stew.

Zach reached over the table with his hand to make a point. "How many book readings have you gone to in your lifetime? It's not an event that our typical circle of friends do. I think it would only arouse suspicion."

Marshall was so enjoying his meal, he was open to payback. "Okay, what do you want me to do?"

"In case Leah asks, just plant the poker game idea in your head and eliminate the book reading one. Get Melody on board and get the house ready for a poker game a week from Saturday."

"That's doable."

Fifty-two

Times Square - New York City

"*Wow*! This place is even busier than Piccadilly Circus!" commented Lance as he and Felicity were walking about Times Square. They had just arrived in New York City, dropped their bags off in their hotel room and were just getting their bearings.

"*Ah*, the New York sights and sounds, it hasn't changed much!"

"City, I thought this was the first time you've ever been here?"

Felicity stopped walking. She quickly thought for a second. "*Oh* yes… I was remembering a scene in *Family Man* with Nicolas Cage," she lied.

"I don't remember seeing it."

Dodged a bullet there.

Felicity's marriage to Lance fell on strained times. Since finding Felicity groping a strange man in Rhodes, Lance had become ornery and suspicious with her. Although he rationalized the trysts he had with his students for many years, he couldn't see passed Felicity's right for pleasure outside their marriage. One of the reasons Lance was initially attracted in Felicity as a wife was her fidelity; now that was in question. The trip gave him some time to focus on their relationship and get Felicity back into his fold.

Felicity wrestled broaching Lance with the subject of attending the book reading. Her feelings about both Lance and Zach were in a tailspin. Her sister and friends were no help, so she left hoping that her feelings would play out once she saw Zach again. Lance surprised her with his receptiveness to the trip. He figured out an accommodating child custody schedule with his ex-wife and cited the accrued vacation time he needed to spend. He had his own agenda of tourist spots listed in his mind, none included anything remotely romantic.

They stopped at the Carnegie Deli for lunch. Lance's eyes were bulging at the site of pastrami piled high into the sandwich stratosphere. While waiting for their food to arrive, Felicity sensed the right moment to discuss her plan to go to the book reading.

"Shirt, let's discuss what we're going to do now that we're here."

Lance smiled. "Okay, we discussed the Museum of Modern Art, Lincoln Center and Rockefeller Center..."

Felicity stopped him from rambling on. "You've discussed them, yes, but I hadn't mentioned anything on my priority list."

He sat puzzled.

She breathed hard for inner strength. "I do have one event I don't want to miss."

"What's that?"

"There's a book reading downtown at the Barnes & Noble bookstore in the Chelsea district tonight at seven-thirty that I'd like to attend."

"Oh, a book reading, *huh*?" He pursed his lips in approval. "City, I hope it's William Taubman, the Pulitzer Prize winner last year. I just read his book on Krushchev; it was marvelous."

"Sorry to burst your bubble, darling. It's not him. It's a new novelist named Duncan Marshall."

"Why does that name sound familiar?"

"Haven't a clue," she misdirected.

"In what genre does he write?" he questioned her with a snooty air.

Their difference in entertainment tastes had frustrated her over the years, especially since those discussions just invited him to talk down to her. "Not the kind of books you read. More me speed: romance, exotic places, Benny Hill-type comedy…"

"You mean your rubbish pulp fiction?" Lance spit out the words like he had a bitter taste in his mouth.

Felicity started fuming. *This is not going well.* "Yes, me drivel, as you say. You can come to the event or not. I read his book and really enjoyed it. So did a lot of other people. It's now on Cindy Perkins' Book Club List here in the States. The event should be well attended and a fun experience. I'm planning to go." She turned defiant. "You can join me or hang out down by New York University, people-watching the pretty girls."

Lance didn't understand her building rage and raised his hand to quell it. "Not fair, City. Let me think about it." He reflected on her recent flares for a moment and felt he needed to be near her to better understand it. "I'd love to go to the book reading. We'll meet the author and buy his book."

Felicity looked away from him. *You've already met him.*

He pulled her attention back to him with a gentle tug of her jaw. "Can we now enjoy our meal? We'll finish lunch and walk around Times Square."

Felicity took a few breaths to calm herself before responding. "Good idea. However, I do want to make it back to the hotel early enough for a nap and a relaxing swim before the event. I guess the jet lag is making me irritable."

The Crowne Plaza Hotel in Times Square gave Felicity and Lance an anchor point for their trip. The hotel carried almost eight hundred rooms and sat fifteen floors above its building's entrance to provide outstanding views of the New York City glitz. It offered a full complement of amenities including a pool and access to the New York Sport Club for workout and spa services.

When they got back to the hotel, the tension between them was simmering. Felicity was well-tired of Lance's overt references to her pedestrian upbringing. He had previously shown no care for her uncivilized friends and certainly not Ellen. In his eyes, Ellen was a classless, fertile baby making machine. Felicity put up with his whining about work and being passed over for Dean of the business school. Lately, she lacked restraint with his obvious sneaking around. She had reached the breaking point.

Prior to Zach's reappearance in her life, Felicity resigned herself to a life without happiness. When her father had his stroke, she interpreted it as a strong signal from God that Zach was out of her destiny. She accepted the sign and moved on with her life. She found Lance after her father's death; he patiently guided her past her feelings of loss with stimulating conversations and motivation to pursue higher education. But her intellectual growth outmatched her emotional stagnation.

Felicity swam laps in the pool while Lance got a massage. While swimming, her mind drifted back to her last month's trip to Rhodes. *I'm surprised how deeply intense my feelings for Zach remain even though they laid so dormant in the recesses of my memory. Realistically, I can't let myself go. He's a married man. To a rabbi, no less. I can't allow myself to think that we would have a future. It's not my destiny. Or is it? I just hope this book reading will answer these burning questions.*

The swim completely relaxed her and freed her mind to see Zach again and to better deal with the mental fencing bouts with Lance. She jumped out of the pool, and went upstairs to shower and relax. She had packed her favorite work outfit for the reading, a dark brown suede leather dress with a tan long sleeved undershirt and matching suede boots. It was stylish but conservative. Zach's novel had already described her breasts in vivid detail. She didn't plan on displaying them for the bookstore audience.

She reached into her handbag and pulled out Zach's book with the event invitation inside. The picture of the beach where they met made her smile. *How am I going to get through this night?*

She finished applying her makeup and checked the time. She knew that it was only a ten minute cab ride to the bookstore from the hotel. The clock read six-thirty and she expected to see Lance return from his massage already. She got so anxious, she pulled on her coat, grabbed her bag and set off downstairs to see what was keeping him. If he created any more delays, she was ready to go without him.

I wish I didn't have to be Lance's timekeeper, the only time he seems to remember these days is his lecture ending times.

Felicity walked through an empty health club weight room. She saw a sign for massage rooms and strutted down the hall towards them. As she neared, she heard sounds coming from one of them. She slowed her pace to a tiptoe as she listened outside the door.

She distinctly recognized one of Lance's signature moans. She fumed as his voice confirmed it. She both couldn't believe it and half expected it. It was evident that some young lady was expertly giving her husband's twig and berries a bit of a sucking.

Felicity punched the door with a battery of fists and screamed out, "Lance, you are incorrigible!"

"*Ow!* You bit me!" Lance screamed. He changed his voice to a mouse squeak. "Felicity? Is that you?"

"You bet, it's me!" Her anger was at a fever pitch.

"Wait for me, I'll be right out!" Lance yelled back.

Felicity walked away from the door and back down the hall into the weight room. She convinced herself to stay and hear Lance's frivolous excuse so she could confront him with her pent-up rage.

Lance quickly followed her down the hall into the weight room in obvious pain and walking with hops while still putting on his clothes.

Her ire disintegrated the governor she typically placed on her controlled conversations with Lance. "Lance, I waited here just so I can hear another one of your inventive excuses. Wait, let me help you... the roof of her mouth needed cleaning. How about...she's starving with eight mouths to feed and you were doing her a favor." Wait, I got it...I was only giving her a tip."

Lance was in a bind and he knew it. "City, stop!" He paused and looked at her pleadingly. "I love you."

Lance's obvious false declaration triggered Felicity's outrage. "Lance Gordon, you love yourself more." She had had it with him. "Okay, here's the revised plan. I'm now leaving for this book reading. The author, Duncan Marshall, is actually Zach Stillman, me Spanish actor friend you met in Rhodes. He's the man I've never stopped loving for the past eighteen years. He doesn't know that yet, but he will tonight. Tata, Lance!" She stormed out.

Felicity heard Lance pleading in her wake but she kept on walking. This latest episode put it crystal clear in her perspective. *Lance is an egocentric, crude and horny old sod that doesn't deserve the likes of me!* She stormed out of the hotel. She was so mad she just kept on walking the twenty blocks to the bookstore so she could to regain her composure before seeing Zach again.

■ ı

After Felicity left, Lance quickly took the elevator back up to his room. He was disgusted with himself. The massage was heavenly and the girl had hands of an angel. *Felicity could never make me feel that way. Once that masseuse got going...I just lost control.* He turned his attention to Felicity and started to put the pieces together. *So this trip and the one to Rhodes was just a clever ruse for a tryst with this Zach bloke! How dare her! I feel like an utter fool and I won't let her get away with that!*

He opened his hotel room door and reached for the mini-bar. He sucked down a scotch to ease the pain of his tooth-marked yogurt slinger and manically paced the room. On the side of the bed he saw a postcard. He walked over and studied it carefully. The contents enraged him as he furiously dressed and stormed out.

Fifty-three

Barnes & Noble, Chelsea District, New York City

The Barnes & Noble bookstore was already filling up when Duncan, Melody, Marshall and Zach arrived. The store had set up their usual thirty chairs for a book reading, but by a half hour before the event, all seats were already taken. The people without seats were milling about looking for a safe spot to stand. In front of the chairs, large, square box speakers sat on pedestals flanking the portable podium. The platform accommodated the size of a powder room.

Duncan Marshall's face was unknown to the audience. The book contained no picture of Zach and this reading was his first public appearance. So when Zach arrived, he looked like any other attendee. Earlier, at Marshall's house, he changed from his poker playing *shmatta* clothes, as Leah called them, into his new Duncan Marshall personae. He wore a brown tweed jacket over a yellow button-down shirt. With his salt-and-pepper hair, he felt like a true novelist.

Zach found a store employee that appeared to be running the event, and introduced himself. She was frantically busy adapting to the overcrowded seating by directing the movement of some bookcases to open up the standing area. She reported that they had found more chairs in the storeroom and that it looked like the crowd numbered almost a hundred people. She confirmed that this event held their largest crowd of the year.

Zach was schmoozing with Marshall and Melody when he saw his father and mother enter the bookstore together. He was wearing a wool coat and a proud smile. She wore an elegant grey wool skirt under her pea coat. Zach walked towards the door to greet them. "It's so great to see you two together again."

Seymour looked around at the packed house and said, "Zach, I'm really proud of you. It looks like you're Elvis Presley. Did you eventually tell Leah about this evening?"

Zach looked at the floor. "I couldn't get myself to do it. I think it's now past the point of no return."

Seymour pulled Zach's attention to his eyes and waved his arm around the crowded store. "Look at all these people. Eventually, she's going to know."

"All these people are here to see Duncan Marshall and not Zachary Stillman," Zach reasoned.

"Duncan *Shmunken!* It's all you anyway. You still can make it right."

The store employee walked up to Zach and told him that the event was about to start. As he turned, he glanced at the bookstore entrance and saw Felicity walking in. He excused himself from his father. Seymour and Helen saw Felicity run up to Zach with a huge smile on her face as she practically jumped into his embrace. Seymour tightened his lip and shook his head. He argued with Helen for a minute, and then walked purposefully out the door to make a call on his mobile phone.

■■■

"I can't believe that you came," Zach beamed. "I hoped…I dreamed…but I didn't expect…." He still wasn't sure he was being honest with himself, but his ultimate wish had come true.

Felicity pleaded, "Zach, I needed to be here for this event. I want to tell you something."

Zach picked up on this thread. "I want to tell you something, too."

Just then, the store employee abruptly barged into their conversation and pulled Zach away to the podium. "We'll talk later," Zach said as he looked back at Felicity.

The crowd was now settled into their chairs. An aisle was created down the middle of the audience to allow Zach to move back and forth during his talk. Felicity, Marshall, Melody, Seymour, Helen and Duncan all sat in the first row set aside for reserved seating.

As the introductions started, Lance raced into the bookstore and saw Zach on stage. He searched for and found Felicity sitting in the first row. His burning envy bled through his veins as he begrudgingly found a standing spot in the back of the crowd.

Zach cleared his throat; now all eyes were fixed upon him. He stared at his loved ones in the first row for strength. He then looked up and smiled into the audience.

"Hi, my name is Duncan Marshall. It is not my real name and I'm not really much of a novelist." The crowd buzzed. "It wouldn't matter to you if I used my real name, but it matters to me. Writing this novel has been a deeply personal adventure for me. The book contains many truths and has uncovered many still unsolved mysteries that compelled me to use a pseudonym. Never in my wildest imagination did I think anyone would actually read the book, much less create such a well-attended book reading event. Thank you very much for coming."

He continued, "I plan to read excerpts from my book, *As the Grecian Turns*, and will have a question and answer session after. Later, I plan to sign books you'd like to purchase and answer any of your individual questions."

Zach read a variety of passages from the novel to suit different audience interests and tastes. He first read a scene and modulated his dad's character's voice to more accurately portray his Yiddish inflections. Seymour even stood up to acknowledge the chuckling applause. Zach then read a passage that took place between Felicity and Ellen's characters using his best Yorkshire dialect. The crowd roared in delight when he said "O' Sis, shut yer cake 'ole." Then, he read the novel's characterization of the black negligee scene. The room quieted to a library's silence. He ended the reading with his reenactment of the doctor and nurse scene in the Rhodes Hospital. He even invited Felicity onto the podium to assist him. The crowd belly laughed uncontrollably.

Just then, Leah walked into the bookstore tired from rushing downtown. When she got the call from her father-in-law, she jumped out of a bubble bath, put on whatever clothes she saw, and drove immediately downtown. Her mind was racing a mile a minute with thoughts that her most intimate relationship was falling from her grasp. She had heard the last of the book excerpts and quietly positioned herself in the standing area away from Zach's vision.

Zach ended his talk and received a standing ovation. He looked over at the first row to try to share the joyous feeling with them. After a moment to take a drink and set up an audience microphone, Zach took questions.

The first questioner was given the microphone. "What research did you do for the sex acrobatics scene?" The audience whistled and cheered.

Zach looked over at Marshall and smiled back to the audience. "I did extensive research. I made sure that I attempted every move personally." The audience erupted with howls.

"Another question, how did you capture the accents

so authentically?"

"I enlisted a whole host of dialect coaches along the way." He smiled at Felicity.

A new person was given the microphone. "How similar are you to Seth, the leading male character in the book?"

"Seth and I are intimately close. We talk to each other almost every minute of the day."

"If Seth was based on you, whom did you base Annie, the female lead?"

"This dear creature," he stretched his arm out to point to Felicity, "was certainly my muse for Annie." The store employee signaled only one more. "I see I have time for only one more question."

Leah slowly stepped out from behind the crowd and grabbed the microphone. "What about Annie and Seth's love story is really true?"

Zach audibly gasped after seeing Leah take the microphone. He attempted to come up with a quick answer but didn't have one. A murmur swept through the crowd, sensing this was no ordinary question. Zach stood in frozen fear for a good fifteen seconds, then glanced over at his father, who nodded his head in understanding. He straightened himself up and turned to face Leah directly.

"Leah, as God as my witness, I've loved Felicity ever since the day I first met her on that nudist beach. And although I've tried to suppress these feelings over the years, writing this book has brought out my genuine sentiment and given me the clarity that I needed today to profess my love for her. Leah, I'm truly sorry in whatever way…"

Lance interrupted the confession by painfully hopping awkwardly down the aisle like he was competing in the Nerd Olympics and leaped at Zach on the podium. Fortunately, Zach saw him coming and deftly feinted to the side making Lance dive through the bookcases behind them. A cascade of books toppled onto him as the crowd gasped in shock.

Felicity jumped up and shrieked. "Lance, no!" She then quickly raced up to the book pile and grabbed Lance strongly by his arm. "Lance Gordon, get your arse out of here, you bloody tyrant! Go on back home to your skin flute sucking pubescents! I'm staying here with Zach!"

Zach pulled his shocked eyes away from Lance as the crowd dispersed. He pushed all the air out of his system in a burst of guilt release and scanned the crowd for Leah. He spotted her shaking her head at him from her place in the back of the room. He moved like a dead man walking over to her.

"This surprise isn't how I wanted it," he offered.

"How could you? We built a life together..."

"That's the thing. I came to realize that I stopped really living many years ago."

"But I love you."

"I think you love the concept of me more. I needed more from our relationship than being your primary administrative support. Once we couldn't conceive... our relationship plateaued."

Leah started whimpering. "Why a book, for God sakes?"

"I really didn't know until now. I guess the book was able to dig through the shield I have been building for many years. I now have to accept the truth."

He reached in and kissed her on her teared wet cheek. She stared down as he slowly walked away back to the podium.

Fifty-four

St. John's Bay Resort, Rhodes Greece

"Look at all those boobs!" Zach smiled at Felicity.

Felicity barked at him, "Oh, shut yer cake 'ole, Zach!" They both laughed together.

They were sitting on lounge chairs overlooking the glistening blue water at the St. John's Bay Resort.

Ellen came out of the resort lobby onto the beach area in a one piece cover-up. She walked up to Marshall and said quietly, "Hey, Marshall, have I changed any?" She then sashayed around him ending with a little *flipsy* of the side of her cover-up proudly exposing the chunky hips that bore six children.

Marshall blushed. Melody spoke up, "You look gorgeous, Ellen!"

Seymour was watching the action from the lobby stairs. He came outside wearing long swim trunks and said to Ellen, "I saw that! Child, please put something on underneath that napkin you're wearing? We are here in Rhodes for the running of the wedding, not the running of the bulls."

Helen closely followed him wearing one of Seymour's button-down shirts. "Seymour honey, stop being such a prude." She came over to Seymour and embraced him. Zach saw them playing and smiled widely to himself.

Zach and Felicity created a destination wedding to where they first met. They readily agreed it could be the only logical place in the world for their nuptials. The wedding was clothes-required, but the after party was "anything goes".

It took four wild months to separate themselves from their spouses, but Zach and Felicity were blissfully wedded together in matrimony.

Felicity stared out at all of her friends and family relaxing in the sun after their wedding, and then kissed Zach deeply. She gently pulled back and said to him, "I guess you and I were in God's destiny after all."

"It's like I always say, it's not where you start, it's where you finish," he replied. He shifted up in his lounge chair to look at Felicity directly. "By the way, I finally found a suitable pet name for you."

"Okay, let me have it, I'm ready," she smiled lovingly.

"Here it is...wife."

—

ABOUT THE AUTHOR

Nathan Jewell lives in the Seattle, Washington area with his wife Natalie, two children William and Renee and his dog Matzah. He is a former New Yorker and proud alumnus of The Bronx High School of Science. He currently spends his work days on completely different topics from the subject of this novel. This novel marks both his first literary effort and the first time he has used the right side of his brain in twenty-five years.

Made in the USA
Monee, IL
12 November 2019